New sounds, new personalities

339-2
62

New sounds, new personalities

British composers of the 1980s in conversation with

PAUL GRIFFITHS

FABER MUSIC LTD
in association with
FABER & FABER LTD
London & Boston

First published in 1985 by Faber Music Ltd
in association with Faber and Faber Ltd
3 Queen Square London WCIN 3AU

Typeset by Goodfellow & Egan Ltd, Cambridge
Printed in Great Britain by Whitstable Litho Ltd

© Paul Griffiths, 1985

British Library Cataloguing in Publication Data

Griffiths, Paul
New sounds, new personalities : British
composers of the 1980s.
1. Composers—Great Britain
I. Title
780'.92'2   ML390
ISBN 0-571-10061-9

Library of Congress Cataloging-in-Publication Data

Griffiths, Paul.
New sounds, new personalities.
1. Composers—Great Britain—Interviews. I. Title.
ML390.G92 1985   780'.92'2 [B]   85-12977
ISBN 0-571-10061-9 (pbk.)

CONTENTS

For this score and some others

INTRODUCTION

The last time an enterprise of this kind was undertaken, by Murray Schafer in his *British Composers in Interview* (London, Faber, 1963), it was possible for a choice of eleven composers to give a fair representation of the whole state of British music at the time. Such a project now would require perhaps five times as many musicians to be interviewed, so enormous has been the expansion of compositional activity in Britain. Certain limitations therefore had to be imposed. The present book includes no subject born before 1932: Alexander Goehr and Peter Maxwell Davies, the *enfants terribles* of 1963, are now the doyens. And though they may not relish the role of father figure, it was indeed their example, and that of their Manchester colleague, Harrison Birtwistle, that helped stimulate the great growth in British music during the last twenty years. Their teaching, too, has played its part, as the interviews with George Benjamin and Robin Holloway may suggest.

Within the post-1932 restriction the choice of composers has been dictated by my wish to include as wide a variety of styles and personalities as possible, and though it would be absurd to claim these are a 'top twenty' of contemporary British music, I hope the interviews do not wholly obscure the real original insights I believe each of these composers to have into what music might be. I ought to add that, although this book comes under the imprint of a music publisher, only one addition (and that readily agreed) was proposed to my original list of names.

Diverse as they are in their views of music, the twenty composers here represent an unusually compact generation, even allowing for the fact that the 1932 limit was contrived: thirteen of them were born during the decade 1943–52, five of them in the first year of that decade, and, most curiously, two of them on the same day of that year (and those two perhaps the most extremely different of the twenty: Gavin Bryars and Brian Ferneyhough). This concentration of composers now in their thirties or early forties may justify the volume's title; it is also, perhaps, evidence of the importance of the 'Manchester school' as models. Most of the composers speaking here were in their teens when Goehr, Davies and Birtwistle were in the ascendant, during the late 1950s and the 1960s. Another feature of that period was the intellectual excitement brought to BBC programming by Sir William Glock, as several of these interviews acknowledge. Bliss was it in that dawn to be alive, but to be a young composer was very heaven. Boulez was conducting the BBC Symphony Orchestra in revelatory performances of Stravinsky, Debussy, Schoenberg, Stockhausen, Varèse and much else; and the Thursday Invitation Concerts on the Third Programme were introducing us to Barraqué and also to Dufay, as well as to the early works of younger British composers.

It may have been partly as a result of all this challenge and enthusiasm that 1969 was such an *annus mirabilis*. The Pierrot Players in that year gave the first performances of Davies's *Eight Songs for a Mad King* and *Vesalii icones*, and his *Worldes Blis* was unveiled at the Proms. Premières given by the London Sinfonietta included those of Birtwistle's *Verses for Ensembles* and Roger Smalley's *Pulses* (his live electronic ensemble Intermodulation was also born that year). And it was in 1969 that Cornelius Cardew formed the Scratch Orchestra, an ensemble of largely untrained performers and composers, with a Utopian view of making music free.

The transformation of the Scratch Orchestra into a grim Maoist cadre in 1972 was perhaps inevitable, but it was part of a wider retreat from idealized visions of progress and ever-widening achievement. Of course, one saw the same thing in other arenas as the rebellion against Big Daddy LBJ turned into a hard-nosed campaign to drive Richard Nixon from office, or as the flowers of the late sixties were exchanged for combat jackets. The problems were found to be more serious, the solutions harder to find and harder to be sure of. And if there is anything on which these twenty composers are agreed, it may be that music is more demanding of imagination, intelligence and care than it might have seemed in 1969. We are not in an age for the instant masterworks of those days.

One other thing that links these twenty composers is their civility. The meeting of a composer with a critic, whose views have occasionally been more explicit elsewhere than they are here, is not obviously destined to be smooth, but for me the pages that follow recall moments of openness and, in most cases, warmth. They do not, however, necessarily record those moments faithfully. I made it a rule to submit transcripts to subjects before preparing them for publication, and while some were returned unchanged, others came back very liberally amended. Thus while all interviews are artificial (who talks in these terms at any other time?), some of these conversations verge into the fictional. I have tried to indicate in the introductory paragraphs where this is so, and to give there too some flavour of the ambience, especially where, as happened in most cases, I was able to interview composers where they work. To all of them I am indebted.

Alexander Goehr

We have arranged to meet at three, and I drive round a corner in Trinity Lane to find the Cambridge Professor of Music out looking for me, ready to guide me to his college garage. The consideration is typical. As we talk later in his rooms in Trinity Hall he is at ease but alert, concerned to make the occasion a conversation and not merely a lecture. A photograph of Schoenberg with some pupils, including his father the conductor Walter Goehr, is the room's only decoration, and its spaciousness is impeded as little as possible by furniture: a piano, a long table for work, bookshelves, three or four chairs. The typescript comes back with no changes of substance, but with hardly a sentence left without some alteration in the interests of clarity and definition.

You've been publishing pieces for more than thirty years: could you say how you now react to your early music?

There's a difference between remembering a piece, remembering something about the intentions and the atmosphere in which it was composed, between that and actually hearing it. When I hear an old piece of mine, or play it through, the notes sometimes surprise me. While composing a piece there seems an inevitability about the notes you choose, but as time passes you forget the background that led to particular choices, and you begin to hear the music as other people hear it; some things seem to survive as images and to work well, while other things disintegrate and just sound arbitrary. The intentions remain clear cut for me, but I begin to become a bit of a critic of my old pieces.

When I began to compose I felt at a great disadvantage: I felt that other people could do much more than I was able, that I wasn't very good, and so I had to invent systems, as many composers do, to compensate for a feeling of lack of natural ability. The attraction to be a systematic composer was there, and it might have been the scorn of my father and his ironical Schoenbergian friends that shamed me from trying to become a Stockhausen-type 'Darmstadt' composer. I don't have a very much higher opinion of myself now, but I do have an autobiography, which I hardly had when I was 20. In my new opera, *Behold the Sun*, there are portraits of people, references to things people said, moments that I have experienced in my own life. The way I am composing, juxtaposing dodecaphony with tonality and modality, is a rediscovery, perhaps from a different point of view, of my own past experience and beliefs. This conscious linking of different modes of thought is something I find happening to me more and more: hence the attraction I feel at present to complexity and free synthesis as I find it in Debussy.

You talked about an inevitability in the act of composition, as if at each point there's no choice.

I do remember occasions like that, particularly in the latter stages of a composition, when I seem to be floating on air; then it's just like writing a letter: everything I put down seems instantly to click. But the starts of pieces are uncertain. I can't always see the way, and there are many choices; but when all goes well, when I'm 'performing' well as a composer, it may just fly home.

What pieces have given you that experience?

The history of individual compositions is very varied: it's a thing which I can't understand, why three or four pieces which adjoin each other in date should turn out to be so different.

In three pieces I made unbelievable mistakes in imagining how long they were. My *Little Symphony* was commissioned for a concert at York in memory of my father, and I was asked for a piece of ten minutes. I had terrible trouble writing that piece, because my father was an ironic man: not the sort of person for whom you lightly wrote a memorial. But ultimately I pushed it out very quickly, in three weeks: it just seemed to write itself. And because I wrote it at such immense speed, with no conscious thought, I imagined it to be ten minutes long. Nothing could have shaken me more than when it turned out to be thirty minutes long. It was because I was imitating a little symphony by Eisler which was eight minutes long.

The second time something like that happened was with *Psalm 4*, which was meant to be a three-minute piece but worked out to be seventeen minutes long. While I was writing it, it all seemed to be telescoped, and even now, when I think of it, I imagine a tiny piece. And *Deux études* also was twice as long as I thought it was while I was writing it.

Alexander Goehr   *photo: Malcolm Crowthers*

I don't know if that answers your question, but it's one example of a particular, peculiar experience in composition.

Yes, it surely has to do with the fact that composing and listening are very different activities: that when you're composing a piece it has an existence outside time, so that you can fiddle with the end before you fiddle with the beginning, and it must be rather hard to convert that into an experience in time.

Very hard indeed. If we name a piece, say Bartók's Concerto for Orchestra, we don't think of it for forty minutes: we think of a synthesized identity presumably made up of features which flash through our minds and combine to make something called 'Bartók's Concerto for Orchestra' that is one second long. Composing begins from instants like that. I think always I can trace what I do back to one moment when I imagined the piece, though heaven knows what it was that I thought, or whether what I thought then had any demonstrable relation to what I composed maybe years later.

That's the way it happens, rather than starting from an opening, or a thematic idea, or some complete segment?

Yes, for me it's a whole impression. I could say to you, at the danger of being completely misunderstood, that I might write a 'green' piece. The 'green' is the total idea which I then evolve: it's a pre-shadow of the whole piece, its slant, and its gesture.

Then how does that begin to unfold? Do you start by planning the form?

No, I never do plan anything: I only tell other people to plan things! But there are quite radical differences between how things unfolded earlier on and more recently. When I based my music quite specifically on twelve-tone rows or something similar, I had a way of proceeding which I almost always kept to. Being a good Schoenbergian I never believed in what's called pre-composition: I don't think there is such a thing, because even the most rudimentary bit of serial manipulation must be part of the composition if it's anything at all. So I never wrote out tables of row transpositions, or I haven't since 1960 or thereabouts, because the choice of a transposition or inversion ought to be made as the idea of the piece expands. I don't want any log tables or catalogues to consult. Earlier on I used to try to plan things, because it was very much the fashion, and older composers told one that one should, but I disliked it for two reasons. It made me feel that composition was too much like a sort of clerical activity, a filling out of something: what I hate most in music is when for some reason of structure or symmetry you've got to go on composing for thirty more bars. That's the enemy of all art: it's mere filling in and it's culinary. One should write as many bars as one's got ideas. I might start with a bit of music of, say, three bars' length, then look at its proportions and add the next bit to it, and so build it up.

Further, I don't like pre-planning because early on I was influenced by something that Boulez said to me, which had an enormous effect on me in an exactly inverse way to what he intended. He was looking at a piece of mine, and he pointed out that at one point I'd reached a kind of dominant seventh, which, he said, created a false kind of tonal anticipation. Because of the wrong accidentals, I'd not realized this (it was like the famous A minor in Stockhausen's *Kontra-Punkte*). You come across such moments coincidentally, in the part-writing, and I've always regarded them as God's gifts. If I hear a quote from the *Ring*, or Janáček, I don't want to cut it out, as Boulez does: no, I want to keep it, and develop it. I'm very sympathetic to Berio's wish to make his music refer to other cultures, though I don't think I do this in the same way: I tend to come across some other music that arises out of my textures.

Even if it's unintended?

Yes, particularly if it's unintended, because it's only unintended until you are aware of it. I've changed the whole development of a piece because I've come to a chord which has reminded me of something, and I've believed that this element of chance should be preserved and cherished in composing. Even in the most stringent pieces, when I've been in the most austere mood of construction, I've theoretically been open to having my piece totally altered by what I've come upon.

Come upon because of the workings of some system?

Yes, or even without a system. With a system it's quite clear: you have some complicated row constellation, and suddenly out of it pops something familiar. But in the way I'm working now, with a more figured-bass-oriented method, colouring chords and transforming sequences, I also 'come upon' things. Take a melody and change its mode, say from Phrygian to major – as Debussy did – and you might suddenly find it contains a memory of something from another musical world. I believe it's an artistic principle to preserve this thing and let it become a part of the piece, because I found it. That's what gives an inner life to the music.

But you've not only got to have the accident, you've got to explain it.

Yes, it's no good just leaving things as if they fell from heaven. You have to develop the reference. I'm very worried about using quotations consciously, because it seems to me slightly affected. The real way to introduce a historical or even autobiographical ingredient into music is to recognize the formulations which arise out of the chance meeting of parts.

You've suggested a couple of times that you've now moved away from the twelve-tone system as you used in the 1950s and 1960s. Has it completely disappeared from your thinking?

No, it hasn't at all. It could never disappear from my thinking because I was so much a child of that mode of thought, and I modelled myself on Schoenberg. I've admired other composers, especially my teacher Messiaen, but I've really felt I belonged to the Schoenbergian family: as if I were a relative (a poor one perhaps). I perpetually walk on tracks. I read books, something catches my interest, and suddenly I come across a reference to the fact that Schoenberg had been interested in the same thing. Consequently there can for me be no thought of throwing off this most powerful love and influence upon my life.

In fact, in my most recent work the twelve-tone technique is making a new bow, not as I used it previously, though in a way of thinking that was foreshadowed in my earlier twelve-tone work. For instance, in *Arden Must Die* there are two central points. One was that everybody told lies all the time, and I represented that by having strong accents fall other than on the beat, so that there were 'false' rhythms. And secondly there was a 'nasty' side and a jokey side to the story; as a twelve-tone composer I evolved what I called a 'soft' system and a 'hard' system: the 'soft' system had nice chords, suitable for parodying Strauss, for instance, while the 'hard' system was more Schoenbergian. Now in a way I'm reorganizing that notion, though in a more Debussy-inspired manner. I'm deliberately exploiting the contrast between twelve-tone music and something generated tonally or modally, the twelve-tone side not now systematized, as it was before, but rather, if you like, used for what Constant Lambert described as its characteristic sound, its particular chords and intervals. To take a similar case, in Mozart's *Adagio and Fugue* for strings, you find formal Handelian rhythms next door to chromatic, modern harmony, and making a powerful effect.

Does that mean that you're now drawing closer to Berg?

No, I'm not drawing near to anyone. But at the end of his life Debussy tried to synthesize seemingly disparate elements, and to get rid of all large-scale designs, relics of sonata forms which can easily sound like a façade covering something completely other.

Isn't that rather a remarkable aspiration when you've seemed so much to revel in sonata and fugal principles?

If you get interested, say, in Beethovenian sonata form, you don't become Beethoven. You take on something, you experiment, and you see to what extent these forms are viable.

There was a famous day in the lives of Maxwell Davies, Birtwistle and myself when we went to see a big Picasso exhibition at the Tate, and we were all overwhelmed by the studies on the works of earlier painters, the variations on Goya, Velázquez and so on. But my attitude to the imitation and re-creation, or variation, of older models was the least explicit: it's not the sort of thing I wanted to do in the way my friends attempted it then. I was much more interested in classical than pre-classical models, and what I was looking for in old forms was not their formality or their schemes: I didn't need them to tell me one could have a recapitulation. I was looking for the way in which the material was dissolved within the structure, which is the aspiration towards musical prose.

At certain stages this did actually lead to things appearing to be rather formalized, and certain of my seventies pieces do have a slightly homage-to-sonata-form feeling about them. But the interest in fugue is rather different, because that was much more a testing of myself, to see whether I could write fugues. There's always been a type of person, and I'm such a one, who feels that fugue, chaconne and suchlike are specific challenges to be met, and the more conventionally they're done, the more fascinating: it's musical chess, if you like.

Yes, but you could have set yourself exercises which you then threw away or put into a drawer.

And I did.

But putting them into a work gives them much more aesthetic force.

Yes, they take on a precise character. I only have to say the word 'fugue' and a certain character comes to mind: it doesn't matter what the subject is. I try to use fugue in the sense that late Beethoven sometimes uses fugue, as it were, to suggest objectivity and formality, seriousness, austerity, counterpoint, harmony arising out of the movement of the parts. It can be one character in a form consisting of many elements. There's no contradiction between sonata and fugue principles and the notion of form as musical prose!

Fugue is indeed one element in your opera Behold the Sun, *which seems to have lain behind much of your recent music . . .*

Yes, I started the actual notes in this room in October 1976, when I wrote the first of the Babylon choruses, and the text and the subject matter came before that. So it's been around for a long time, but the pace of work accelerated as other things fell away.

Do you keep your sketches?

Yes. Every work has a large amount of paper: I use any paper that I come across, and I'm unbelievably mean about paper, so that I'll jot down something if there are two lines that haven't been used.

Might you sketch ideas for future works?

No, I carry everything in my mind until I actually start on the piece. In fact I'm extremely superstitious about that. I'm thinking at the moment of a piece that I might write in a year or two, but I would absolutely shudder to write down anything, because I believe in that chess player's rule that if you touch a piece you've got to move it. If I write something down, then all my thinking has to be in terms of what I've written down: I lose my freedom. So I try to carry whatever there is of a piece in my head for as long as possible, and if I forget it then it probably wasn't any good anyway.

How do you start when you do get to writing things down?

This has varied at different stages in my life. I think the order in which I do things is most important, and if I can teach anything about composition, I think it's to do with the order in which one does things. Many years ago I had a conversation with Eisler on this subject, and he told me that Schoenberg and others had told him that Mahler could sketch one of his enormous movements in a matter of days. The question is: in what terms did he do that?

For the last twenty-five years I've been trying to devise ways in which I can notate something that is the whole piece, all at once. And that's not easy to do. I try to write down something which is the whole piece in embryo, and then evolve gradually from it, expanding rather than continuing. *Deux études* is a case in point. One of the reasons why I thought it was so short is that the whole first movement consisted of a conventional sarabande (like Brahms, I have a soft spot for sarabandes). I just sat down and wrote it, roughly in Bachian form, with just a few chords and bits of tune, and it took me two and a half hours. The first chord of this sarabande is the first chord of the *étude*, and the last chord is the last. In between I did all sorts of other things, but in a sense I'd written the whole piece on that first morning.

Having got that embryo down, would you then start at the beginning?

I can start anywhere, but probably at the beginning. I fiddle around in all sorts of ways: it's a question of getting the right flavour, the right texture, the right weight. There are many ways to write, and each piece demands its own atmosphere, its own way: whether you write it straight into score, or into piano score, or on to six staves. These are difficult decisions, but once you've got it right, you may have answered the most important questions about the piece.

Once started, do you ever abandon works?

Oh yes, often: there's about a one-to-one ratio. But very often I write something, and I don't abandon it, but I can't go on. Then I start again, and at a later point I can bring that false start in, because I've understood it in a different way.

Because of that experience I once wrote that I thought composition was like the movement of a pendulum. I might write something down and then think: no, that's just the sort of music I don't want to write. And so I swing to an opposite extreme. Reaching some kind of balance where ideas are brought together . . . I thought that was a dialectic of composition, every idea having its opposite. But I'm not sure I know what that means . . .

2

George Benjamin

Benjamin is young. There are white hairs scattered among the black curls, but one does not believe their message: he is brimful with eagerness to please, like one's image of a 10-year-old (but like few 10-year-olds in fact). In his spruce London flat he demonstrates his latest toy: a pair of electronic keyboards tuned in quarter tones. Over the more normal piano, a white upright, a coloured photograph of Messiaen smiles in benediction. Eventually I settle him to talk, which he does while feasting on orange juice and Twiglets. Later he only slightly amends my plodding transcription of his bubbling enthusiasm.

You went to study with Messiaen at a very early age. How was that?

In 1978 he had to leave the Conservatoire, and if I hadn't gone during my last year at school I would never have got to study with him. I always thought he was a great composer, and the idea of studying with him had been, when I was 13 or 14, an incredible dream. I'd heard some of the organ music and *Turangalîla* in concert, and I had the Larousse encyclopedia, which had a picture of him surrounded by his pupils in class. But what enabled me to go was having Peter Gellhorn as my teacher, for piano, composition, *solfège* – everything. He knew Messiaen through his work at the BBC, and he wrote to him; we went over to Paris to visit the Messiaens in their flat, and he literally handed me over.

That was when I was 16. I suppose I'd thought Messiaen was the kind of figure you saw in history books and on record sleeves, and actually to meet such a kind, natural, gentle man – not at all the difficult mystic I was expecting – was the most exciting thing that has ever happened to me. I played him my pieces, and he accompanied me in the pedal part of an organ piece we played at the piano, and he sang the bits he liked. I remember I played the first piece too fast, because I was so nervous, and he said, 'That was very nice, but it should go at *this* speed.' Then I knew that we were going to get on. Peter Gellhorn and I stayed so long we almost missed our plane back, and I was just overjoyed.

George Benjamin   *photo: John Carewe*

Had he been an influence on what you were writing?

Not really, except for the second mode of limited transpositions, which had got into one or two things – though I'd always been attracted by that sound, and I was perhaps attracted to it by Debussy, Ravel and Stravinsky before I knew any Messiaen. But there was no real influence, because at first I found his music difficult to listen to: there seemed to be no real tension, no forward motion. Only when I really studied it, and got to know him, did I begin to understand it.

Of course, while I was studying with him there was bound to be a lot of influence, because he would explain his techniques and his way of listening to music.

I'd thought his teaching was mostly based on music of the past, that he'd take you through opera, or Mozart piano concertos, or whatever.

He did do that – and it was fascinating – but he also analysed *Des canyons*, *Chronochromie*, *Poèmes pour Mi*, *La Transfiguration*, the *Méditations* . . . a whole load of pieces. And he showed us his rhythms, his melodies, his harmony (that was the thing that fascinated me the most), his way of orchestrating, his way of thinking about form. I lapped all this up, and took what I could from it; and though I was sensitive if my own pieces sounded too much like him, in a way I didn't care. The pieces I wrote in Paris were very Messiaenic in detail, but not in spirit: I always tried to twist his techniques into pushing on and being different. Now I don't use sounds like his any more, but that's not because I've rejected his music; I hope I've always tried to remain true to it, and add to it.

How do you react to the pieces you wrote in Paris and immediately afterwards: the Piano Sonata and the Octet?

I don't like all my own pieces, though I do like my three orchestral works. I enjoy playing the Piano Sonata from time to time, because it has such gusto and it's exciting to play. It really means what it does, and the chords are quite true and colourful. But in terms of form and depth . . . well, it's a dramatic showpiece, and it's plastered with faults.

You wouldn't be tempted to revise it?

No, I'd have to recompose it. And I think it works as it is: it's just a bit haywire, which I don't necessarily mind – better that than that it should be frigid and calculated. Which the Octet to some extent was: that was an attempt to order myself and my musical sounds after a period of very intensive study with Messiaen in my second year. I think it was very important for my development, but I don't think it's a particularly interesting piece.

After that you went on to Cambridge and studied with Goehr.

Goehr wasn't as spontaneous a musical personality as Messiaen, but a man of absolutely extraordinary intelligence and integrity; and I think it was the right thing to go from someone who instinctively responded to music through every pore to someone who was much more intellectual in his approach.

With Messiaen I used to take him chords. I had a collection of thousands of chords, and for six months I just took him chords, asking him, 'What colour is this? What sound is this? Is this a good chord?' And gently he would bend me towards the areas that he thought were my personal ones as sounds. I couldn't write music with them – they were too static – but it opened my ears, cleaned them out, and built up a relationship with every interval and type of chord, every register and density of sound. When I went to

Goehr we talked about concepts of form, and above all counterpoint. He made me think a lot, and I'm sure helped me develop away from Messiaen in many ways.

Also I studied with Robin Holloway, who was marvellous. Robin has an instinctive love for music that hasn't been tarnished by years of being an academic, and he was almost like an oasis. I used to go and play duets with him and show him my pieces, and it was wonderful to be with someone who was so instinctive, even waywardly instinctive.

Even so, Cambridge was in some ways an anticlimax after Paris – but then anywhere would have been. And it did give me four years to digest what I'd learned in Paris; it also gave me the chance to perform, conduct as well as compose, when my neighbours weren't playing records or I wouldn't disturb them with my piano.

Do you regularly compose at the piano?

I have never written a single note away from the piano. Without any question, I think fundamentally in terms of harmony right from the start of a piece: if I can't find some sort of harmonic *raison d'être* to a piece, then I can't write it. And I can't do that unless I'm actually feeling the sounds on my piano. It doesn't matter if notes are out of tune or strings are broken; I can't imagine composing without a keyboard. That's why I've now got a Yamaha quartertone keyboard, because if I'm going to write microtones I have to feel and hear them.

I suppose it's also because I drifted into composing from mucking around at the piano. I don't muck around any more: I spend most of my time thinking – walking around in circles or whatever – but when I come to write my harmony, I won't do it without a piano. The feel of the sounds is the joy of composing. And if you have a sequence of complex chords, then they have a harmonic relationship with one another, and I'm not sure that the inner ear in isolation can really pace and feel that.

Would you sketch a harmonic background in advance?

I try and keep my technique as malleable as possible, but many moments of a piece will have a harmonic plan – like the last movement of *At First Light*, which is basically one big harmonic succession that grows and becomes ever more resonant. There's one passage there lasting for about one and a half minutes, which is the culmination of the work, and where I wrote the harmony before I wrote any of the detail at all. It was just a sequence of chords in which all the music was latent. Other places I might first attack rhythmically, melodically or contrapuntally, but I would never write just one line and then fill it in.

How does a piece start?

I can't start a piece unless I have a sound that comes to me, often a harmonic idea. It's usually not the first chords in the piece but rather something to home in on. For instance, in *At First Light*, which I think is my best piece, there is at the beginning of the third movement a sequence of very slow chords bang in the centre of the orchestra's register: they're very rich-sounding, and I think very sensual. And that was the first idea, which I had two years before I started the piece – I start with so few ideas it's frightening. Eventually I realized they had to appear about two-thirds of the way through the structure, and that everything before would be preparing for that point.

Similarly in *Ringed by the Flat Horizon*, there are slow chords almost in a similar place in the piece, the first moment where the bass really comes in; and that again was the climax, even though it's very quiet. At the beginning of this piece I was very lost, as I always am, but I had that sound which I'd discovered about a year earlier and which had gradually enlarged in my imagination. I knew that was where I was heading for, and the whole piece evolved around that.

What processes do you go through between the original sound and the finished piece?

I sketch a lot. I have an idea of how the harmony develops, colours, transforms, and of what happens to the rhythm, shape and motion of the lines, the form. But I don't necessarily follow the logic of the paper as I'm writing. I try to find a way of communicating in sound that is as direct as possible, and that pleases me. Often I'll sketch a very rough harmonic outline of a passage, and then the details will accumulate: there will often be up to ten sketches at that stage.

Do you hear colours in your chords?

Sometimes. But more generally they *mean* something, perhaps in relation to natural resonance or diatonicism. And I can't write harmony unless I feel it's going somewhere, unless it creates a sense of passion, of pushing forward. Once you've got that going, then you can contrast it with colder sounds, more static sounds. But the biggest joy is to find music in which the harmony takes off, as happens in the second minute of the piano piece I'm writing at the moment. There's a pair of chords that brings the piece to life, and I was really thrilled when I found them.

For me, music without a harmonic structure doesn't have a meaning. I could calculate and create all kinds of complex shapes, but if there isn't a harmonic meaning – not one on the page, but one that I hear – then I'm not interested. All the gestures and events, all the lyricism in a piece must spring from harmony, and gain meaning from harmony: that's the origin of the music's force. When a piece is flowing harmonically, as so rarely happens, then everything you ever imagined for it becomes possible. If you haven't got that harmonic heart . . . well, I've written pieces like that, and I don't like them any more. My cello piece, for instance: that was constructed and contrived. It has the chords I like, but I *used* them; they didn't evolve internally.

Is it twelve-note?

It sounds it, but it's not. I never have used serialism: it's very foreign to the way I think.

Do your sounds have an origin in something else: a poem, a landscape, a picture . . . ?

My pieces have pictorial allusions, but they don't always start out like that. Often I only know what a piece is about half-way through, when a certain image keeps coming back to me and getting involved in the piece. But the start is very difficult. I might spend the first three months making notes purely in words: how to put the piece together, what to construct it out of, how it will progress, what will be its ideas. When a piece is finished, you have the impression it's always been there; but at the beginning I feel totally lost, especially with big pieces. I don't know anything. I have perhaps one idea, and I have to force myself to get even that down.

Do you ever abandon pieces, or make false starts?

My word! I've just spent eighteen months writing 650 pages of orchestral score, and it's all abandoned. I have long periods when I don't write well, and I can't do anything about it. With this orchestral piece, there are all sorts of exciting ideas there, but no push: none of the sketches gets beyond page 13.

Now I've gone on to a piano piece where I'm experimenting with all sorts of rhythmic procedures and techniques which are new to me, and the music is therefore more contrapuntally agile than before. Also, a lot of the harmony is less complex than in my recent pieces – almost modal in a funny sort of way – and I hope that this is helping me to evolve a much simpler melodic style.

Do you think in terms of performance and listening while you're composing?

When I'm not at the piano I often walk around conducting, and imagining the instruments. And I think of the listener, sure: I want to express what I have to say as compactly, powerfully, directly and accurately as I can.

How do you feel at first performances?

Paralytically nervous: I can't listen. But I enjoy rehearsals and later performances. I remember the very first rehearsal of *Ringed by the Flat Horizon* at Cambridge, when it was badly played, but just to hear the sound of my own notes, and especially the big chords, was like a dream come true. At a performance, though, I'm terrified of wrong notes and mistakes, because I want people to hear the piece as it is.

Does it worry you that the audience is going to be relatively small?

Yes, but I don't think it is always small. Composers in the past often had tiny audiences, whereas nowadays one might get a thousand for a big piece. Also, I've been very fortunate to have my pieces played quite a few times, whereas past composers often had only one performance.

But some of the bad music of the last thirty or forty years may have turned people away, and also the way modern music is presented may have done so. My main job at the moment, apart from composing, is teaching: doing educational things with the London Sinfonietta and other organizations. We're trying to give young musical people the chance to hear today's music in their schools, before they decide that Brahms is all there is. And I've found them extremely responsive. I greatly enjoy teaching, and if you show them the things that you really love, and do that in an unpretentious, non-condescending way, there's no stopping them.

What contemporary music do you really love, apart from Messiaen?

I've always liked Ligeti (ever since *2001*), and I've grown to admire Carter enormously. I think the opening of his Concerto for Orchestra and the slow section of his Double Concerto, especially its end, are visions of genius, though sometimes I find his pieces too abstract and confusing in sound. With Ligeti, I love his sound, and I've learned a lot from his orchestration and his notational technique. Both composers' sense of time and space fascinates me.

Are you conscious of more detailed borrowings?

Oh yes. I can't imagine there are many bars of my music that don't contain a reference to something I've heard. For instance, the big chords in *Ringed by the Flat Horizon* come from a mixture of *Chronochromie, Wozzeck* and *Peter Grimes.* And in *At First Light* those special chords come from a moment that haunted me in 'Hommage à Rameau' by Debussy. There are also things in that piece from *Tapiola,* Skryabin, Varèse, Xenakis, the younger French composers . . .

But going back to the living composers I admire, I find Boulez's orchestral music scintillatingly beautiful to listen to. I'm very fond of certain works by Dutilleux, Copland and Tippett. I'm interested in Donatoni's and Nancarrow's music. Then among the young French composers, I admire Tristan Murail and Gérard Grisey. I find the standard twelve-note sound of a lot of contemporary music very incommunicative, but Murail's sound is refreshingly different: his *Gondwana,* the pure sound of it, just knocked me sideways. English music I don't always get on with, though there are certain figures that I greatly admire. However, I sometimes find that the relationship with sound in English music is a little bit too cerebral: it doesn't seem to throw itself into the noise.

That idea suggests to me electronic music, which you haven't done at all, have you?

Not yet. For me, most pure electronic noise is dead noise, I'm afraid. I like some works, especially Jonathan Harvey's *Mortuos plango,* and some of the sounds of modern pop music are very exciting, but for me the sound of people crashing and blowing or whatever is essential; I like music to be live. I value the drama of performance: the tension, the danger, the ritual . . . all of it. However, I've worked at IRCAM [Institut de recherche et coordination acoustique/musique, Paris] and found it extremely productive in opening my mind and ears up; and I'm going to go back there to do some research (including perhaps a brief tape piece) that will eventually be incorporated into a big piece for voice, orchestra and some kind of live electronics. In fact, I'm about to use synthesizers for the first time, in a short piece for huge forces I'm doing for the ILEA Symphony Orchestra, where I want low bellowing sounds that you can't get from acoustic instruments.

As electronic sounds evolve, and get away from the drab, nasty sounds of the past, they definitely will find a place in the orchestra. Another interesting possibility is to get rid of twelve-note temperament, because you can't get quarter tones and microtones from conventional instruments except at slow speed. With synthesizers I can imagine some pretty amazing sounds coming out, especially as the means of performance become more sensitive and supple. Of course, you'll lose the sense of the force of the arm or the lungs actually present in the sound, but there is a mechanical side that can be exciting and can be used expressively. You could lose the electronic sounds in the orchestral fabric, perhaps, then bring them out, like pillars or iron girders across a landscape.

3

Peter Maxwell Davies

Davies prefers the inaccessible: a clifftop cottage on Hoy, or in London a dapper, newly converted penthouse flat reached by climbing innumerable dingy stairs. We talk in his tiny study, where there is just room for a couple of small bookshelves, a clavichord, a fine seventeenth-century portrait, some seating and a little table stacked at present with sketches for the Third Symphony. He talks easily – he always does – and in half an hour enough has been collected. The typescript comes back from his agent unchanged.

Could we start by talking about how your music starts, where the ideas come from?

It's very hard to say, because I think there's an awful lot that goes on in your mind without your being aware of it, at the beginning of the process. You can be thinking of something entirely different, and then you tune into a process that's going on somewhere. Or it might be a thematic idea, or a purely structural idea, with its main pivots: a big time span, with departure points and arrival points, but you don't know what's between them. I suspect that before you write down anything on paper, you've probably got, with a big work like a symphony, some small ideas and a big design. Then you start thinking through things in terms of the ideas going into the design, and then you start sketching.

Might the ideas or the design come out of some previous work?

Particularly as far as the architecture's concerned, there may very well be something left over that you feel you've not done as well as you might, or that's capable of further extension in a different way. For instance, I thought there were possibilities in the scherzo of the Second Symphony – the way it all works into itself, sections coalesce as the thing goes on, and there's a big point of departure where two things become one – I thought this was capable of extension, and in the Third Symphony there are two scherzos. The first time it's straight; the second time its centre of gravity is shifted and its time-scale becomes a bit skew-whiff, and I've introduced windows in it that look out on the kind of landscape that the last movement's going to be (which I pinched from Mahler's Ninth Symphony). That's a slow movement, and there's a big quick movement for a start, with a slow introduction and one of those long accelerandos towards the main tempo that I seem to do time and time again without thinking about it.

What form does your sketch take?

It's a short score on five, six, seven staves as necessary, with an instrumentation, though that may change. There are different pieces of paper all stuck in, with ideas besides the central ones.

But I know full well that once a work's out of the way I'll never look at the sketches again: anything that's going to be of value for another piece you hold in your mind. I do keep the sketches, though, so that checks can be made if there's any doubt about something in the second score.

Do you sketch the whole work before making that second score?

No, I do it movement by movement.

So what happens if something you've done in the last movement makes you want to change something in the first?

I can't, because it will already be at the copyist's. Anyway, it's a good discipline, and if you have a new idea there's plenty of time to write another symphony.

Do you ever feel you want to go back and revise?

In a way, old ideas don't interest me so much that I want to go on chewing them over: there are always enough new ones. I'm not a perfectionist in the way that Boulez and Stockhausen are. Once a piece is done it's part of the past, and it really doesn't concern me very much any more. I've already got an idea for another symphony, and, all right, I'll go to the rehearsals and hear No. 3, but the next one's much more interesting.

Do you like hearing old pieces?

When they're well done, yes. But there's nothing like the actual writing: that is totally absorbing and fascinating. When you get a good idea down on paper – and usually you know when it's good – then you're walking seven miles high. But at a performance or rehearsal of that very same thing you're so worried about whether it's going to work, whether the players are going to be able to do it

Peter Maxwell Davies at home on Hoy *photo: John Carewe*

or want to do it, whether the audience is going to get the point, whether it's really as good as you thought it was . . . With *Worldes Blis*, for instance, the audience didn't get the point, and in a strange way that threw me off course so that it took *me* a long time to get the point. I just left the piece alone. And still I don't know if the form of that piece is satisfactory, just working up and working up to a climax: it's a very simple form, and these days I'd want to do something a bit more complex. I don't think it could have been changed, but it could have had more movements added.

Presumably it's even more difficult to get the form right when you're writing a work movement by movement.

It's rather like doing a painting on a ceiling, where you have to get it right immediately. I wouldn't have been happy doing that ten years ago, when I would have needed to go back and change things, but I think now I've got enough technique and enough confidence.

Does that mean composing has become easier?

Not at all. Certainly not.

Yet you're composing much more quickly these days.

I think that's partly to do as well with getting some foundation of technique. One's not struggling to find the words one wants in order to express things, but rather with finding the right material to work with. One's concerned less with the minutiae of syntax than with the whole expression. And I think the larger output recently is due at least in part to having accustomed myself to work hard: it takes a long time to become able to concentrate so that one's working to the absolutely best effect when one's sitting at the desk.

Do you try to keep to particular hours?

No, I just *do* keep to particular hours. When I'm writing a big piece, I work many hours a day, from the idea I get when I wake up until I've worked it into some satisfactory shape, which may be twelve hours later, with a few breaks.

How long do you keep that up?

Probably for several weeks. Then have a few days off: read books, go for walks, write a carol.

Do you interest yourself in other people's music during these periods?

I certainly listen to it as much as I can, and get scores and look at them.

Do you prefer to acquaint yourself with new pieces through the score or the sound?

I would attend a performance if I could, but when I'm in Orkney – and that's where I concentrate best – obviously I can't, so I get scores and tapes sent. But I don't really think about other composers very much. They're irrelevant to the central process which is going on inside my head musically, and I think that course was set probably thirty years ago: the tree's just going on growing as it was going to grow anyhow.

I remember when I was very young at Dartington, in 1957, and John Carewe's ensemble did *Alma redemptoris mater*. The other composers there were much, much more 'experimental': I was considered terribly old-fashioned. But I was aware that I was finding out things that were going to stand me in very good stead for a very long time, that I was building up a solid enough foundation of technique to be able to support fifty, sixty, seventy years of composing. I thought that was very necessary. And though *Alma* doesn't go very far – it just works through a limited kind of modality in relation to the plainsong – it was laying out ground work, and I knew that anything I might learn from Darmstadt or whatever had to be grafted on to those very basic germinations which were beginning to happen.

Yet you've continued to be open to influences that probably didn't seem important to you in the 1950s, like Sibelius.

Yes. I think when you're dealing with large forms you're inevitably going to look at somebody like Sibelius. Of course there are all sorts of influences, but I regard them as having helped the growth process rather than been fundamental to it. Without such nutrition it would have died, but the thing itself was already growing.

Could you see yourself at the time of Alma *one day writing symphonies?*

No, but I could see myself writing large orchestral pieces, though I knew it was going to be difficult, because it's hard to get big orchestral pieces played, and yet it's only by having them played that you learn. It took a long time to get confidence.

You keep saying that, though surely the works you wrote in the late 1960s – Worldes Blis, St Thomas Wake – *are quite as fully achieved as the* First Symphony.

In many ways I don't think they are. In other ways, yes: they make a young man's statement, quite proudly in a way. But some of the orchestration is a bit rough and ready.

But then you're critical of all your old pieces.

Any old piece I find I'm bored with.

But let's talk about some more old pieces: the three chamber orchestra pieces of 1982–3. Do they form a triptych?

They've got gestures in common, and one or two cross-references, but the connection has more to do with architecture and shaping than with thematic content. For instance, the second movement of the *Sinfonietta Accademica* and the second movement of the *Sinfonia Concertante* are basically working through the same idea, though the *Accademica* does take off towards the end. There the form gets quite complex. It covers a whole range of architectural perceptions: that kind of wedding together of fairly disparate elements by making a rigid kind of architecture – that appealed to me.

Do you mean disparate thematic elements?

No, it's the kind of gesture. My own performances with the Scottish Chamber Orchestra brought that out, because we were playing and rehearsing the piece enough to be able to characterize and shape the material. That gave me the confidence that one can, within the confines of a carefully considered architectural structure, make very big and various kinds of gesture, which I'd never done before within one movement.

What about St Thomas Wake?

Oh yes, but that goes between different levels, and it sidesteps the issue by not attempting to integrate them at all. And that's a criticism of it too.

Another thing about these chamber orchestra pieces: they've been widely remarked as easier to listen to than other things of yours.

I think that has partly to do with the fact that as you get older you realize that a complex surface is not necessarily a complex piece of music, and that there are many pieces that have very complex surfaces but are actually very simple-minded. In the chamber orchestra pieces I tried very consciously to make the surface as transparent as I could, so that it allows one to perceive the relationships within the architecture.

I'm reminded of something you said in an early essay, about the latent complexity of harmony, rhythm and so on within an innocent Mozart theme.

And I feel exactly the same now, probably more strongly. I know now that I can write music as complex as anybody else's on the surface, and there's no point in doing it again. It's much more exciting to try to conceal the art with the art, and write something which allows the listener to perceive the inner relationships as clearly as possible. I think in those pieces this is beginning to be so.

It's a matter of harmonic consistency, isn't it?

That's right, and I hope that's coming: I think it is. The possibilities of harmonic organization are very exciting, and I want to make them as clear as I can. It's not a return to tonality; it's not nostalgic. It really is finding out how music works in terms of our own experience, and it's totally wrong to say that this is turning one's back on what happened in the 1960s and 1970s. As far as I'm concerned, it's the inevitable conclusion out of my experiences of that time, looking forward.

And there's no question of return when the music doesn't sound like anything one's heard before?

Not at all. Though I don't feel there's a tremendously different approach between my orchestral pieces and things that are tonal in a more traditional way, written for schoolkids on Hoy.

Indeed, back in the 1960s there was the same kind of relationship between your carols and your more developed pieces.

Oh yes. I think I can hear it very well in the harmonic vocabulary of *O magnum mysterium*: it seems to come out in a way that's consistent with the Quartet, the Sinfonia and the other pieces I was writing at the time.

And of course within O magnum mysterium *there are the straightforward carols and the complex fantasia with the sonatas in between.*

Yes, they're very odd. I must say when I hear them now they make me smile.

Do you see where your new harmonic consistency is leading?

I can only hear it in terms of quite specific things. I think it will make possible a very high degree of harmonic coherence, where one might expect all the musical faculties of memory, expectation and contradicted expectation to be brought into play. But I think there's no short cut to that. It might well happen after my lifetime: I don't know. But I can smell it in the distance.

Do you think this new harmony might make it easier to compose opera successfully, since it perhaps will give a strong narrative thread?

Yes, I don't really think that operatic and symphonic development are all that different, deep down. An orchestral piece has got to have a great deal of theatre in it if it's going to grip the imagination, though obviously you can't have abstract symphonic development in an opera.

Well, Taverner *does.*

Yes, but I wouldn't do that again: I've done it once, so I don't have to.

So Resurrection *will be of a different nature.*

It's not going to be so big in scale. There's no point: it just gets in the way of pieces being performed. You can see for yourself: *The Lighthouse* gets put on everywhere, but *Taverner* doesn't; and you do like people to hear pieces. *Taverner* was a one-off. I had to write it, and I learned an awful lot doing it. But I've been asked for another large opera several times, and I don't see the point. Also I feel – as I felt about symphonies once – that I'm not quite ready to put my eggs in that particular basket. I might. Give it another twenty years and I might write a whole series of operas, but at the moment it's symphonies.

4

Simon Bainbridge

Bainbridge divides his time between London and an Oxfordshire cottage, where he has a small, light upstairs studio furnished cleanly and briskly with what is necessary: a large white table under the window, scores, textbooks, records and sound equipment, and just two of his father's canvases, as well as chairs on which we sit relaxedly and ramble, the ramblings later to be judiciously expanded by him with local colour.

Your father was a painter. Was the family also musical?

I remember when I was 8 my father asked me what I wanted for Christmas: a clarinet or a box of paints. I decided to go for the clarinet: I'd started on the recorder just before that, and I became very interested in the sound of the clarinet. I decided that was what I wanted to play, and I think that was probably the very earliest recognition of something musical. Then shortly after that I made my first feeble atempts at childhood composition, writing pieces for solo clarinet.

I played the clarinet right up to the time I left the Royal College of Music. In fact I entered as a clarinettist, and composition really started to take off after I began having lessons with John Lambert. Gradually, during my three years there, composition became more important than playing the clarinet, partly because of nerves: I had a couple of engagements playing in orchestras after I left the College, and I nearly had a nervous breakdown.

Had you known much contemporary music before you got to the RCM?

Oh yes. I think I can thank Olly Knussen for that, because I'd known him since 1965, when we went to the Central Tutorial School for Young Musicians. The first thing he ever said to me was, 'Do you like Schoenberg and Stravinsky?' To which I replied, 'Do you like *Tosca*?' I had a lot of pieces to learn! He had the most remarkable record collection – he still does: it just gets bigger and bigger – and it was a great opportunity to hear so much for the first time. The CTSYM (later the Purcell School) was situated at

Morley College, and almost every day one of the London orchestras would be rehearsing in the Emma Cons Hall. I remember sitting in on a lot of those rehearsals: particularly I recall Boulez (in dark glasses) rehearsing *La Mer* and Colin Davis conducting *The Rite of Spring* with the LSO. It was quite an experience for a callow 13-year-old. Also, that was the time when Boulez was doing things like *Gruppen* at the Proms and introducing us to the important works of the Second Viennese School. I remember too hearing the premières of Peter Maxwell Davies's *Eight Songs for a Mad King* and *Revelation and Fall* at the time when the Pierrot Players were getting off the ground: that made a tremendous impression on me. I think back on that period with great affection, because there were so many exciting and innovative things happening in London. It makes the situation nowadays seem fairly depressing.

How did John Lambert teach? Were you showing him things or doing exercises?

It began with showing him things, but he was, and is, a very good teacher because he doesn't exert his personality on your work. It was a question of discussing points, and talking and talking about music. At that time he was discovering things; we all were. I remember, for instance, Berio's *Sinfonia* and Ligeti's *Atmosphères* were big talking points. But allied to that, he would give me lots of very strict sixteenth-century counterpoint exercises. He was a Boulanger pupil, and had a very strict training. And I remember doing these exercises for weeks without really seeing the point of it all, until suddenly it all came together and I saw why these things were relevant and related to my work and to what we'd been talking about. That was a main transition and awakening for me, and for the first time I began to have an inkling about what I was doing. To this day, the way I go about composing relates very much to that time of working with him on sixteenth-century models, just to control the thought processes, giving me a sense of line and knowledge of where the piece is going.

Were you still seeing Olly Knussen?

Yes, he was very much present during my three years at College, although not as a student! Queen Alexandra's House, the girls' hostel, was nearby, and that was a great meeting ground for us.

Our musical development, too, went very much in parallel. Olly had been to Tanglewood, and in 1973 I submitted some scores to Gunther Schuller and was invited to study with him that summer.

Simon Bainbridge   *photo: Malcolm Crowthers*

It was an amazing eight weeks. Both Ligeti and Maxwell Davies gave seminars. Michael Tilson Thomas was doing extraordinary concerts with the Boston Symphony Orchestra and the Berkshire Music Center Orchestra, and I met many interesting young American composers, some of whom are good friends to this day. It was just a wonderful enlightenment. I went again the following year, again studying with Gunther. After the first summer it was a bit of an anticlimax, but it gave me a good opportunity to write and have performed a piece for viola and ensemble. I later withdrew it, but it was an invaluable sketch for writing the Viola Concerto.

In 1978–9 I went back for a year on a US–UK Bicentennial fellowship, and I had the opportunity to meet composers living in downtown Manhattan: Steve Reich, Philip Corner, Phil Niblock, Bill Hellermann . . . I didn't have a great deal of sympathy with their music (except Reich's), but I did admire some of the ideas that were coming out. And I suppose I did pick up a lot from the process aspect of composition. Some of the pieces I wrote shortly after that attempted to use the discipline of process music. I found it increasingly frustrating because of the harmonic limitations it imposed: that wasn't for me at all. But what I've found more recently, in the last year or so, is a way of using some of those techniques to my own ends: using them not on the details, where I like a certain amount of flexibility, but rather as a control over large-scale structures.

Do you not see also an Americanness in your orchestral sound?

It's not something I'm conscious of, but obviously over the years I have been bombarded with lots and lots of American music. Also, I'm half American and have some of my roots not a million miles away from where Charles Ives was born.

How were you earning a living? What were you doing between the summers in Tanglewood and your return to the US in 1978?

Anything. Copying mostly, but I also played the saxophone in a band that had Jonathan Lloyd on bass guitar. Unfortunately it came adrift pretty quickly. In 1976 I became Forman Fellow in Composition at Edinburgh University: it was the first time I was on a salary.

How do you feel about the music you were writing at that time? Do you ever want to go back and revise things?

No, though I did revise *Spirogyra* and *Flugal*, a little piece I wrote at Tanglewood in 1973, to make them the first two of a set of *Three Pieces* for chamber ensembles in 1982. More than revision that was mostly a matter of notational changes, producing the same effect in a more intelligent way. And I did that really because I thought it would be interesting to make a set of pieces for different instrumentations covering eleven years.

Then my early Wind Quintet was done at the 1983 Huddersfield Festival, and I was a bit worried about hearing it again, but it seemed to work, and I saw in it things that still exist today in my music.

Like what?

There are the same interests in colour, harmony and form. I think my harmony's now got a longer range, which I couldn't cope with then, but I saw I was trying very unsuccessfully to do that. It's very difficult to remember how one composed a piece, but I remember with that quintet I was very concerned with the slow expansion of intervals, which determined the shape of the piece. And that's the sort of thing I'm still interested in.

How do pieces start?

It's a very visual thing. I have almost to be able to see the piece on the stage, to be aware of the space that it's going to be performed in. There has been a spatial element in a lot of my pieces, and the first seed is the combination of a visual image with a very nebulous sound world. Gradually both become clearer. There will be lots of sketches for the shape, and gradually each piece brings forth systems and processes that are uniquely its own. I've never used the same process twice in the same way.

What form might such a process take?

Well, in the first movement of the *Fantasia* for two orchestras there's a series of chords filtered initially from a low E flat pedal, gradually ascending and fanning out to the highest instruments in both orchestras at the centre of the platform. That was the first idea, both spatial and harmonic, and I had to work out a way of controlling that process. I achieved this by calculating the overall length of the section, keeping in mind how long the material needed to be fully developed and reasoned with, and then set about plotting harmonic areas within that timespan, creating a massive expanse of harmonic movement. This was calculated at first in minutes and seconds, and then transferred into bar lengths.

That sort of planning has come to me only in the last couple of years. Before that I was working very much by intuition: the Viola Concerto, for instance, was composed almost entirely intuitively. I wasn't really aware of the second movement until I'd finished the first. I just started with one particular sound and let it shoot out in all sorts of directions. Since then I've analysed it in classes, and it makes quite a lot of sense, but at the time it was just composed through. I couldn't work like that now.

Do you work on only one piece at a time?

Yes. I may jot down ideas for future pieces: I carry a little book around with me, because you get very interesting ideas when you least expect them.

What sort of ideas?

Melodic ideas, rhythmic ideas, or just instrumental combinations that I'd be interested in exploring.

Most of your works have been instrumental.

Yes. I've always been scared of setting words. There are poems I have a great love of, but I don't want to get in the way: they're perfect as they are. And it probably stems also from the fact that instrumental colour is so important to my initial ideas.

Would it ever happen that a poem would spark off an instrumental piece?

No, because the original idea has so much to do with the sound world of the instruments involved. On one occasion, however, a piece was triggered by an amazingly bleak landscape seen on the coast of Essex. This was *Path to Othona*, the third of the *Three Pieces* for chamber ensembles. The image of walking slowly towards a beautifully preserved Anglo-Saxon chapel, which gradually came more and more into perspective through very barren, flat, grey surroundings became a slow acceleration of pulses, bell strokes and attacks, while the spatial image was preserved by having an alto flute and three recorded alto flutes play circular music: melodic phrases being slowly repeated around the auditorium.

I've always been very turned on by landscape and colour, and this probably goes back to my father, because we used to have a lot of discussions about the relationship between music and painting. In his paintings there's always a point of focus, and that's something that's stuck in my mind: the idea of moving towards something.

Do you use the piano at all?

Just to check chords and phrases. I can't actually compose at the piano: I need to be immersed in the abstract instrumental sound. I always sketch on large paper – not in full score, but I have to have the orchestration there. Then it may change. You find ways of doing things better as your knowledge of the piece improves, because at the start there's this terror of the blank page and not having anything to generate music. That was probably why I became interested in processes, because I couldn't stand the stress of working in such an intuitive way.

Might the orchestration change again after a first performance?

Yes, definitely. In performance I often find that certain instrumental balances don't always work and need revision. I think the BBC's policy of doing a studio recording of a new commissioned orchestra piece prior to the concert performance is marvellous, and a true luxury for the composer.

Orchestration is not the only thing I revise after a first performance. Recently I've undertaken some minor surgery on my *Fantasia* – just taking out the odd bar here and there to tighten the continuity. These are things that would have gone unnoticed before hearing the piece in the concert hall.

In a way it's a shame there is such a thing as a first performance, because one would like the opportunity to change things before the work is presented in public. You go as far as you can with what you know while you're composing, and then it ought to be possible to work closely with the conductor, who may have some very intelligent ideas, and see things you haven't seen.

Do you enjoy first performances?

No, I hate them. I wouldn't say I hear a first performance, because I just can't concentrate.

Are you ever surprised by the length of a piece when it's being done for the first time?

That tends not to happen because of the way I work, starting with a timed process as I described with the first movement of the *Fantasia*. I don't make an arbitrary decision about that: it's a matter of trying to hear the whole process, in real time, before committing a note to paper.

But then when you get down to writing the detail, that may change the plan?

Yes, it could, but not so much now in my recent music. It wouldn't drastically alter my original structure but would hopefully give the music that moment-by-moment feeling of spontaneity which can often be achieved paradoxically by having a fairly rigid ground plan.

Do you have any ideas for big pieces you want to do in the future?

Yes. Recently I orchestrated a movie score for Stanley Myers, and that gave me the opportunity of working with the remarkable Fairlight computer synthesizer for the first time. I'm beginning to see a way of pursuing the sounds that are in my head with the computer hardware that's available today, and that's the only way I would go into electronic music: as an extension to what I've got in my head at the moment, rather than going into a studio and trying to generate sound for sound's sake.

I have a large piece brewing in that direction. Also, I have an idea for an opera, something that really fired my imagination while reading an extraordinary novel some months ago. I'm afraid it's early days and I don't want to go into details: I'd be terrified of giving the idea away!

5

Jonathan Harvey

I meet Harvey at his publisher's headquarters, where a small office is provided for us to talk before going on to a Stockhausen concert. The ambience is neutral, then, but coloured by the gentle melodies of his voice: the whole of his part in what follows really should have superscribed neumes in the manner of early chant notation. He himself, however, is satisfied with only a few minor changes to the wording.

How did you start composing?

I started when I was about 6, by sheer imitation. My father would sit in his armchair and I would sit at the piano, write a few notes down and play them, and he would make some suggestions, and I would try that. He was a businessman in Walsall, but he composed in a very small way pieces that are quite original and beautiful, I think: on a miniature scale, but very distinctive, a mixture of Fauré, Busoni, the Russians like Medtner and Skryabin, Debussy, and quite a lot of English influence as well. My first pieces were quite imitative of him, and of the many records he had. I was very keen on his compositions, on this rather mystical nature music: the forms were very anti-German, very fragmentary and fugitive, nothing solidly composed in the classical Viennese tradition. I think I did start off, not with such a complex style, but imitating him in my own way.

Then when I went to choir school, when I was about 11, I started having lessons with the choirmaster. That was St Michael's College, Tenbury: it was rather a special place, permeated with music through and through. Nearly everybody learned an instrument, and the choir sang matins and evensong every day, with hardly anybody to listen: it was glorious, in a wonderful Victorian chapel, almost gaudy in its colouring. I did write church music, but they didn't perform anything: I'm sure it was rather clumsy. However, they did perform a piece for three flutes and piano, and that got printed in the college magazine: that was my first frisson of being acknowledged.

Jonathan Harvey   *photo: John Carewe*

At that time the most pressing influence on me was sixteenth-century church music, but beyond that it was still my father's record collection that was the really exciting thing. In a way I feel I did all my listening up until the age of about 15. I was a really fanatical listener: I listened to everything on the radio, got the scores, went to the local library and record library. Many things I haven't heard since then: the popular concertos, ballet scores and so on. Many of them I don't hear now, even avoid.

What don't you avoid?

Well, of course there's an enormous amount. If we take opera to limit the answer, I find medieval Latin church drama very powerful, what I've heard of it, then Monteverdi, Mozart, and then there's quite a gap until Wagner: I find him a problem to be solved. There's something there to be discovered and understood, and until we've understood Wagner properly we can't really go on. Because he was totally uncompromising in his search for what one might call redemptive music, music that speaks of the most important things that music can speak of. He wasn't doing a job: he was deliberately setting out to seek something in a Holy Grail manner.

That's rather an interesting challenge. I don't say that Beethoven didn't do that in his own way – of course he did – but with Wagner it's more explicit.

I think he's trying to find what the nature of the will is, what are man's instinctual roots, and what it means to get beyond this will. The end of *Tristan* is an attempt to find release from the will, though in that work he comes to the pessimistic conclusion in the words (but not in the music) that there is no release, only an endless cycle. What interests me more is *Parsifal*, and how his solution for a transcendental music is to go back to thirds and third-dominated progressions, particularly in the Grail music and its expansions: the thirds within that theme are, I think, expanded to vast dimensions. And this seems to refer, semiconsciously perhaps, to music of the fifteenth and sixteenth centuries, where the roots tend to move in thirds – in so far as one can talk about root structures at all, but Wagner would have understood them in those terms. So the music of the Holy Grail, liberated, freed from sin and oppression, is a move back to modal Christian polyphony's harmony. It doesn't seem to be terribly satisfactory. But what does happen is that timbre – though I have doubts about whether timbre actually exists – but timbre becomes the main salvation of a work like *Parsifal*. This is the great discovery: beyond the suffering of Amfortas, chromaticism pushed to its emotional extreme, beyond the pseudo-religiosity of the Grail music, comes the radiance of the sound, the sheer light of it, the light-imbued alternation and fluidity of timbres.

But what are your doubts about the existence of timbre?

It's a very useful word for talking about instrumentation, but when you come into the electronic studio . . . I think we've come to the point where timbre has been dissolved, because vertically it's a matter of formant spectra, a subcategory of harmony, and horizontally it's a matter of both the evolution of spectra and the evolution of the fundamental pitch as melody. And culturally it's a matter of mental picture, of associating a sound semantically with an instrumental type. Everything really belongs to a more basic category, and you can't find timbre any more. Once you've studied timbre, as I have at IRCAM, you find that even the most innocent sound has surprisingly unique formal properties, and I think these will be more brought out and composed with. So one talks about form – form of the spectrum, form of its evolution – rather than timbre.

Going back to what you said about Wagner, it isn't surprising that a conversation with you should immediately be touching on questions of the spiritual in music. Was that always important?

It was very important to me as a choirboy. Music was associated with this wonderful ritual, and I did get quite into it: I felt very inspired, and I have beautiful memories of it. Then there was a long lapse until when I was at Cambridge and read Evelyn Underhill's *Mysticism*. After perhaps five years' holiday that book struck me forcibly, and from that moment forward I became rather preoccupied with mystical ideas. But I think my music was much more concerned with personal emotions, such as have been the main theme of Western music, because I was using that language. I wasn't conscious of trying to find a different feel, a different tone of voice, until quite a bit later.

In those days I was influenced by Schoenberg and Berg, and even a bit by Britten in one or two pieces. I was going to Erwin Stein for lessons while I was at Cambridge and from that moment on I began to get much more interested in the Viennese tradition: he made me study Mozart and Beethoven in a way I hadn't, to my shame, thought seriously necessary. At Cambridge I could quite easily have got away without studying any of the Viennese classics: in fact I specialized in the period 1400–1600. But Stein was giving me exercises in the classical style, following the Schoenberg methods, and then when he died I went to Hans Keller, who made me aware of this tradition and its rigours, its depths and its riches. Thinking about both the first and the second Viennese schools became very important for me. But in Cambridge I learned the usual things, which were not very useful, except for ear training and acoustics.

Then after Cambridge I went to Glasgow University, because I'd proposed what was rather too mystical an idea for a thesis: 'The Composer's Idea of his Inspiration'. It turned out to be quite factual, based on composers' letters and theoretical works: a categorization of opinion, relating it to contemporary thought, taking composers from the eighteenth century to the present day. But I went to Glasgow to do it because Cambridge wasn't keen on the idea.

Were you beginning to get performances by then?

A little bit. I think I was a slow starter. I did win a string quartet competition and had that played in London, and some things were done at Glasgow University. Then in 1964, when I left Glasgow and went to Southampton University, the SPNM performed my *Triptych* for five wind and piano, which is the first piece I still acknowledge. A little later I was taken up by Novello, and things began slowly to start off: *Ludus amoris* in 1969 was the first piece that really drew some attention.

But the lack of notice before certainly didn't stop me writing: I just love to write, and I'm not very happy when I'm not writing.

During this period, the mid-to late sixties, you became influenced by Stockhausen.

In 1966 it happened, the great Stockhausen conversion, when I went to Darmstadt for the first and only time, and Stockhausen was very much dominating proceedings. The entire set of piano pieces (the *Klavierstücke*) was performed by Kontarsky, and works of a less determinate sort: maybe *Plus-Minus*, *Telemusik* – I can't remember. Then I went to Royan the next year and heard a lot more: he was there with his group. And I became absolutely inspired and lit up by the sounds, which obviously I must have understood in some part of me, but which I didn't admit to understanding. It just seemed very exciting: those occasions are wonderful, when you come across a new dimension. I shall never forget that.

So I was impressed by those works of the 1950s and 1960s, works sometimes of a very obscure and harsh nature, like *Klavierstück VI*, but with new rhythms: long silences, strangely disrupted shapes, things not following in the rhythms one had been accustomed to. And yet there was sense to be made of it: it seemed somehow to mean something. And I began to try out some of these things myself. I've always been very open to influences like that, as must be obvious, though I've also always tried to incorporate them into myself.

I remember saying quite definitely to myself that I wanted to take things steadily, to develop a complex and powerful language step by step. I didn't want to do things where I was completely at sea, and it seemed to work out to plan. I'd thought of that quite early, as a student at Cambridge: I knew my style then was conservative by comparison with some of my friends, but I didn't want to rush things. I wanted just to elaborate by a natural process, like an organism: spontaneously, intuitively, nothing forced. So I didn't have that experience of plunging into incredibly complex scores.

Then I had a similar kind of encounter with Babbitt a few years later. I was supervising a thesis by Stephen Arnold, and he was going in very great detail into those pieces. I found it fascinating: the depth of structure Babbitt was using and the extremely intricate, elegant patterns, which seemed to match the kind of thing I'd been discovering in the first and second Viennese schools. So I very much wanted to investigate Babbitt: that was one of the main reasons I went to Princeton in 1969. It wasn't so much an emotional experience, being overwhelmed with new feelings, but being overwhelmed with the tremendous power of integrity and respect for the possibilities of music. I think for a while I went under, and I had to fight a little bit to retain my sense of simple spontaneity within an intellectual framework.

Did you see Stockhausen and Babbitt as providing indications in your own quest for a spiritual music?

Yes, certainly that was one of the great things that appealed to me about Stockhausen. Here was a man who was quite explicitly seeing in music the language of some greater consciousness. There was a feel to it that seemed to me right. A very striking thing was the quality of the sound, in the electronic pieces and in the music he made with his group: one heard this immersion in sound, this famous exploitation of the static sound. One heard values of an absolute nature, as opposed to the relative nature of music, which has an argumentative grammar. One heard sounds that were extremely beautiful, that sucked one in, in which one could exist as if they were another kind of reality. And I felt even in the more serial and strict works this love of sound for its spiritual nature, for its paradoxical ability both to speak of something beyond and to be itself more intensely.

But Babbitt and serialism: that was another stream. I did feel that this language brought with it a release from the problems of Wagner, the problems of a music that seemed to belong to an age that was passing. I love tonal music – needless to say – and I write it quite often, but it does seem not to belong to what I would like music to belong to. I'd like music to speak of, to herald and to prophesy a better world, less entangled with personal egoistic emotions.

Serialism and electronic music, with its ability to get into unknown sorts of sound, both suggest a new world which could be called spiritual; or one might speak of a greater awareness of what is. It's a matter of the expansion of the narrow self. Of course, there's no magic in making new sounds – anyone can do it with a toy synthesizer. The magic is in the composer inviting people to expand their individuality into a new region and thereby experience selflessness, egolessness, without losing the sense of a connection. It's the function of art to make one expand one's consciousness, so that a narrow, insecure, individual self disappears and a larger self, the absolute, is brought to consciousness.

I think this can be achieved when unfamiliar sounds take one, literally, into an unfamiliar world. The art of the great composer is to make music so strong that it takes people ever further towards this egolessness which is not nevertheless a loss of the larger self. And it can only be achieved by lengthy attempts, sometimes succeeding but very often failing, to create things that are genuinely new.

There's also a specific thing which I personally am after. I have the feeling there's some new type of music hovering on the horizon, which I can glimpse very fleetingly now and then, and which does seem like a change of consciousness, as the move into tonal music was around 1600. There's a change back to a certain objectivity.

You say this is a personal intuition, but I wonder if it isn't shared by other composers: Stockhausen, for example.

And perhaps Boulez most of all. Boulez particularly seeks balanced universes of sound, poised without any rootedness, and this to my ear tends to come closer to the objective musics of our own distant past and of the East – objective in that they're more concerned with collective and spiritual existence. But that's only a change of emphasis, an emphasis more on the absolute than the relative, more on the 'being' qualities of music than on the 'becoming' qualities of climaxes, tension, relaxation and all the rest.

Isn't this a change more in the way music is heard than in the way it's composed? Can't one have the kind of experience you were describing when one listens to Bach or Beethoven?

I'm not sure. If you question composers you might find they are less interested in finding a music concerned with the life of the emotions than with reflecting a more expanded experience. I think Stockhausen would say so, and Boulez. Such experience includes hearing Bach and Beethoven through new ears too.

You mentioned a vision you have of a new kind of music, but how do individual works arrive?

In general it's the feel of the whole work that I get first of all. I jot down things in notebooks – fairly general, often in words rather than musical shapes. The work has to be about something: it has to have a split-second identity even if it lasts two hours. It has to have something you can sum up in a quarter of a second: this charged moment which explodes. Usually it would be a moment in the work, or it might be quite an extended passage, but everything will grow from there. Sometimes an idea will sprout two quite contrasted ideas, and then I might try to integrate them into a piece: they might be the beginning and the end, or I might alternate them.

Might the original idea be a melody, as in recent Stockhausen?

Yes. Obviously one has to have the inspiration that it's going to be that kind of melodic, singing piece: it depends on the instruments and what one wants to do with them. Though I do increasingly feel melody as the bearer of feeling, whereas earlier it would have been harmony: it seems more and more powerful, the idea of a line as strong and expressive.

But I don't plan things out the way Stockhausen does: it's quite a dangerous model, to be so systematic. It's all right for him. He has an exceptionally logical mind and an exceptionally emotional nature.

Presumably an electronic work will require more advance organization.

Yes. For instance, *Mortuos plango* I did plan out in outline. I did an analysis of the bell before I went to IRCAM, and that provided me with a clue for the structure of the piece: I took the eight lowest partials as dominant notes of eight sections, and I simply made the higher ones shorter. That was planned out, and also the percentages of bell and boy to feature in each section, and a few strategies for computer work in transformation and hybridization – but that all became clear only when I got to IRCAM and could find out what was possible and what was artistically interesting.

Often the composing at IRCAM is slipped in between programming, scribbled down in the odd hour and then put to the test. And the odd thing about the work there is that it's very slow. I feel very much at the edge: it's absolutely new, and it's very exciting to be slowly, inch by inch, doing totally undiscovered things.

6

Oliver Knussen

The scene is his den in the Knussens' ground-floor London flat. One wall is shelved with records, another with scores and books, but these things also tumble in massive piles all over the floor. I ask if this is the kind of chaos where everything has its known place. 'It used to be.' There is, however, room for an upright piano, a table under the window and two chairs, where we sit, plied with tea and huge slices of cake. Tiny toy owls stare on benignly from across the room.

Thereafter Knussen becomes a regular character in the life of our telephone, as we are brought up to date with his revision of the transcript, which eventually arrives just as the book goes into production.

You had a very early public beginning to your career, and I wonder how you now feel about the music you were writing in your teens, like the First Symphony.

I still find the First Symphony quite interesting as an early example of the odd relationship between means and ends in my music – it sounds something like a 'tonal' American symphony written by a Russian who knows his Britten, though in fact the first three movements were composed almost exclusively with twelve-note procedures of a rather basic variety. Whether it's actually any good or not, I haven't decided! It's withdrawn for the time being, but at some point I may trim it and make it into a piece for youth orchestras.

Considering that I wrote it when I did, the First Symphony is not bad, but it was put into a context that was I suppose inevitably too big for it. In retrospect, the long-term advantage was that I got a few years of extremely beneficial and practical orchestration lessons out of it: both from that piece and the two or three I wrote immediately afterwards (the Concerto for Orchestra especially), simply by hearing straight away what I'd written down, played well. That experience was nearly unique in our day, and I'm still very grateful for it. The disadvantages – the PR hype, and the understandable resentment of some older colleagues who *deserved*

Oliver Knussen   *photo: John Carewe*

those performances – fizzled out after a short while, as these things tend to. The potential danger of the situation was not entirely lost on me at the time, and I simply decided to go away and start again from scratch somewhere else.

The only thing I regret is that although the demand for sizeable orchestral things forced me to stretch my legs very early on, it also possibly made me a bit too cautious. It's difficult to take big risks under a spotlight at that age, and the smaller things which I was writing for myself at that time were in some respects more interesting, more exploratory than what I allowed myself to do in those larger 'public' pieces (*Processionals* and *Masks* are the surviving examples). Luckily, these tendencies were encouraged by my teacher in America, Gunther Schuller, to whom I owe a lot: the Second Symphony, which I think is my first really characteristic thing, was written while I was working with him, and my orchestral thinking certainly owes more than a little to his example.

Apart from Ives, which I've always adored, the American music which most affected the way I compose was Elliott Carter's. The first time I went to New York I bought the two-piano score and record of the Piano Concerto (which had just come out) and a score of the Double Concerto, and spent a lot of time trying to unravel them. I'd never seen anything that looked so fearsome but was actually built practically from very basic materials – pulses and intervals. And I was especially impressed by the attitude of treating individual intervals (or pairs of intervals) with respect. It's harder to rationalize *why* one particular note choice is made than *when* it occurs, and yet the details all contribute positively to a very powerful, monumental sense of large form. I learned from Carter's music that for me the crucial things to sort out precisely and hold to are the big shape of the piece, and a clearly defined vocabulary for it (Britten had told me almost exactly the same thing when I went to see him for advice much earlier). Once those are in place, you can compose with any degree of stringency or freedom called for by the moment.

But I've never consciously restricted myself to any one type of compositional grammar for long. I've always allowed each work to dictate its own rules, as it were, and then moved on – though of course it would be strange if certain approaches, at least, were not retained across works. You see, I've always had the feeling that composers of my generation were *encouraged* to be myopic, and to do one thing too much, perhaps. If I find myself faced with a compositional situation which is familiar, or that I've dealt with before, I'll try to find a quite different way of articulating it, of solving it.

How do you start a piece?

I usually have a very specific idea of the sound of one moment, like a photograph, which I then write down. It might be just a pair of chords, or a line, or a bit of layered polyphonic texture, but always instrumentally conceived from the beginning – I can't conceive pitch in the abstract, divorced from timbre. Then I try to work out the background of that idea, where it's come from and what it implies, and design the rest of the piece out of that. I've always tended to feel a responsibility to this original idea, to finding a form which the 'given' belongs in – though sometimes things don't work out the way they are supposed to, and a work can hang fire because altogether the wrong route was chosen.

I sometimes think that I don't ever really finish: I tinker endlessly with matters of detail because the textures of my music, though they're often very elaborate, are also transparent to a large degree, and audible detailing is critical. Aside from which, in order for a whole to be convincing, its components must function properly.

What sort of details might bother you?

Imagine a situation where a slow chordal processional is unfolding across a highly detailed texture with a very rapid internal rate of change. If the balance between the two kinds of movement isn't right, you get a sort of bad counterpoint: it doesn't have the maximum amount of tension between the parts. These concerns – and the other one of changing notes to improve a line or clarify harmony – lead to the sort of corrections you might make to a sixteenth-century counterpoint exercise.

Except that the rules are your own.

True, although one's own rules are frequently hard to rationalize, and therefore to bend! But there are always contextual harmonic concerns to be taken into account, or odd rhythmical number workings going on. For example, sizeable sections of some pieces are scaffolded by big polyrhythms which govern overlapping cycles of short phrases: say, one phrase will recur six times while another recurs five times over the same period of time (this is again a Carter-derived thing, of course), so that one implies a tension between two units which begin at the same moment, pull apart and meet together at the end.

But the repetitions won't be exact?

Apart from the basic scheme of cross-pulses, which will usually be kept intact, we're not really talking about repetition at all (I have a basic guilt complex about unvaried repetition, except in very special circumstances!). It's probably closer if you picture continuous, simultaneous stretches of through-composed music which have been arbitrarily cut into short slabs and then separated according to the pulse scheme, although of course the composition may have been conceived in the reverse of that procedure. And I may find that these slabs are too close for too long, or too far apart for too long, so that there's no tension: in almost every case it's actually a question of tension between parts that will bother me. I'll spend days puzzling over a problem like that, and then when it's played people say, 'But your music sounds effortless!' It's quite ironic, really – but then I suppose one doesn't 'hear' the effort in Brahms, or Debussy either, to take two favourite composers of mine – though I think Berg is probably the composer I feel closest to, and one certainly senses it there.

But I don't regard a high degree of self-scrutiny as anything less than necessary. I was fortunate in that my first teacher, John

Lambert, insisted on the avoidance of easy formulae or padding –
unjustified literal repetition of any kind in particular – which is an
attitude I suspect he partly inherited from *his* teacher Nadia
Boulanger. I think this is probably the root of my obsession with
following through the implications of what you could call musical
cross-hatching. For example, in the first interlude of *Where the Wild
Things Are* there's a long horn melody over mixed piano and harp
arpeggios on each beat. The arpeggiated chords start at two notes
and build to twelve, while the actual harmony shifts gradually.
Now the way those chords are distributed and arpeggiated each
time was more than a week's work. It may seem nonsensical to fuss
that way, particularly as this is only one of three or four layers
operating in that section, but the point to me is that you can focus
your ear, if you so choose, on that accompaniment figure and find
that those arpeggiations are doing something constructive.

*Is this a feeling of responsibility to your material in itself, or of
responsibility to the listener?*

In an ideal world, those would be one and the same, of course!
More realistically, I suppose, one's approach must be to ensure that
the idea and broad design of a work is crystal clear to anyone who
wants to be receptive to it – which implies also a willingness on the
part of the listener to try to get on to its wave-length in return. The
working out of other, less immediately perceptible levels *must* be
carried out with the same degree of care, obviously to facilitate the
clearest possible articulation of form, also to try to achieve a model
balance between order and spontaneity or fantasy, and finally
because I think any other attitude amounts to a contempt for the art
itself. There is absolutely no justification for applying mass-
production criteria to the composition of serious music today:
alarmingly few people want it, and the sheer quantity of music
being written far exceeds any real demand for it, particularly in the
orchestral field.

That particular problem is awesome, and is probably one reason
why I take my performing very seriously indeed – even though I
don't regard conducting as important to me careerwise, because
basically I do it to subsidize the composing. But I do feel a
responsibility to hammer some of the vast body of contemporary
music into performance. In London now, orchestral programming
has got to the point where the problem isn't so much the difficulty
for performers or audience of new music as the unfamiliarity of the
composer's name! Unfamiliar music that is potentially popular – or

at least 'mainstream' in some way – is relegated to contemporary-music channels, where it doesn't really belong either, or only tangentially (I'm thinking of composers like Holloway, Del Tredici, Ruders or the recent work of Takemitsu). There is no route any more for suitable works to enter a central orchestral repertoire here. The blame for this, I feel, lies fairly and squarely with orchestral managements, who are scared – no doubt for perfectly sound financial reasons, these days – to risk anything at all for new work. But where does that leave the *really* difficult composers? In America, even the most conservative major orchestras feel obliged to do a reasonable amount of unfamiliar music each season, partly because programming responsibility is still largely in the hands of the music directors, and some of these conductors do still have a conscience. I suppose I can afford actively to worry about these things because I've been quite well looked after, performancewise, by some of those American orchestras and by my association with the London Sinfonietta (which is probably the single most bene-ficial thing that has happened to my musical life since I began in this profession). But despite the very active compositional scene here at the moment, the provision of a backbone of large-scale perform-ances is left almost entirely to the BBC and the Sinfonietta, who have a nearly impossible corrective task to do.

Are you optimistic that things will change?

I don't think it can get much worse, so in that respect I'm very optimistic indeed.

Perhaps change might come through the opera houses, where these days the repertory is often far more adventurous than it is in the Festival Hall.

Well, from the *audience*'s point of view the musical theatre is a good place to open the ears to unfamiliar symbols, because the 'story' and the theatrical spectacle can function as access points – provided the relationship between these and the music is coherent, and natural enough. Reciprocally, a good libretto will draw from its composer the widest range of real expressive gesture possible within the confines of his language – often, I suspect, more than the composer is aware of himself, at the start. But I'm not sure that most of those responsible for determining what is and isn't played (thereby decisively influencing taste) think quite so positively about these things. And one does make the same kind of mistake oneself, sometimes: I remember warning my American grandfather – who was a music-loving osteopath – that *Moses und Aron*, for which he had been offered a ticket, was probably much too difficult and heavy-going for him. He took that as a challenge, went to *Moses* and relished telling me that he had 'loved every minute of it'. (It wasn't Peter Hall's production, by the way!)

I must add a little story about my own experience with *Wild Things*, which is – I think – a very accessible piece anyway, partly due to the subject matter and partly to the wide stylistic net thrown out by the music. When Glyndebourne did it at the National Theatre, the only people who – in my earshot, anyway – complained about the difficulty of the music were some music teachers! Strange, isn't it, that the children present apparently accepted the music on its own terms as appropriate to what they saw, as did most of the adults! But there seems to be something triggered off – some negative, judgemental thing – in certain people who are in the uncomfortable corner between the actual production of work and the audience (be they administrators, programmers or middle-men of other kinds) which *over*reacts to music they feel incapable of judging, regardless of the actual response of the people they are 'protecting'.

Did you write it for children?

I certainly had always wanted to write something for children to *hear*, as I'm not particularly good at devising music for them to participate in (I have tried, on several occasions), and *Wild Things* is certainly the best present I could think of for them. But Maurice Sendak, you know, says he doesn't write his books for children: he writes them for himself, and as expressions of his own inner world, and I would have to say that I felt exactly the same thing writing *Wild Things* – although a lot of feelings I had forgotten from my early childhood spontaneously returned during the composition, which made me realize with even more force what a profoundly truthful artist Maurice Sendak is.

I was thinking of the comparison that's been made with L'Enfant et les sortilèges, *which wasn't written for children at all.*

But *L'Enfant* is sophisticated, witty and also poignant in quite a different way from what Maurice and I are trying to do – in fact we discussed that very thing in our very first conversation together, that while we both adored the Ravel, we wanted to avoid the 'knowingness' so characteristic of it. That, in my view, is from Colette – what is heart-breaking about *L'Enfant* is the sincerity and simplicity of Ravel's response, however sophisticated the musical means employed (the very beginning and end, and the scenes with the Cinder and the Princess are the best examples of what I mean). It is, however, a superb model in terms of scale and pacing, and those children lucky enough to know it well certainly do adore it, myself included.

I approached the composition of *Wild Things* by remembering what 'magic' music I liked best as a child, which was the early Stravinsky ballets, *Daphnis*, the Debussy *Nocturnes*, parts of *Boris Godunov* – all of which I knew from records – also Mahler 1 and the Britten *Sea Interludes*, which are equally magical and nostalgic for me. And then there were other pieces I heard on the radio at that time – I was about 9 or 10, I suppose – which sank in somewhere deep: things like Schoenberg's *Herzgewächse*, Stravinsky's *Orpheus*, perhaps even some early Henze and the Boulez *Mallarmé Improvisations*. I realized that it was *all* those immediate responses I could begin from, and then I simply started to build the best piece I possibly could, without stylistic inhibition. Obviously, you wind up with music that half-consciously refers to things a hundred years apart within a few bars, but in practice that doesn't seem to matter, because the view of them all is mine, I hope.

In fact, these stylistic worries only do matter if you have an *ex*clusive view of music; I tend to regard something I don't 'get' as *my* problem – and if it's well-made music by a composer who is intelligent, *I'd* better do something about it (within reason, anyway).

Do you try to do that, to expand your sympathies?

I'm told by well-wishers that they are too wide for my own good already! But there are some indisputably great composers who I have problems with, Haydn being one and Verdi the biggest block of all – I don't understand what it's doing, and I don't even like the way *Falstaff* sounds. So *Falstaff* has been bedtime reading quite a lot lately, as I try to work out what I'm missing.

Simply for the exercise, or because it might be useful?

Well, I'm setting a libretto with an awful lot of words to get across and that moves very fast, and *Falstaff*'s a fairly good example, to put it mildly! Sometimes I'll come up against similar problems when I'm conducting. Often, in order to do a work you like, you also have to do things which you wouldn't choose to do (and hopefully one can't tell which is which in performance!). So I try to approach those as a discipline – to devise a good rehearsal method, and to approach the work as if I'd written it myself.

Do you enjoy conducting your own music?

I enjoy doing early performances, because some pieces of mine
have suffered from early performances which were much too slow:
a lot of my music is very fast and hard to play, but it doesn't make
sense as shape if you do some parts under tempo. So I like to
establish the tempi and have a tape made. Also I can make
immediate adjustments (to dynamics, doublings, etc.) much quicker
if I'm in the driving seat. (I think composer-conducted recordings,
for example the Elgar or Stravinsky ones, are the best possible
guide to the way the music should be *articulated*, whatever the
performance conditions and however variable the tempi from
performance to performance.) I have been very lucky, however, in
finding early on conductors like Michael Tilson Thomas and
Simon Rattle who have an intuitive understanding of what I'm
after, in their quite different ways. Many of my colleagues have not
been so lucky, and that's one reason that I like to conduct their
music also. As well as the fact that preparing performances efficiently
in a short period of time is the best possible antidote to being a very
slow composer – or one who works fast in short bursts and then
thinks a lot.

Do you keep regular hours for composing?

I'm trying to learn how to. My regular hours used to be from 11 at
night till 4 in the morning, largely because that's when the phone
doesn't ring and there are less things to think about. But it's very
difficult to keep regular hours if you're under a lot of psychological
pressure because you're late, as I often have been. You tend to
work extremely hard for two or three months on absurdly little
sleep, and then stop dead for the same amount of time because
you're exhausted.

Do you work on more than one piece at a time?

Not exactly. I have a big piece on the go for three to five years: the
Concerto for Orchestra, the Third Symphony, *Wild Things* and
now *Higglety Pigglety Pop!* Other pieces are composed against their
background presence, in gaps between periods of work on them,
but never at the same time.

What's the next big piece?

A large orchestral triptych, rather along the lines of the Debussy
Images, which I tend to think of as a more successful single unit than

most people seem to, although I agree to a certain extent that the three don't quite knit, which perhaps is the challenge.

I wrote three chamber pieces in the mid-1970s which were conceived quite independently but wound up as three different aspects of the same thing, which is what I suppose attracts me to planning a piece that way. I knew that one of them was going to be a purely technical exercise, to find out how much variety of harmony I could extract from rotations of a single tetrachord: that was *Autumnal*, the violin piece. Another was planned simply as a sequence of seven different arcs spun out between repetitions of a chordal refrain, but the notes were completely intuitive: that was *Sonya's Lullaby*, which sounds just as harmonically tight as *Autumnal*, because it benefited from the experience. And in the oboe *Cantata*, which I wrote all through that period, with the two other pieces in the gaps, I was simply desperate to write a good piece for a combination I didn't like. I had terrible trouble with that piece, with much starting and stopping, and as a result it became a thesaurus of virtually every harmonic usage in my music to date.

If you listen to those pieces in sequence, they somehow actually fit, but that wasn't planned at all. There's probably something emotional that binds them together, too: I don't know. I don't like to think consciously about those things.

Yet you must have to when you're writing operas.

I think the expressive character of music is very dangerous stuff to be dealing with *consciously* if you're a composer. Obviously you make certain observations as you go, like the dreaded supernatural function of A flat in *Wild Things* for example, which was obvious to me almost from the start of my work on it. But otherwise one decides *what* it is one wants to write, and then simply does it as best one can, often learning *how* to compose it as you go. You don't plumb your depths to write a terribly self-expressive piece. You do it with technique, and hope that it talks back to you when you finally hear it.

I suspect Brahms felt the same way, or Tchaikovsky or Berg, who certainly all approached the actual composition technically, however affecting the end product.

Everything you've said suggests that you see a gap, and a necessary gap, between means and ends.

Yes I do. There are an infinite number of ways, for example, to build up a crescendo from a single low note in the bass to a climactic tutti, everything from simply adding a chord note by note over a tam-tam roll, which would be the commercial solution, to making some incredible elaborate polytextured, polyrhythmic layering machine. The choice of *how* must be made just as carefully as the choice of *what*, in relation to context and intention. Also, for that matter, the choice of length, which is crucial: decisions like that I make very objectively before I've written a note. You have to be constantly alive to the implications of what you do within the world which you're putting together.

I also feel very strongly that one has a responsibility to the performer, if you're writing for instrumentalists and singers, as I have done exclusively. I try very hard not to give a musician something that doesn't justify the amount of time needed to learn to play it, and also take into account the musical characteristics of the people I'm writing for – if I know them, that is. Some composers regard that as an intolerable straitjacket; I find it the most stimulating restraint in the world.

Might you compose something electronic in the future?

If you deal in slabs of time which you then divide in certain ways, then you're always going to come up with rhythmic things which you have to modify or renotate for practicality. I have many ideas which I'd like to realize, where the result would still be almost impossibly hard from an ensemble point of view (*Coursing* is an example of what I mean, I suppose), and it would be nice, one day, to let the numbers run wild. So I might, yes.

7

Brian Ferneyhough

Ferneyhough is our king over the water: teaching in Germany, and performed much more on mainland Europe than in England, he is not to be available in London during the period of these interviews. He suggests a postal dialogue, whereby he will respond to questions I submit, and to help me in my part of the task he is good enough to send me offprints of a couple of his recent essays; a book of further writings, in Italian, arrives from his publisher. The questions are duly composed and dispatched, courteously acknowledged and then answered: 'I have tried to be as spontaneous as may be,' his covering letter assures me, 'standing at the keyboard and thinking directly into it without much meditation or subsequent revision.' The result is a sheaf of pages bristling with single-spaced, double-sided typing. I raise one supplementary question, on Walter Benjamin, which 'threatened to unleash quite a flow of ideas completely unsuited to the proposed context, so that I finally came up with a paragraph not all too desiccated'. I become convinced of what he might call an 'analogical correspondence' between a composer's music and his prose style.

Can you remember when you started to compose, and why? What sort of musical experience and education had you had at that time?

I probably still have the original score of the first piece of mine ever to be performed, albeit not in public. I seem to remember that it was a march for brass band, written when I was 13 or 14. This was just before my 'official' studies in harmony began, so the piece must have been quite primitive, although I remember the general sound as being reasonably idiomatic. Since I had begun conducting the band in which I played on odd occasions, it may have been this which led me to begin composing too. One of the advantages of the band system was the high level of interpenetration of roles. Anyone interested more in the organization and layout of the whole than in a specific instrument has plenty of opportunity to observe as much detail as he wants over the space of a few years. By the age of 18 I had played most of the band instruments, apart from the very extremes of high and low, and this had given me quite an (unordered) insight into all sorts of compositional techniques and textures. Allied to this was the complete catholicity of style, ranging from soft-core pop up to quite demanding pieces by Holst or Vaughan Williams, for instance. My first confrontation with the 'classics' occurred in this fashion, in fact.

When and how did you come to know the 'avant-garde' music of the fifties?

My first encounters with major 'advanced' scores of the fifties and sixties were completely fortuitous. If I am not mistaken, the Coventry City Library did not exactly distinguish itself in this regard, but did contain Searle's very Lisztian Piano Sonata – a neglected work, in some ways, although very ambiguous in its relationship with serial technique, of course. Entering the Birmingham School of Music brought access to the music section of the municipal library, which contained a lot of items collected according to principles that still remain unclear to me. Alongside single scores by several post-war neo-conservatives there were interesting examples of the Schoenberg circle, such as his own Wind Quintet (in the piano–flute transcription) and the Piano Variations of Skalkottas, which latter impressed me quite a lot. Aside from one or two Webern works there was a mass of quasi-serial symphonies and suites which I quickly laid aside. Coming across at least one Webern score there led me to buy as many others as I could afford, in particular those having a more lasting influence, such as the Bagatelles and the opus 5 quartet pieces. My earliest efforts at twelve-tone writing came after reading the *Grove* entry (as the only literature accessible to me), and reflect the Webern influence quite strongly.

Stockhausen's *Kontra-Punkte* entered my growing library quite early, as did his *Klavierstücke I–IV* and Boulez's Flute Sonatina. All these works made a lasting, if still diffuse and half-digested impression, being more important for reasons of motivation than of actual technique.

All this was of a purely visual order, since performances were few and far between. My earliest key experience in terms of actual sound must have been hearing a 45 rpm record of the second and third movements of Varèse's *Octandre* when I was 15 or so. I remember being tremendously impressed by the uncompromising clarity and cleanness of sound, and it was at that moment that composing became my definitive goal in life. The radio provided sporadic nourishment, of course: in this way I came across *Gruppen* and was struck immediately by its obvious strength and fecundity, even though I had no idea at all as to its aesthetic or mode of

Brian Ferneyhough   *photo: Manfred Melzer*

construction. I must have heard a lot of English first performances too, although no specific pieces come immediately to mind. Lack of scores and of direct contact with other composers made the construction of a satisfactory overview practically impossible, of course.

Several books were quite important at the outset. *Die Reihe* on Webern in particular, also Leibowitz on the second Viennese school provided a first tentative insight into questions of form and basic issues of technique. As far as teachers were concerned during those years, I drew a complete blank, since Birmingham provided no instruction in composition. Even more important was the lack of direct interaction with other students with similar interests, so that my early development – up until the age of 25 really – was very slow and insecure. At the time this was naturally very depressing; later I came to the view that the obstinacy and creative independence thus fostered were quite valuable properties to have, and might not have been gained in any other way.

What led you to study with de Leeuw and Huber? What did you learn from them?

My first venture outside Britain as a composer was to the 1968 Gaudeamus Week in Bilthoven. More than any other single event this first intensive encounter with like-minded individuals encouraged and strengthened me. It was quite a revelation to be able to defend a radical point of view without reserve and to be accepted without prejudice. Being able to hear live performances of quite complex and demanding works meant a lot to me too, so that I resolved to move across to the Continent at the earliest opportunity, and the chance came through the award of the Mendelssohn Scholarship for that year. My first stop was in Amsterdam, in the class of Ton de Leeuw, since I had wanted to return to Holland above all. This winter stay was not altogether fortunate, since it was not a fruitful time for me compositionally: nevertheless, the continual contact with a thoughtful composer of an older generation was very important, even though discussions were not always centred on my own compositional activity (or lack of it).

My money soon ran out, and it was only the intervention of Klaus Huber (whom, like de Leeuw, I had met in Bilthoven) in gaining for me a stipend of the City of Basle that allowed me to continue on the path I had chosen. I stayed in his masterclass at the Basle Academy for two years, until the end of 1971. Although by that time my own technique was more or less fully formed, I still remember that period with warmth for the supportive attitude of Huber towards my projects. I was composing *Firecycle Beta* – a work with no hope of performance at that time – and the lengthy period of continuity thus afforded enabled me to bring that massive fragment to an end only shortly after my official studies had been concluded.

What is the nature of musical influence? Do you still feel yourself to be influenced by elders and contemporaries, or indeed by younger composers?

I don't think that my music is particularly influenced by others in a pinpointable stylistic sense, since the impetus of my own collection of ideas and techniques must surely be more weighty than momentary points of coincidence or sympathy. My teaching involves me so intensely with the thoughts and stylistic preoccupations of other composers that I have evolved methods of draining it off immediately after teaching activity has finished for the day.

Influence doesn't have to be all that concrete, though, does it? I mean, sometimes one can be decisively influenced by a simple attitude of optimism or creative energy without identifying with the ultimate product. Of course, I can't at all eliminate the possibility of subconscious influence of whatever sort, but, given my extremely slow rate of composition, this is, I assume, minimal.

Not that influence is always necessarily a bad thing, of course! I can think of many composers who have benefited enormously from exposure to the works of others. It may be that, as one gets older, the possible damage arising from such absorptions becomes more specifically threatening, and this would have to be taken into account.

What do you learn from teaching?

The infinite variety of nuance comprising human personality; flexibility in appreciating and thinking through the insights of others; how to avoid imposing my world-view and musical aesthetic on others; and – not least? – patience.

In many respects your music is remarkable for its consistency over a period now of twenty years. Does it seem so consistent to you? What is your present attitude to your works of the 1960s and 1970s? Do you have an urge to go back and revise? Are you writing the kinds of works you might have expected to be writing?

I like to think that my works have remained consistent but not immobile. Only in retrospect is it possible to assess the real degree of coherence in passing from one work to the next, since as the composer I of course can't extricate myself from the web of memories and associations woven during the period of writing. At the time I often feel the differences between two pieces to be larger than they later seem to be. Even quite small shifts of technique or aesthetic emphasis take on enormous significance when seen close to.

On the whole I suppose my career has carried on much as it began, with the need continually to reformulate and reassess the field of forces lying between more innovative and radical compositional tendencies and those qualities tending towards a more recuperative, consolidatory profile. Several swings of this sort can be distinguished without difficulty in my progress over the last two decades. Like most composers, I expect, I have several times tried travelling back into the past in order to 'rewrite history' via the revision or recomposition of an earlier, rejected work. With me this has never once been a successful enterprise – largely because each work is so firmly embedded, for good or ill, in its particular biographical and stylistic developmental context that any attempt to create a latterday 'creation myth' for it synthetically is pretty absurd. I haven't tried this for quite a while, anyway, although I do on occasion look back through works written many years ago, since I find them to contain – in spite of all embarrassments and obvious inadequacies – facets of myself which, because of inevitably increased goal-consciousness and refinement of means, have tended to fade into obscurity. Sometimes I've found the odd point there which has given me a hint to follow up in my encounter with current creative issues. Sometimes, too, I find remarkable parallels with former ideas or manipulational techniques of the present time, albeit in a nascent state.

As regards the final part of your question, I'm not sure twenty years is the sort of timespan that allows for coherent and concrete prediction. In the late sixties my horizon was necessarily limited far more to the acquisition of a technique adequate to the sorts of sounds I had in my head than so many years later, where the perspective is obviously wider (although not necessarily more authentic, of course). On the whole, I think my younger self would have recognized himself in the sort of thing I am aiming at today. At least, I hope so.

Do you recognize anything English in your music?

There have been so many attempts to define the nature of English music that I am not about to embark on another! Most such definitions revolve around the premise that Britain has a genius for keeping a weather eye open for new developments, while eliminating from them many of their more obviously *outré* qualities. This may have some truth in it: on the other hand, the essence of a great talent is always to evade such neat and conveniently vague pinning-down. Probably every country has its share of composers who, by being less innovative, display all the more clearly whatever the common denominators of a 'national consciousness' might be.

There seem to be three main issues here. First there is the nature of originality and its role in imposing new definitions of national qualities by *force majeure* (that is, how the fingerprints and idiosyncrasies of one individual can be adopted, so to speak, on a higher and more abstract level). Secondly, there is the type and intensity of relationship found between English composers and the totality of social institutions that engender, support and live from compositional activity. I'm convinced that this has a vast influence on a young composer's nascent stylistic awareness and his subsequent development, but it is something that affected me relatively little, since I left Britain without having come into close contact with these regulatory mechanisms. Then thirdly there is a sense in which any stimulus, however accidental, received in and through the English environment leads to the formation of an English composer.

As I said at the beginning of this interview, the works and styles I ran across early on may not have originated in Britain for the most part, but it was the British musical infrastructure that conditioned the order, quantity, as well as availability of secondary information of this input, so that one could plausibly argue that I am a child of my place and time at least in this respect. On the other hand, I never felt intensely moved to take upon myself some reintegration of aspects of the English past such as was rather current in the late sixties. There is much English music from previous epochs that I admire intensely – Tallis, for example – without this fact having had much to do with my musical sense of identity, I think.

How does a work begin – from a vision of the whole, from a particular idea, from a particular sonority?

When does a work *begin*? There have been occasions when I experienced a sudden sensation that a work was *there* – not specific musical materials, necessarily, but the sense of active possibility. More often, a piece has crept out of a mass of loosely interrelated ideas, taking on concrete form almost at the last moment. This can go so far that I literally have no idea how a work will end until shortly before the moment of having to decide between a number of more or less equal possibilities. If a certain instrument is involved right from the outset, that is a different matter entirely, since it is clear that the suggestive power of a particular sonority leads to a form of spontaneous generation over and beyond any more abstract ideas present. Normally I come very soon to a sort of 'mental sculpture', which has a certain mass and external shape, and which can be turned round in my mind and modified if necessary. The ideas of 'energy', 'weight', 'mass' and 'momentum' thus have an important role to play in my initial formulations. Other pieces emerge only after protracted battles with an already extant idea, such as the piano piece *Lemma-Icon-Epigram*, or the *Time and Motion Study* series. This is usually much more agonizing, since the idea is constantly undergoing mutations caused by the development of the purely musical techniques and it is easy to get the feeling of the project chasing its own tail.

What processes, mental and written, may be involved between conception and completion?

Usually long periods of unfocused thinking for a start. This allows ideas to order themselves 'under the horizon', leading frequently to the most astounding Jungian 'synchronicities' when the active phase has begun. Then follow sporadic bursts of experimentation with new and already used techniques, during which sudden intuitions as to further developments are followed up, and the vital lines of communication established along which disparate ideas and forces can be channelled. After that, I usually know what the piece is 'about', and have become familiar with the current state of my tools, so that a period of interpenetration between the concrete and the more formally dispositional can begin. This might again last a long time. Once the large-scale form has finally been established I begin tentative composition, often not at the beginning of the piece. Bit by bit, the details of the mosaic become more firmly outlined; rather more slowly the elements take on that aura of secondary properties with which the *real* act of composing has to concern itself. The work emerges, under increasing pressure, from this slow self-liberation from the initial matrix of constrictions, against which its expressive world will be reprojected.

Do you ever abandon works?

Not recently, although there have been a lot of times when ideas for pieces have taken on concrete form – usually two or three bars of fully worked-out material – without my being able to find the key to their continuation. A composition almost always 'begins' long before the first notes gather enough energy to appear on paper, and many projects are abandoned or considerably modified at this preliminary, gestational stage. It can happen, too, that several distinct projects are gradually 'boiled down' to something which finally becomes a finished work. At a later stage in the composition of most pieces, too, there is a period during which I let the actual work of writing come to a stop. Such periods can last for several months, providing time for a final reorientation before the intense effort involved in bringing the composition to an end. At this stage there are often a number of outstanding, unresolved problems or tensions facing me, so that I sometimes feel at such times that the piece will *really* never get finished. In reality, though, once this stage is reached, there is very little likelihood that completion will not be achieved. It has not happened yet, anyway.

Do you keep sketches that may be of use for future works?

My sketchbooks are full of notes of various length, ranging from the gnomic, frequently indecipherable half-sentence up to whole pages of diagrams and pitch materials. Since I frequently note down ideas on any surface available, there are bits of old newspapers, hotel stationery, etc., glued in as well. I know that there are some composers who enter all such *Einfälle* into a card filing system when they get home, but this seems a bit too much like a conceptual banking system to me! In fact, I very seldom refer back to these notes; I can only suppose that they act as some sort of psychological back-up strategy, enabling me to move freely from one area of interest to another without losing contact with things that, at any given time, don't seem obviously relevant. The recycling process is so continuous that I sometimes catch myself reinventing an idea years after I first thought of it, having lost track of it somehow. Since the context within which this act of rediscovery takes place is usually vastly different and often significantly more highly developed, I find such spiral movement quite exciting, since I feel myself to be gaining extra insight into those parts of my musical universe which are slowly accumulating structural significance, becoming permanent signposts.

Do new works grow out of ideas or forms from old ones?

There *have* been occasions when the idea for a piece has come upon me unexpectedly from behind. It's not often that such sudden visions are actually realized, though, unless, after further reflection, they seem to bring together other, already extant ideas in a new and innovative fashion. Mostly there is a constantly mutating vista of future projects before the inner eye, which is so clearly defined that it allows for little possibility of major modification. By the same token, though, there is a much greater potential for the gradual development of materials or means of treatment from one work to the next. One of my more firmly held tenets is that, in the face of the high level of stylistic plurality, the term 'style' itself needs to be seen as an essentially diachronic function – that is to say, the composer needs to pursue the goal of a slowly developing, quasi-organic linguistic usage capable of providing for some equally gradual semantic enrichment of musical vocables which only some form of historically linear perspective would seem to afford. Although I don't of course wish to deny the possibility of other, divergent approaches, my own way of working and my artistic world-view demand this sort of concentration upon the concept of 'individual style' as the presupposition for any sense of ordered evolution. This means that all works are 'infected' to a greater or lesser degree by their predecessors, sometimes to the extent of sharing actual materials (as in several current projects) or passing back and forth different approaches to the same type of organizational background. In the *Carceri d'invenzione* cycle, for instance, the three pieces of that name share all their initial chordal material in a literal form, while the nimbus of smaller, surrounding works offers quite a kaleidoscope of transformational and form-building devices.

Do you write regularly during particular hours?

I suppose that most composers are *always* composing in one sense or another, even if not with tangible, visible results. One of the defining qualities of *being* a composer seems, in fact, the propensity actually to reconstruct the external world according to this almost unbroken stream of inner preoccupations. I imagine that many such 'compositions' have been created via such interactional ritual without ever coming to be transformed into sound! As I said before, on the other hand, I quite often have periods during which a particular piece comes to a standstill.. Since I work on at least two pieces simultaneously, this doesn't necessarily imply total inactivity. There is always work of a more mechanical, preparatory nature to be done, in any case.

In general, I try hard to be at the desk for between six and seven hours a day – more if things are flowing well, less if I come up against obstacles that I feel need to be slept on. Although the number of hours I teach composition may seem less than onerous, in fact the sort and quantity of energy thus expended usually prevents me from teaching and composing on one and the same day. Since I travel a fair amount, too, I have to be careful when calculating what sort of compositional activity will be realistically possible in alien and anonymous environments. Miscalculations are sometimes inevitable, of course. In the most unfavourable of cases, there is always something to be copied or corrected, and this activity tends to flow over almost imperceptibly into composition proper. Perhaps that is one of the most fascinating things about composing – I mean the permanent fluidity present in the individual division of artistic labours.

Do you learn anything from hearing your music? Do scores change during rehearsal or after a first performance?

Of course one always learns something from live performance, particularly under intensive rehearsal conditions. Witnessing the gradual growth into maturity of a particular interpretation can provide decisive impulses for the future, although this remark applies largely to those works for one performer only or for quite small ensembles – small enough, that is, to permit individual contact with each player. Beyond a certain limit this is no longer practicable, and, what with the invariably insufficient amount of rehearsal allotted to a work, there is sometimes no time to 'grow into' the sound of a work emerging for the first time into the real – phenomenal – world of the senses. I have often had the desire to separate out this or that texture, to listen to it by itself, to focus in on a group of instruments which only I (as the composer) am aware of as forming some sort of unit. Instead of this, one is often left hanging in the air after the performance, oppressed by the conviction that the work should really only now be beginning.

I very seldom change much, apart from the inevitable elimination of notational inaccuracies or the accidental omission of performance indications. The main reason for this lies in my actual way of composing, since I tend to copy out the definitive score (the one later published) step by step with the act of composition itself. For most of my pieces this means there is no rough score as such, merely a vast and unordered convolute of single pages of various sizes and shapes. Copying the score as an integral part of the composition process arose in the first instance from my habit of always writing in ink as opposed to pencil: later I realized that it also allowed me extra time to work through ideas while not interrupting the continuity of creative activity in any violent or arbitrary fashion. Working slowly and in this way may, indeed, not eliminate all errors of judgement, but it does tend to weave errors much more seamlessly into the overall fabric of the work, making their ultimate correction not only vastly more difficult but, often enough, actually undesirable. A lot of my more detailed methods of working are centred around the absorption and effective redeployment of the energies that systems errors generate.

Do you have any intention for your music other than that it should exist?

I'm not sure that I completely understand the question. I have always felt the old 'art for art's sake' against 'engaged art' to be a false and dangerously oversimplifying dichotomy. In a world where we have all become more 'decentred' in the interest of all sorts of nebulously powerful social pressures, there seems to be a significant role to be played by a view of art that transcends such black-and-white definition. What is music 'about'? Possibly, about the relationship pertaining between the realm of the senses and the ordered object of their perception seen as an extended metaphor of possible forms of life. The idea of a work *acting out* the conditions for possible worlds of order which are not immediately subjected to external cost/efficiency categorization seems a reasonable point of departure, although each individual instance will, by definition, expand and distort this basic position in hitherto unimaginable ways. A truly 'experimental' music is not necessarily one that juggles half-digested ideas and materials in order to be surprised by what comes out: rather, it is a form of living discourse, which, at every moment, offers many possible paths towards its own future. One of the reasons I have been so attracted towards the Piranesi etchings has been their quality of being capable of throwing their perspectival trajectories across the edge of the page into the world outside. It is this sort of matrix that I try to compose, not necessarily the once-for-all definition of the precise forces which encounter each other there.

If all this seems rather vague, it is because, in the context of the work it is really rather concrete. In any case, whatever intentions for his work that a composer has are usually directed more at getting the piece *written* than speculating too much on its ultimate function. Beyond that, one could argue that the term 'exist' used in your question implies a far too passive mode of being for an art work: I hope that my compositions suggest a more active interpretation since they, too, are setting out on a long journey of their own.

Is an audience necessary?

I'd say that *resonance* of some sort is quite necessary, since it would seem rather difficult to maintain the Adornoesque 'message in a bottle' metaphor in this age of instant transference of cultural information. Naturally, there is little use in imagining some 'ideal listener' when composing, since the sort of mass audience that makes any generalization of that sort useful is hardly a characteristic of *any* species of contemporary music. There is no such thing as *the* new music audience, but rather a chaotic mesh of special interests – something true of life in general, of course. There may be the man or woman fascinated by Stravinsky while being left cold by Mahler. The same person may love *The Rite of Spring*, but heartily dislike the *Symphony of Psalms*, so that, if one looks closely enough, one's imagined listener dissolves into a shimmering and impalpable mass of currents.

In a certain sense, the sort of traditional concert where a relatively small number of listeners congregates in a back-street hall has been overtaken by the new reality of the record industry, radio and so on, so that it is hardly to be wondered at that the composer's sense of direct relationship with a specific, identifiable group of listeners has taken some hard knocks in recent decades. Probably the fetish of large numbers is a quite recent symptom of the same thing, since the history of art has frequently shown that major artists have exercised an influence largely divorced from their annexation or not by organs of mass dissemination. In the last analysis every composer works for himself, since only he can gather and maintain the impetus necessary for the creative act. Otherwise, I suppose one writes for the dozen or so individuals whose personal opinion and esteem have importance, without this implying that other facets of the problem are being ignored. Whatever the more abstract categories of listener being aimed at, this sort of basic 'targeting' towards known individuals seems to me to be the starting point.

Do you intend your programme notes to baffle?

To tell the truth, I've often been somewhat baffled myself on observing the seeming unwillingness of the listener to reconsider the purpose and format of programme notes. All too often the fireside-chat tone of voice many composers feel impelled to adopt switches the ear and mind automatically into more secure, familiar channels whatever the nature of the music itself. The ubiquitous ideology of good common sense giving rise to such phenomena is a pretty good example of how social pressures know very well how to defuse even the most potentially explosive art. On the other hand, providing no accompanying notes at all strikes me as being a rather defeatist gesture, and ends up being interpreted as a particular – even less individually differentiated – form of comportment open to grave misinterpretation on the part of the uninitiated.

The texts I sometimes offer (only when asked!) are certainly not intended as *descriptions* of my music in a direct sense: after all, there are a number of stages of the compositional process associated with verbal, conceptual activity, each of which is capable of making a specific contribution to the work's unique ambience. This many-layered aspect of creativity should surely be emphasized, not eliminated. Also, a text can stand in all sorts of relationships to the work with which it is nominally associated, even to the extent, for instance, of collecting together aspects of the original ideational 'background' *not* expressed directly in the music itself – remainders, if you like. These, too, are by no means irrelevant. Another possibility I have sometimes made use of has been to generate a text utilizing identical techniques to those employed in the piece itself, without necessarily making these techniques objects of discussion as such. In other words, there is a sort of verbal 'double' of particular central aspects of the work which, I hope, might prepare the ground for the subsequent intuitive sifting and reordering of musical impressions.

While the text is in no way conceived of as part of the work, there is a sense in which it exercises an *exemplificatory* function, suggesting the existence of fields of force between work and world through which the resonance of the music can be projected into other dimensions. Music does not exist alone in the world; there were periods when it was a self-evident fact that it formed a centre of gravity around which all sorts of cultural experiences were clustered. It is only relatively recently that the art has become shamefaced about some such vision, taking refuge in some anony-mous and unreflected ideal of 'communication'.

That said, perhaps it is useful to emphasize that composers are not primarily wordsmiths – a fact apparently often forgotten or ignored by critics who content themselves with regurgitating the programme note (a prime proof of some of my theses if ever there was one) or treating it as the object (rather than the piece) of a form of debased literary criticism. One of the main problems seems to be that, in contrast, say, to the visually orientated arts, the language of critical speculation on music has become overly conventional, not to say impoverished. My texts are certainly not setting out to baffle, as you put it, but, rather, strategically disorientate, in an attempt to subvert this sort of formulaic reaction.

Are you ever moved to write music in response to external stimuli that you can recognize: words, other works of art, natural phenomena, ideas, etc?

Yes, almost always in fact. Over the years I have developed a 'nose', I think, about what is likely to stimulate me and what not. Sometimes other works of art (usually not music) have acted as catalyst, not directly leading to the piece, but acting as focus points for the collecting and ordering of all sorts of fragmentary impressions, speculations and so on. One of these was the Matta painting *La terre est un homme*, which served this purpose on several levels at once, such as the actual configuration of the elements, the title and its implications, and the sort of surreal animism that lends the painting its specific life. The same is true of the Piranesi series to perhaps an even more far-reaching degree. *Transit* was a case in point too, since the layout of the orchestra was a close reproduction of the concentric circles seen in an eighteenth-century pastiche of a

Renaissance magus penetrating the outer limits of the heavens and hearing the music of the spheres. Quite a lot of correspondences were built up around this convolute of images.

At the same time, I would need to emphasize that my music has nothing in common with programme music. There is a tight web of analogical correspondences attached to an extramusical idea, it's true, but no 'story line' being followed outside the musical action of unfolding and revealing itself. Later works tend to dispense with specific external images in favour of more fundamentally music-immanent considerations – although, in asserting that, it immediately occurs to me that quite a few of my recent compositions have had quite clearly formulated parallels of that sort: *Lemma-Icon-Epigram*, for instance, with its connection with Walter Benjamin's theory of the allegoric.

Sometimes I think that if Wittgenstein and Benjamin had met at the ends of their respective careers they would have regarded each other as creatures from another universe. Still there are often points where even the most idiosyncratic of trajectories intersect and, at the end of the *Tractatus* where he speaks of the limits of the sayable, Wittgenstein comes closer than one might expect to the admission of real forms of meaning which transcend verbal encapsulation. Earlier I said that I feel emotionally close to anything that defines a border in the act of crossing it; the same is true here, where we sense that the showable and the sayable are not *really* so far apart. The obvious immediacy of the indicative image remains firmly embedded in our linguistic culture, just as the word itself (*pace* the more recent ideas of Derrida) is always being drawn back into the maelstrom of pre-logical sensibility. Music, for me, is an art form that – more than any other? – partakes of both worlds in a vital and elemental manner, and Walter Benjamin (like Adorno in a different context) is relevant to the extent that his primary concern was always the moment of modulation between one manifestation of meaning and another.

In his *Ursprung des Deutschen Trauerspiels* Benjamin first formulated what I hope to be forgiven for calling the concept of 'pictorial synaesthesia', according to which he unearthed endless varieties of interconnections between images and concepts. This has been interesting for me in so far as, in *Lemma-Icon-Epigram*, I was deliberately searching for a sort of *non-discursive argumentation*, and the formal organization of the baroque *Emblem* (consisting of verbal superscription – the 'lemma' – pictorial image and concluding exegesis in the form of a poetic epigram) seemed immediately useful and suggestive. In fact, it was via Benjamin that I came across this whole world of subcutaneous significance. I see the Emblem-form as a sort of 'frozen rhetoric', so the idea of the piece was to bring the tripartite structure of the Emblem into frenetic motion, to dissolve its conventionalized immediacy into a new species of communion between musical object (always on the brink of disappearing) and chain of transformatory processes, itself teetering on the brink of dissolution. In keeping with the original layout of the three parts of the model, I chose techniques and approaches that emphasized first the scriptive, linear aspect, then the rigid, object-bound side of things, finally (although this not entirely literally) the argumentative, exegetical.

Only years later did I come across several tractati (Gracián in particular) that underlined the close relationship between classical rhetoric, the art of memory and the image that conjoins them. Seen as a continuation of this line, Benjamin seems to me one of the few cultural critics of the pre-war years truly to have a foot in both camps.

What is music, and what is it for?

I find it interesting that you automatically couple these, for me, distinct and independent points. Art in general seems to be a basic definitional quality of being human. One might as well ask, 'Why breathe?' As to what it's for: off the cuff I can only suggest that it serves to keep the tenuous lines of communication open between different areas of our selves. As soon as we start looking for catchy phrases to nail our experience down with, we end up in exactly the position that I sense art to be opposing. I have always been attracted to works that straddle boundaries, without sitting on the fence: the rule-bound quality of sensuality and the sensual aspect of the intellectual seem to be getting further and further apart in most people's minds. Perhaps music, by incorporating both these extremes in high degree, can hope to bridge the gap, if only as a form of favoured special case and for a limited period of time.

What music would you go out of your way to hear?

Almost anything from the Italian renaissance, primarily Monteverdi, the Gabrielis and their contemporaries. The exuberant pleasure in the architectural play of masses in the latter and the mannerist intensity of every detail of the former – not to speak of his amazing timing – have always exercised a powerful pull. Little from the eighteenth and nineteenth centuries; my central interests begin again with early Schoenberg. The Second Quartet, for instance, seems one of the century's masterpieces, and I would always make an effort to hear a performance.

There's not a great deal of more recent music that I would go far to hear, but that's probably because I hear a lot anyway, and like to spend as much time as possible with my own things. I seldom feel greatly attracted to first performances, although things were different a decade or so back: since then the 'aura' of expectation attached to such events has largely dissipated, along with the adventurous spirit of most of the composers.

What music do you detest?

Would it really be very illuminating if I offered my personal hit list? As far as contemporary music is concerned, I try to suspend judgement as long as possible, since it is very often rather hard to judge quality before entering into the stylistic ambience of a piece. I'm afraid there *are* areas that leave me fairly cold – most minimal music (of the repetitive sort), most social-critical or overtly political music, particularly the sort that offers a thoroughly middle-class view of what the masses *should* like. Opera is mostly a closed book, too, apart from Schoenberg, Monteverdi and some Strauss, but that may be due to other factors apart from musical quality or content, I suppose. Apart from those specific points I suppose there is a certain sort of 'festival music' that makes me distinctly restless, since there have been many occasions when I have been over-exposed to interminable concerts containing only minimally individual works. There again, though, it could be that the mass desensitization involved in the very act of listening for such a long time is more worrying than the pieces themselves. Sometimes I think contemporary music concerts should consist of no more than five pieces, each no more than four minutes in length, with the pauses between them being calculated in inverse proportion to the length of the works they separate. Really *listening* to contemporary music of quality demands such an intensity and involvement that present-day concert practice is either a reflection of the decay in our hearing capacities or one of its prime causes.

How do you react to such phenomena of the age as the New Romanticism, minimalism, Neue Einfachkeit?

I wrote an article last year, published in various Continental journals (including *Darmstädter Beiträge*) that deals extensively with this issue in terms of what can and cannot be expected of *style*. My personal view of the necessity of continuity of personal style as a presupposition of 'depth effect' was there contraposed to the various brands of neo-historicism now current. I suggested that the view of musical 'history' often implied in such music is a necessarily limited and limiting one, and that the view that musical gestures can effectively reflect the emotion of the composer in some sort of direct depictional manner leads to all sorts of problems when thinking of form, particularly when bound up with the now ageing polemic against the so-called 'serial' (in the sense of 'total serial') tendencies of the fifties. The main argument against most New Romantic phenomena is that the iconic representation theory (on whatever level) leaves the single gestural unit of significance on a rather isolated and formally ineffective island. Indeed, the more effective the depicting act, the less the resultant gesture is in need of continuation! This leads more and more to a return of textbook forms such as fugue, variation, etc., which schematic and over-simplified models are frequently at crass variance with the type of hyper-expressive material employed. There *are* things to be done in the field of 'trans-stylistic' modulation, I imagine, but not without extensive reflection on the part of the composer. Some sort of inverted commas are inevitable.

Do you feel yourself to have any affinities with composer colleagues?

There are a lot of composers whose attitude towards the importance of compositional ambition and its connection with other areas of experience I respect very much, without necessarily sharing their belief systems, which may be of a religious, philosophical, social or psychological sort. It is extremely important, I'm sure, that reflection be carried out in intimate alliance with sensation in a way possibly pointing to a path beyond both.

Are there colleagues whose works you follow with particular interest?

My teaching activities bring me into contact with a wide spectrum of composers from all over the world, and I like to keep in touch with as many ex-students and their activities as possible. This keeps me quite occupied! Apart from that, as I said earlier I think, I don't really have much opportunity in Freiburg to follow at all continuously the careers and development of others. Some colleagues and I occasionally exchange scores, and this helps one keep important threads unbroken. Anyone attempting to keep up with even the tip of the growing production of new music scarcely has time to compose himself, I should think. My activity in the Institute for

New Music at the Musikhochschule involves me in ordering scores and records, it's true, but I can't order only what I like, of course, but have to see that a wider selection of styles and composers is at all times represented. The best composers are not always the ones most pedagogically instructive either.

8

John Casken

Living near Newcastle, Casken suggests a meeting during one of his infrequent visits to the foreign south, and by phone we efficiently arrange a time and a place: the Festival Hall bookshop before a concert. We talk over coffee there, he with total assurance and straightforwardness, concerning himself more than any of his colleagues with the practical business of making compositions. He returns the typescript with no more than a few second thoughts.

When did you start composing?

I started rather late: I was probably in the lower sixth when it dawned on me that I was never going to make anything as a performer – at that time I was playing the organ, and trying to learn the double-bass, and I learned the flute as well later when I was at Birmingham. But during that period at school the most important thing was art: I had a marvellous teacher, Roy Kearsley, who exposed me to new ideas and ways of looking at things. He encouraged us to do quite experimental things, and to take an active interest in twentieth-century painting and architecture: in a way that encouraged me to be more radical in making things with my hands at that age than I was in terms of music. Even though my music teacher had encouraged me to listen to Berg's Violin Concerto, I was writing pieces which were, I suppose, mid-Delian, but I remember rehearsing a piece at school which went terribly wrong: all the notes went out of alignment, and it sounded so much more interesting.

So my compositions were chasing hard on the heels of my paintings, and it was a bit like going through the experience that the painters and composers must have gone through in the first decade of the century. You begin by doing representational things, but then you put the object on one side and try to see a different kind of reality. Shortly after I began to take painting rather seriously, I realized that there was a musical parallel, and I started to write pieces that were pseudo-early-Schoenberg; I remember

John Casken   *photo: Geoff Holt*

writing a piece with a mandoline in it because Schoenberg had done that, but I didn't really know the Schoenberg piece.

Why did you elect to study music at Birmingham rather than go to an art college?

I suppose I must have felt that a degree in music would be more use to me in the future than a qualification in painting. But for the first two years at Birmingham I regretted that quite frequently.

Were you still painting?

Yes.

Do you paint now?

Not as much as I used to, because of the pressure of other things, but it's something that I still hold as very important to me.

When I was at Birmingham as a student, though, I didn't feel at all comfortable with the academic side of music. The only thing I felt capable of doing was composing, and certain challenges arose from that. Other people didn't have much confidence in what I was writing, and I can remember thinking that I would stick at it; perhaps it was this struggle which determined that music came first and painting came second.

Were you having composition lessons?

Not at first. It was only at the end of my second year that I showed a composition of mine to John Joubert, who became my tutor in my final year and then as a postgraduate. Peter Dickinson joined that tutorial circle, and he was a great eye-opener to me: he pointed me in the direction of Messiaen, Stockhausen, Boulez and Cage, and just said, 'Go.' I'd been very interested in Prokofiev as an undergraduate, and suddenly at a very late stage to discover Messiaen and the avant-garde . . . It makes me shudder to think how late in the day it was before contemporary music suddenly hit me as a huge wave of new sounds and possibilities.

As a postgraduate student I wrote a piece for chamber orchestra called *Improvisations on a Theme by Piet Mondrian*, and parts of that are a bit Messiaen-like, parts a bit Lutosławski-like. I was very excited by such composers, because they were making the sorts of gestures and dealing with the flow of musical time in ways that I was only just beginning to see the possibilities of.

How did the particular interest in Lutosławski develop?

Peter Dickinson exposed me to it, and it just clicked. He himself had been very interested in the Polish school in the late sixties and early seventies, and he had a lot of the scores.

John Joubert was a different sort of teacher. He was more likely to ask you to have a look at how Debussy, Ravel or Stravinsky had done something. At the time I thought that was rather old-fashioned, but now I realize how wise this approach was. In fact, I tend increasingly to refer to such past examples when trying to solve compositional problems.

You went to Poland straight after Birmingham?

Yes, there was a choice of going to Bucharest or to Warsaw, and I decided on Warsaw because it seemed a more lively place. I said I wanted to study with Lutosławski, and they smiled politely. Then it took me about six months to pluck up courage to phone him, in my best Polish, and ask to come and see him. That started a series of visits, during which we chatted about all sorts of things: we didn't actually talk very much in detail about his scores, or if we did, we talked about them from memory. I think if I'd asked him to show me how he'd made a piece, he would have done so, but I thought that was impertinent.

But I was given Dobrowolski as my teacher. A committee of professors looked at your music and decided whether you were a Dobrowolski-type composer or a Rudziński-type composer, which is very interesting, because Nigel Osborne, who'd just left Warsaw, studied with Rudziński. Dobrowolski was the first teacher I'd had who would be very specific: he'd ask me what I meant by a single A flat, whether it ought to come a bit later, whether it was in the right octave. It was an extremely useful education, because it made me try to develop a technique for myself so that I could answer his questions. I stopped writing completely, and started again very slowly.

In the first year I wrote only a short piece for cello and piano, and then towards the end of my stay I started writing *Kagura*, in which I discovered certain principles of pitch organization which made sense to me, in terms of how you organize notes one to twelve horizontally and vertically, and how you apply systems of duration that can be heard. It was the first piece of mine that I thought Dobrowolski approved, but it was a crisis piece, because it changes direction half-way through. The first half basically has two ideas: one based on a trill, and the other a polyphonic cantilena, which is non-metrical. The two play off against one another and form a huge crescendo, which comes down on to a central G. And that G was the point at which I left Warsaw, or my immediate contact with Warsaw ceased: the piece was finished when I got back here, and even though subconscious Ligeti hovers in the background throughout, the second half becomes more like Birtwistle or

Stravinsky. It's like two pieces joined by a single thread, the single G, and I think in that sense it's a very unsuccessful piece, though it was very important to me, because I discovered ways of going about things, and because I discovered the dangers of the Polish texture music.

Unless you carefully control the harmonic rate of change, the music is just busy, not really fast or energetic. I didn't realize at first that the more static, *ad libitum* blocks you have, the slower the rate of harmony, and the more metrically inclined the music becomes, the faster the harmony – which is low Lutosławski gets out of it.

But you did go on writing that sort of aleatory counterpoint.

I did, in the chamber piece *Music for the Crabbing Sun*, but I think there was less of it, and it attracted more attention than it deserved. There are other things in that piece: for instance, I tried to apply something of what I'd discovered about Babbitt, but rather unsuccessfully, and it's not something I've pursued. The ensemble was rather austere – flute, oboe, cello and harpsichord – and I thought that this rather austere approach would be suitable for parts of it.

By the time I got to *Amarantos*, in 1977, the Polish thing was definitely on the way out, and if there's any Polishness in *Tableaux des trois âges* it's the Polishness of Szymanowski. There I was interested in harmony which resonates with thirds and sixths, with a very strong fundamental. The idea was that it should open with a very bright dawn and should get much darker, harmonically and orchestrally, and composers like Skryabin, Szymanowski and Richard Strauss were very important initially. I think it was in that work that I decided it was about time I put present-day composers aside and see what I could produce by absorbing the colours of earlier composers.

I think composers are like magpies. They find things that interest them, and pick at them hard, and then retreat. It's a selfish determination: you know what sounds you want, and it's a question of looking for help and guidance in achieving those sounds. The uses of quotation in *Ia Orana, Gaugin* and *Firewhirl* are other examples of my magpie-ism.

You mentioned finding principles of twelve-note organization in Kagura *that worked horizontally and vertically. Was that a matter of making the harmony work functionally?*

It depends what you mean by making the harmony work. I like to think that now there is a certain inevitability to my harmonic progressions: I've always got in mind a point of departure and a point of arrival, and for that you could read the word 'tonic'. The music progresses in carefully considered steps between these points. But what harmony meant in *Kagura* was simply a rational organization of the twelve notes within a chord, sometimes regardless of the chord next to which it was placed, sometimes moving by symmetrical steps. It might work in terms of intervallic progression, but there was little of conventional voice leading, of tension and resolution. What I discovered in *Kagura*, and what surfaced later in *Amarantos*, was that one could make exciting chord formations based on symmetrical relationships, as in Bartók or Lutosławski.

Maybe I absorbed all this through Dobrowolski, but it's quite different from the harmonic processes in a piece like *Tableaux des trois ages*, where I built up six twelve-note chords in the first movement with the same fundamental, and with intervals that have strong tonal implications: there might be a first inversion in the bass, followed by a diminished chord, followed by an augmented chord, followed by a major chord at the top. Having heard that first chord, I move on to the second chord and make sure that each voice follows some logical linear progression, that it's not a repetition of the same note or a series of oscillating thirds, that it has a nice chromatic curve to it. So I have a grid of six-by-twelve chords prescribed before I begin to compose. What I then did was to filter it from the bottom upwards, because it was a part of the work where I was trying to get the sensation of things rising and coming to life, so it seemed natural to lift off from the bottom. So I might start with the first chord and sound just its lowest note, and then the lowest two notes, and then move on to the second chord and take the lowest three. But at some points it would be possible to sound larger areas of the chords, so that you were reminded of the main struts of the harmonic fabric. Then the problem was what to do with the curving lines of the individual voices: you couldn't have them repeating ostinato-like. And so they began to be decorated, and they began to attract notes from neighbouring chords, but nevertheless with a focusing on the main chord that was being shimmered at that point.

That first section of *Tableaux* was particularly important in opening a way of developing a harmonic movement between chords that had a strong degree of consonance, and an orchestral colouring to match it, a method of working that I tried to pursue in the Piano Concerto and *Orion over Farne*.

Do you frequently start with a very abstract idea and then develop it into music?

It's different with each piece. In that instance with *Tableaux* it was a question of knowing what harmonic language you want to adopt, and then trying to develop the technique that will realize the sound you have in your mind. I knew it was going to be a very rich section, but I couldn't just sit down and compose a rich section: it had to have some kind of harmonic structure to it. You plan that before you set off, and then your music grows out of the progression.

In *Amarantos*, for instance, the instrumentation was prescribed for me (it's a mixed nonet), and I knew the sonorities, accents, densities I was going to want; it was a question then of finding the technique to realize that energy. A lot of time was spent working on that, almost divorced from the music itself: it's like doing your scales.

But some pieces are more spontaneous, like the brass quintet *Clarion Sea*, which I've just finished. It's a much freer, looser piece with regard to pitch, and wasn't worked out in large chunks beforehand. With my more recent music I've been trying to define a general harmonic area, with certain scales and chords, and then perform it more spontaneously: I feel when I'm composing a work that I'm performing it in incredibly slow motion.

Does that performance go through many different stages?

I change an awful lot. I never know whether what I'm producing is going to be useful or dire rubbish in terms of the final piece: it comes to a final sketch, where I've got a very good idea of what there is to do in the piece to make it musical, and that's the point at which I throw things out and change things. With *Orion over Farne*, for example, I had the whole piece sketched in full score, and some bars I would copy exactly into the final version, whereas other parts would have to be changed in order to sound right.

Do you sketch ideas for future works?

I'm beginning to, though having said that, I can't work on more than one piece at once. But sometimes you have visions of pieces you'd like to write, even though nobody's asked for them, and that can be quite refreshing, because I tend to write pieces that people have asked for. I don't know whether I'm practical or opportunist, but if someone suggests I might be interested in writing a piece for a certain ensemble, that lays a seed, even if I'd never thought of writing for that ensemble, and maybe some time later I'll want to do it.

Where do the basic ideas come from? Are you ever stimulated by landscape, paintings, poems . . . ?

All those. I'd hate to say I was a romantic composer, but I find it very difficult to write a piece without knowing why I'm writing it. Simply to write a piece for four instruments, to be played by four players, is for me not enough: it's got to have a life of its own. And I feel my pieces have to have that sort of identity almost before I begin to compose them. Even if I'm going to apply rigorous structural ideas, the piece has got to be related to something beyond itself, in the way that the whole concept of *Tableaux* demanded a certain way of thinking of form and structure largely determined by the paintings of Gustave Moreau, on which the work is based. When the ideas behind the piece and the ideas within the piece came together, then I was off.

To get this kind of energy going within me, and then hopefully within the piece, I have tended to be stimulated by poetry, by paintings, or by little schemes of my own devising – like *Masque*. It's an oboe concerto, but I couldn't simply say that I was going to have a first movement in ABA form: why should I compose in ABA form? But having thought of the oboe as a character on a stage, quite capable, perhaps more than any other instrument, of mimicry, of pantomime, then I developed a kind of silly scenario, where the soloist begins singing offstage and then gets chased on stage by the rest of the orchestra. They have a little tussle, and there's a jig at the end of the movement. The danger of that sort of thinking is that it takes over, and the piece doesn't work as music. It has to work for somebody who knows nothing of your programme and can apply their own ideas, because if they're doing that then it's exciting their imagination. And one of the main reasons for composing is the hope that some of your listeners will be excited by it, and at the same time entertained in the best sense of the word.

What are the other reasons for composing?

I hoped you wouldn't ask me that. But if you feel capable of making something, I think you have to do it. You can't rest until you've seen that project to its conclusion.

Does that mean you don't abandon works?

Yes. And more than that, even if something doesn't work, I work as hard as I can to make sure it does work: the String Quartet I revised twice, and *then* did a radical rethink of the whole formal shape. There are other works, like *Arenaria*, which I'd like to go back to.

The String Quartet's rather a rarity among your works in not having a very poetic title.

Yes, and even with that piece I referred in the programme note to a nocturnal landscape: I could have avoided saying that. But I think if you're going to spend so much time thinking about a work in a certain way, then you're withholding something if you don't disclose that. The title just says something about the ambience that surrounded you and the piece while it was being composed.

The title of *Music for the Crabbing Sun* comes from Dylan Thomas, and *Music for a Tawny-Gold Day* was an autumnal variant of that, because it's for a similar quartet, but of more mellow instruments. *Amarantos* has to do with 'amaranthine'. *Melanos*, which I thought of as a companion piece to that, is a sort of miniature tuba concerto: it was written for Melvyn Poore and a group called Anomaly, it starts with a song (*melos*) and it's rather a dark piece, so everything seemed to come together. *Clarion Sea* I imagined as a warlike odyssey; *Piper's Linn* is for Northumbrian pipes and tape, and 'linn' is the Northumbrian word for 'waterfall'.

There's been quite a Northumbrian flavour to your music of the last few years. Do you feel you belong to that area?

Yes. I live there, and I teach there. I identify with the north of England very much: I'm a northerner, and I've never belonged to the south. The north has a quality I admire, a tough resilience. But the Northumberland connection wasn't self-conscious: it began with the coincidence of being commissioned to write a piece for Northumbrian small pipes and being recommended to look at the poetry of Basil Bunting, who was a great discovery for me.

He provided most of the words for *To Fields we do not Know*, an unaccompanied choral work, and the title of *Orion over Farne*, where possibly something of my knowledge of the Northumbrian landscape comes out in the music, whether it's the end, where you get this brilliant starscape, or the feeling elsewhere of monumental hills. I don't know that I've created that in the piece, but I would like to think I were able to, because those are qualities I admire: the feeling that you've got nothing between you and the distant horizon, that you are completely alone.

9

David Matthews

David Matthews occupies a flat in an undistinguished 1930s block over-looking Clapham Common, not far from his brother's house. It is inevitable that I should visit them both on the same afternoon, but perhaps that only emphasizes to me the contrast between Colin's burgeoning family establish-ment and these brown, serious, high-ceilinged, donnish rooms. We sit in a large study which puts a penitential distance between the small desk under the window and the upright piano at the other end; there are also many books and, almost the only ornament, a minute framed example of Stravinsky's musical handwriting. But the conversation is relaxed and easy. I am concerned only when he holds on to the transcript for several weeks; however, though he takes the trouble to retype it, there are no changes of substance.

How did it come about that your family produced two composers? Were your parents musical?

Not especially. We were an ordinary suburban family. Our mother would have liked to play the piano, which is why she made us have lessons – I'm afraid without great enthusiasm on our part. We both gave up eventually, I when I was 13; then there was a gap until in the summer of 1959, when I was 16, I happened to hear the overture to *Tannhäuser* on the radio and for some unaccountable reason it made the most tremendous impression on me. I started to listen to other things on the radio, and going to concerts; then I was given a record of Beethoven's Choral Symphony for Christmas, and I immediately wanted to write a symphony. It was the sound of the orchestra that seemed so exciting, and I felt I must do something like it myself. So I borrowed scores from the library, to see how it was done.

Colin started composing too, soon after this. We were in a state of complete ignorance. I remember seeing woodwind staves with two notes, and assuming therefore that woodwinds could play chords. We didn't know anybody who was a musician, to consult them. But I plugged away at my symphony until it was finished: it was about an hour long. It doesn't survive: inspired by Brahms I made a bonfire of all my early works when I was 19. But it was quite adventurous. I remember at one point I divided the strings into sixty-four parts: I glued three pieces of manuscript paper together and had them all playing trills in a cluster. I thought I'd invented the effect. Then I found it in a symphony by Gerhard and was most annoyed.

At the time I'd only got Colin with whom I could discuss things, but it was terribly useful, because we could teach each other, and we had a mutual enthusiasm for learning all we could. Looking back, it was of course an extremely unusual experience, but at the time it seemed perfectly natural.

What were the musical influences on you at this time?

Well, 1960 was the Mahler centenary year; I got to know all the symphonies and they were a revelation. I think he was the chief influence; but also all sorts of people I heard, Berg, Stravinsky, Skryabin . . .

Then you went to Nottingham University to study classics?

Yes, really because I didn't know how one went about studying music: there hadn't been any music at school in any organized way. Also, school was just something fairly dull that I got on with, and I couldn't associate that kind of routine with my music, which was the real world, the world of the imagination. So it wasn't something I thought of doing publicly, in the sense of going to a music college or reading music at university.

But I had a movement of a string quartet played while I was at Nottingham, and I showed my next symphony – I'd now completed two – to the music staff: I thought they might be rather surprised, but nobody seemed very interested. It was a very conservative music department at the time. And I didn't write very much while I was at Nottingham. After I came down I wrote another quartet and sent it to the BBC, and it was eventually broadcast. Around this time I felt I must have some proper tuition: I thought that what I was doing was too undisciplined. I would have liked to study with Tippett, but I gathered that he didn't take pupils and that he recommended either Priaulx Rainier or Anthony Milner. So I studied with Milner for about three years, just showing him things I was writing: he didn't make me do exercises. I sometimes feel I should have studied harmony and counterpoint properly – I think when you're self-taught you do tend to feel like

David Matthews   *photo: John Carewe*

that. On the other hand I've always been able to do counterpoint fairly naturally. As for harmony, Nicholas Maw, whom I'd got to know, influenced me a lot. I never had any official lessons with him, but I had a lot of unofficial ones, and the way he'd worked out a coherent system of harmony impressed me, and I've tried to do the same.

How were you earning a living after Nottingham?

I managed to start work in music through Deryck Cooke, who introduced me to various people – in particular Donald Mitchell, who gave me copying work for Faber. And then I started working for Britten, because he needed someone to finish off the rehearsal score of *The Burning Fiery Furnace*. For the next three years I was associated quite closely with Aldeburgh, and of course that was very useful, to be in contact with him and to see how an absolutely professional composer operated. One of the things I did was to copy out the full score from his draft score, so I certainly got a lot of ideas about instrumentation from him. And because I went to the first rehearsals, I could immediately see how things worked, which was a new experience for me.

At the time I also had ideas of becoming a music journalist. I did some articles for the *Listener*, and I've always done odd bits: I enjoy writing words, though it's even more difficult than composing.

Did you teach?

No, I was determined to stay out of teaching, because I knew it would use up most of my energies. And I've always avoided any 9-to-5 job, because I need a lot of free time to compose. I need time to brood, to go for walks, as well as for working.

How will a piece start?

It varies. Sometimes it will begin with a thematic idea, which for one or two recent pieces has actually come in a dream. Very romantic. That happened with my Violin Concerto: I got up in the middle of the night and wrote down about ten bars. In the morning I looked at it and it seemed to be a violin melody with orchestral accompaniment. That's unusual. But I often get ideas and write them down, then maybe use them later. I also reuse thematic and harmonic ideas from pieces that I've discarded. For instance, I wrote down the opening idea of my Second Symphony in 1971, then used it in a piece which got discarded, then reused it five years later in the symphony.

When I've got a musical idea to work with, I make a lot of sketches for the beginning of the piece: it's always very difficult to work out the first page, and I do endless sketches and drafts for that. Once I've got it roughly right, then I can through-compose, sketching the piece and working out a draft score more or less at the same time if it's an orchestral work, because I hear things in full score as I go.

When did you write the first piece that you haven't discarded?

When I was 25. That was a pair of orchestral songs which were done by the SPNM in 1970. They showed me that at least I could write for the orchestra, which has always been one of my chief aims. I do think it's vital that the standard orchestra doesn't become a museum; yet writing the kind of orchestral music that stands a chance of getting into the repertoire, as opposed to having just one performance, is in danger of becoming a lost art. You have to learn how to write gratefully for the players as well as imagining new sounds, and for various reasons this has become very difficult.

The other thing I've especially wanted to do is to write string quartets, where the repertoire is also conservative and it's hard to get new pieces into it. The technical problems are a great challenge, especially achieving the kind of transparency one finds in, say, Britten's Third Quartet. In fact I'm only just beginning to solve them.

It was highly unfashionable at that time, around 1970, to write the sort of thing I was doing. But I didn't worry overmuch: partly because of being isolated, it didn't really affect me.

You weren't impressed by, say, Boulez or Maxwell Davies?

They did impress me, but it wasn't the sort of thing I wanted to do. At least, not the language they used: the architecture of their pieces I've found much more interesting. But to me, post-Schoenbergian languages in general seem too narrow. A totally chromatic language is absolutely right for *Erwartung*, but to use it as a kind of lingua franca, without regard to its expressive quality – which is what many composers do today – seems illegitimate. I think it's important to find a language that's appropriate for your temperament, and for the kind of things you want to say. I've always felt close to Tippett, because like mine his music has a lot to do with the expression of physical energy. Musical ideas often come to me when I'm feeling most physically alive: that's when I most want to compose.

Perhaps you're dissatisfied also on formal as well as expressive grounds.

Well, I'm unhappy with music that's just static. Whether they're called symphonies or not, most of my works are symphonic in character, which for me means music that contrasts dynamic energy with passivity. True stasis is achieved through energy and movement. Sibelius's symphonies are fine examples of how to do this: I've learned a lot from his control of pace, his welding together of different kinds of movement, his imperceptible transitions from fast to slow or slow to fast.

How do you arrive at a musical form? Taking the example of the Violin Concerto theme you noted down, how did that find its form?

The thing about that work is that it didn't start off as a violin concerto. I first wrote a single movement for violin and chamber orchestra. I'd just read a Dostoevsky story, 'White Nights', which suggested a rather nice formal idea. The story is a triangular one involving two men and a girl, and I turned the characters into instruments: the main character, who tells the story, became the violin, the other man a clarinet and the girl a flute. In the story the main character loses the girl to the other man, but the experience has, one feels, given him the resolve to become an artist. And what happens in the piece is that the girl's and the other man's themes become his at the end: the violin takes up their material. So that gave the form, which as you can see is related to sonata form. I extended the idea of recapitulation to the cadenza: there is a cadenza at the beginning which is repeated at the end.

Then this seemed to be a possible first movement of a full-scale concerto. So I rescored it for larger orchestra, and wrote another, longer, movement, which was a scherzo with episodes. The piece became uncannily autobiographical, because as I was writing the second movement the story began happening to me. Things don't usually happen in quite so Hollywoodish a way.

That piece is an exception, too, because it's programmatic. Although I'm a romantic composer in that I'm concerned with the expression of emotion, I usually have a very detached attitude towards pieces: when I'm composing them my almost exclusive concern is with form. I work out the overall shape before I start, with approximate durations of sections. I often draw the shape, like a cross-section of a landscape. There will be changes as I compose, but the basic shape generally remains.

Do you change things after a first performance?

There are always details of balance: you never get everything right. I've occasionally rewritten pieces completely, but that's not usual. I could probably go on making small revisions for ever, but at a certain point I'm willing to let a piece go, and live its own life.

Are you satisfied at that point?

I'm satisfied with bits. I'm not sure I'm ever satisfied with a whole piece. You start off with the wonderful excitement of a vision that you have, and gradually you realize that you're never wholly going to achieve it; but by that time you're committed to your material and you simply have to go on, otherwise you'd just keep giving up and going back to the start.

What are your criteria for finding a piece acceptable?

Each piece will have its own internal logic, which you gradually discover. I have my own rules about harmony: it's important to me that the music should always make vertical sense. I still feel that th bass and the treble should obey the traditional rules, and I'll play them through to see that I'm not breaking them. It does seem to weaken the piece if I am.

My concerns are with what music has always been about, rather than with substitutes – which was the Stockhausen way. At one point it looked as if that was the only answer for the future, and everything else was tired, but now it's clear that a lot of what happened in the 1950s and 1960s was an offshoot: the main branch of music has continued to grow, regardless. There's no substitute for real composition, and to be convinced of that is itself liberating.

Colin Matthews

Looking down the line of Victorian terraced houses, I bump into his wife extricating two or three children from the car: one small boy is detailed to lead me up to Daddy's study. I knock, enter and squeeze myself around the grand piano that occupies most of the space in this book-lined sanctuary. There is just room for him to sit at a little desk by the window, challengingly supervised by a photograph of Schoenberg's head in severe quadruplicate, and for me to perch on a chair. There is something a little uneasy about the dialogue, which may be my fault as much as his, or Schoenberg's. My script is returned with emendations made carefully but alarmingly in red.

Can you say how it was that you and your brother David both became composers?

We always did things together as children: we were the only two in the family, and there was just a three-year gap between us. We were usually interested in the same things, and I think both of us have the same attitude – that if we're interested in something we have to follow it right through. We'd learned the piano early on, but it wasn't until I was about 13 or 14 that we became seriously interested in music. David took the lead, but I think that both of us felt that, if we were going to take an interest in music, then there was no point in doing anything else except write it. There was no point in being passive, just sitting and listening.

What music, though, were you listening to?

Everything that I could; but I was particularly obsessed by Mahler. The BBC had broadcast all the symphonies in the centenary year, 1960, and in 1961 I was at the first performance of the Third Symphony in this country. I'd been particularly fascinated by the broadcast of the Tenth Symphony, and I immediately wanted to get hold of the manuscript facsimile, which was almost impossible to find. Eventually I went to the BBC Library, and the librarian was very helpful and even let me borrow Deryck Cooke's recon-

Colin Matthews   *photo: John Carewe*

struction which at that time was banned from performance by Mahler's widow. I transcribed the whole thing myself and then compared it with Deryck's, and when in 1963 I heard that his complete version was going to be done I wrote him a letter saying that I'd found a few mistakes. And Deryck, typically, instead of ignoring this letter from a schoolboy, wrote back and asked me to let him know if I could find anything else. I then sent him my own orchestration of the fourth movement, even more presumptuously. But he was terribly friendly and welcoming, and oddly enough nobody else had shown much interest. It amazed me that more people hadn't looked into the facsimile themselves.

Was Mahler influencing your own music?

No, I've only found lately that Mahler has come out in the wash, especially in my orchestral piece *Landscape*: it was a great surprise to find how much Mahler there is in it. A lot of it's dark; there are bits that actually sound like Mahler; and it's got a Mahlerian shape. It's a big half-hour movement, not so distantly related to the finale of the Sixth, which along with the first movement of the Ninth is my Mahlerian highpoint.

How were you learning to orchestrate, to the extent that you could score a Mahler movement?

I used to read scores absolutely avidly, because we had a very good public library with things like a full score of *Daphnis et Chloé* and lots of Strauss. I used to read them and absorb them totally, between the ages of 14 and 18. I was going to concerts too, hearing whatever I could, and the BBC wasn't doing too badly then either.

Writing for the orchestra was always what I wanted to do, and I enjoy scoring both my own and other people's music. I do a fair amount of film orchestration, which is not only a useful way of earning money, but enjoyable as well. It's one of the most exciting things: scoring something and then hearing it two days later. I've learned a lot from that.

What were you composing while you were at school?

I was quite cautious at first. David started on a large scale: knowing little more than the rudiments he was immediately off writing symphonies with great confidence. But I didn't write anything of any substance at all until I was 18 or 19, and studying classics at Nottingham; though by that time I was writing with reasonable competence, and it attracted the attention of the music staff. Arnold Whittall arrived at Nottingham after my first year, but before he came the students were very conservative – Hindemith was regarded as avant-garde.

The first piece of mine that was at all representative was a very Bergian piano piece, very influenced by the Berg Piano Sonata. Then I got much more serial, and some of my pieces of that time were quite intensely serial in a Webernian sort of way. But I didn't find that very constructive: it was a bizarre mixture of Webern and Tippett, as I remember. Tippett's Second Sonata, in particular, was very important structurally.

What other music has been a creative influence?

Early on I learned a great deal from Skryabin, especially his harmony, but also the concentrated single-movement form of the late sonatas. Schoenberg was always a powerful influence, although now I only care for the early works, up to opus 16. But it would be easier to list the twentieth-century music I *haven't* learned from. As far as contemporaries are concerned I'm particularly interested now in Birtwistle, because I think what he's doing now is very exciting. In the mid-sixties I was very influenced by Maxwell Davies – *Taverner II* and *Revelation and Fall*, and later *Worldes Blis* – and I was writing in a similar style. There were a number of large-scale pieces that never got finished.

Then you had lessons with Nicholas Maw.

I didn't have very many lessons, because he was ill and out of action for nearly a year (this was around 1968–9). I admired his music a lot: I was very impressed by *Scenes and Arias*, and I liked his use of harmony. It was the first close contact I'd had with a composer: that was the most rewarding thing. The lessons weren't all that substantial in themselves because rather few and far between, but I turned out some useful pieces, and it's been a lasting influence.

Then in the early seventies I found myself in a total rut and unable to write anything. At about that time I came across process music – Steve Reich and the rest. It seemed like a breath of fresh air, although the pieces I wrote under the influence were almost ludicrously simple, and it was some time before I found out how to use processes purposefully. That's to say I found how to use the technique to get the music going, without making the technique the be-all and end-all of the piece. And that's been retained: it's been quite a useful thing, and has helped to sustain quite a number of large structures. But I couldn't possibly write large-scale process pieces, because there's no substance there: it's all technique.

What's the difference between music and technique?

If technique was all that mattered then there would be more composers. It becomes music when there's something extra – imagination, expression perhaps.

Are you conscious of expressive quality as you're writing?

No, I don't recognize that until I hear it. I certainly don't *try* to express something, but that doesn't mean that I'm not aware that it does express something, however abstract or intangible.

Also, I don't like technique to be too audible, or too binding. If I'm using a series, then if the note doesn't sound right I'll change it. And I do write quite serially, which I don't think is audible. My recent Cello Concerto was composed fairly freely, but *Night's Mask* (which was written at the same time) is almost totally serial. Quite by chance I found two amazingly combinatorial rows with all sorts of harmonic possibilities, and I just let myself go on that. I hardly needed to change anything, because everything fitted in the most extraordinary way. But if it hadn't, then I'd have changed things.

When you say 'serial' what quite do you mean?

I suppose Berg might be closest, using lots of forms of the series simultaneously.

Which means you can use practically any note at any time anyway?

It can do, yes.

How do you start a piece?

With difficulty. Usually the harmonic aspect is the first thing to come, but sometimes I start with a single line and elaborate. I always find pieces terribly slow to start, so that the draft at the beginning will be complicated and full of alternatives. Then as it speeds up I can't necessarily keep pace with it to the extent of elaborating the whole texture. But at the start I might be ostensibly composing for a whole day and produce only two notes. There'll be a mound of sketches for the opening, which I'm very particular about keeping. There's always a lot that I don't use, and I do look back on sketches and sometimes rework material: the piece I'm writing at the moment for the London Sinfonietta expands on material from *Night's Mask*.

Do you begin with an idea of the whole piece?

Yes, but that doesn't necessarily mean that it's going to stay that way. For instance, with *Landscape* I had a very clear idea of the overall shape, but it's a piece I spent ages on, and it was in the background of a lot of other pieces. I started it in 1976 and took nearly five years over it: in the process it kept changing direction, but the general shape stayed the same.

Might the shape be influenced by traditional models? Several of your earlier orchestral pieces are called 'sonatas'.

That's just a useful hold-all title. I find titles rather difficult: I try to keep away from the 'Osmosis II' syndrome and prefer to be abstract. The shape is nearly always different with each piece.

Some of your titles are very visual, like the subtitle of the Fourth Sonata: 'Green and Gold and Blue and White'. Do you see music in terms of colour?

No, but I always think of composing as being rather like painting, in the sense of filling in various areas of colour, and that was certainly what that piece was about.

Do you get ideas from paintings, or other things you see?

Not directly: I don't think I could translate paintings into music. And much as I love landscape and being in the country, I never want to work there in the sense of being inspired. I just want to get home: I can only work up here in my own room. So that piece *Landscape* isn't about any geographical landscape. It's a sort of journey, a journey through a landscape, where you continually see things from different perspectives. In any case that title was imposed quite late on – my original title was *Light Music*, which everybody told me was asking for trouble. It follows on to my *Night Music*: it starts off in the darkness and becomes a journey expanding towards light. It moves forward in three big zigzags, ending right up in the air.

Is the Cello Concerto another journey?

I don't know. I'm too close to that piece: I don't like it much at the moment. I tend to go off pieces almost as soon as they're finished. I'm usually pretty dissatisfied.

Does that make you want to change things?

No, because that would mean a wholesale revision and I'd rather go on to the next piece. There may be structural things that have gone slightly wrong, so that the argument isn't carried through in the way that it should be, and I just accept that I've got to learn from it and not do it next time.

But one of the few pieces of mine I do like without too many reservations is *The Great Journey*, of which I've only written half, and I'm very frustrated about that: I want to finish it off. I rather like the idea of coming back to a piece and being able to continue it at a distance, but I don't know when I'll be able to.

Generally, though, pieces are a history of possibilities that are lost. I do have a very clear vision when I start, and I'm aware of how far I've strayed from it when I've finished. Then when it gets to the first performance, I'd much rather not be there. It's better if it's in a studio, without an audience, but I don't like the thing happening in public. If I'm aware of a weak part of a work, then I'm just sitting there wincing, wondering how it is that everybody isn't getting up and walking out.

11

John Tavener

It is an ordinary suburban drawing room, except that it thinks itself a Greek chapel. The coffee table carries devotional literature; the alcoves are shelved with tiny icons and photographs of holy men; the light is dim and the scent of incense. The black grand piano bears more pious images, sanctus bells, candles and a huge offering of white flowers. We sip at peppermint tea and talk, he slowly and with difficulty in pinning facts, the large face drawn to peer as if into the sun. But when he speaks, he is direct and authoritative, so that the task of transcription is straightforward. He returns the typescript with only one change, to set right a spelling mistake.

Could you say when you started to compose, and when it became clear that this was going to be your life?

I was composing or improvising from a very young age, 3 or 4, and then I composed a lot at school. But there was one work in particular, Stravinsky's *Canticum sacrum*, which was a musical revelation to me: I must have heard its first performance broadcast from Venice in 1956, when I was 12. I didn't know at the time why it made such an impression, but it's remained a key work of the twentieth century for me. And probably it was through that work that I came to the Orthodox Church. I felt when I was received into the Church, in 1976, that I'd come home.

Was there anything else that was important to you at an early age?

Really nothing as much as that. In my teens I wrote a series of works that sound terribly like bits of the *Canticum sacrum*, which I think gave me a first sense of the Byzantine world. How much Stravinsky knew about Byzantine and Orthodox music I'm not sure, but it's certainly there.

Then more recently I feel I've come into contact with what icon painting is, with the primordial kind of Orthodoxy that the West never had: the fact that the Byzantine tone system is practically unchanged, the fact that Greece never had a renaissance. I think a lot of people are feeling the importance of this: one of them is the

John Tavener   photo: Malcolm Crowthers

composer Arvo Pärt, who is someone I always feel absolutely in tune with when I meet him. Whereas I feel very out of tune with most contemporary art, even though I was very impressed by parts of Stockhausen's *Donnerstag*. And it's not just contemporary art. Since this confrontation with Byzantium I've felt that, however impressed I am by Michelangelo, the simple peasant Greek icon means much, much more to me. Or to give a musical example, I'm deeply moved by the very simple harmonic music they sing at the Russian Orthodox cathedral: it's really just common chords. Then the other day, unknown to me, they sang my setting of the Lord's Prayer, and even that, which is simple enough, seemed to stick out.

Does this mean that there's something in your earlier music that you're trying to get away from?

I think there is. I find now that *Ultimos ritos* is too much: it isn't a truly meditative art, like an icon. I do feel remote from my earlier music, so that it's like looking at pieces brought by a student. I certainly felt that when *The Whale* was done at the 1984 Proms.

It sounds very extreme, but I think sacred art has gone downhill since the middle ages. I think one has to compose in the manner of an icon painter, but the problem is that there's no tradition for it. The Greek chant hasn't changed: they haven't harmonized, though they do in Moscow Road in London and it sounds like Theodorakis. But in the monasteries in Greece where I sometimes stay the chant hasn't changed, and it's so beautiful one wouldn't want it to. That music means so much more to me than so-called great Western music, which is quite a problem for me to deal with when I'm writing myself.

But you do go on writing works within the Western tradition.

Just about. There's going to be a combined Anglican Orthodox service, attended by a Greek patriarch and a Russian patriarch, and they asked me to compose a setting of the whole vigil service, which is about three and a half hours in length. I couldn't think what on earth I was going to do. There's no English Orthodoxy: I suppose the closest one gets to it is in Celtic art. But I made a study of Byzantine chant, acquainted myself with the Greek tones and the Russian tones, allowed them to sink into me.

These are modes?

The Greek ones are modes – they're almost scales – but the Russian ones are much more difficult to recognize: you identify them by their melodic characteristics. The Greek tones are much easier to work with, and with them I somehow managed to put the vigil together. That seemed nearer to painting in an iconic manner, because there were strict rules laid down.

Is it a pure chant line or is it harmonic?

It's harmonic, but I've virtually avoided polyphony because the Orthodox Church doesn't allow it. Certainly I've never allowed it to obliterate words, because the Orthodox have this great imperative that the word must be heard. And I have this strong feeling that they're right, even though it does cause such compositional problems. I just wonder if I'll ever compose music again outside that tradition.

You don't have any plans for more operas or orchestral works?

I've got an idea for an opera, but it's a Desert Father story, and I would use chant a lot in it. I don't know about orchestral works.

But there isn't entirely a break with what you were doing in the past. For instance, you've always avoided any very energetic polyphony.

That's true. Stillness attracts me, and I think that goes through my music from *Ultimos ritos* to *Akhmatova Rekviem* to *Prayer for the World*, which I think is my most radical piece. It's just a setting of the prayer 'Lord Jesus Christ, Son of God, have mercy on me, a sinner', and it lasts seventy minutes. I know when it was done at the Round House for the Contemporary Music Network I felt very uncomfortable, with those circumstances and this very quiet, meditative and austere music. It doesn't have the whiff of the Pacific that *Stimmung* has, and it's not at all sensual.

Were you feeling some alienation from the normal sort of contemporary music concert?

Yes, I do feel that.

Did you feel that when you were younger, when works like The Whale *brought you very much to the forefront of what was still considered the avant-garde?*

I don't think it ever lay very happily on me. But I owe an awful lot to David Lumsdaine, who was associated with that world, and who opened up technical vistas for me. Also, and I don't know whether he's religious or not, but he has a very deep feeling for the magic and mystery of music, which communicated itself to me.

Were you religious as a child?

Not particularly. Perhaps it was going to come anyway, but again Stravinsky was important there, through his music and through things he said – not in those late books but in earlier ones – about childhood experiences of Orthodoxy.

Yet in the 1960s and early 1970s your works were much more Catholic.

Yes, but I now find St John of the Cross doesn't mean to me what he meant to me then.

What about Messiaen?

David Lumsdaine introduced me to his music, and of course that was an enormous influence. But now I don't want to listen to Messiaen, whereas I could listen to almost anything of Stravinsky.

And what else?

The Mozart of the Masonic works. I think *The Magic Flute* is the greatest opera ever written. But the Requiem always seems to me odd.

Is there any similarly unfinished Tavener?

No. Very often there are long periods of nothing at all, but once started I don't stop. Something will happen – it might be the death of someone – and music will come to me almost full-grown: that's happened a lot during the last three years, but also before that up to a point.

Then how do you begin writing it down?

The first idea will often be melodic, or it might be a chord, and it will hang around for a long time while something is going on inside. Then I have to know from beginning to end what is going to happen. Very often on the way things will change, but I have to know before I start. Then I need to know when it's right – I don't know what 'right' means in this context, but right as far as I am concerned, as right as I can get it. This might sound daft, but I used to go into the country and look at a tree, and connect what was in my mind with the tree. If the tree and the music seemed to be one, then that was right: that was a way of checking it.

So that it felt organic.

That's right. Now I suppose I would look at an icon: that would tell me.

Might you then revise your thoughts at a later stage?

Very little. Though sometimes I get it wrong. I remember once I went with a group of British composers to Denmark, and I gave a lecture on a piece I was going to write: I even thought I knew what the subject matter was going to be. But the piece turned out to be *Ultimos ritos* and nothing to do with the lecture.

Do you keep sketchbooks and go back to old ideas?

Not really, because I feel that everything I do has to be new – which I know rather contradicts what I said before. But otherwise it's not worth doing. If one sees music as a spiritual journey, as I do, then it must always go forward, and I think it must eventually end in silence. I never understood that with Stockhausen: why it didn't end in silence. Perhaps it will.

It doesn't show much sign.

But I think it must end in silence, and go on to prayer, which is a higher form of creativity.

Is the act of composition then primarily a spiritual exercise for the composer?

That's interesting. You did imply that in your review of *Akhmatova Rekviem*, that it was essentially a rite for the composer and didn't need an audience. I was very taken aback by that, and unable really to answer. I don't know.

What's your feeling when works of yours are performed: pleasure, anxiety, embarrassment?

I think embarrassment. And when *Thérèse* was done at Covent Garden, acute embarrassment. I didn't want to be in the audience, to have to listen to what people next to me were going to say.

But perhaps that was partly also because I'd recently moved away from the Catholic to the Orthodox world, and towards Greek art. I feel a lot of sympathy with Greek artists, with the painters and poets I know there. They've got very anti-Western, and they're trying to get back into what is Greek. There's a big revival of interest in Orthodoxy: artists are going to Mount Athos and spending weeks there in study.

You mentioned another opera. Will that be for a large house as Thérèse *was?*

I think for smaller forces. It really isn't anything yet because it hasn't formed itself, but it's based on the story of St Mary of Egypt, who was a prostitute in second-century Alexandria. She took a boat to the Holy Land and went out into the desert, where she spent sixty years. And there was a certain Father Zossíma, who had reached a very high spiritual state through asceticism but had not really known eros, and he met it in Mary, when she was an old woman with her skin scorched by the sun and ferocious winters.

In *Ikon of Light* I worked with the concept of uncreated light. In this new piece, if I can, I'd like to do the same thing with uncreated eros.

I'm not sure what you mean by 'uncreated'.

There's the light of the sun, but there's a light beyond the sun which is the light that was present at the Transfiguration of Christ, or the light that lightens certain very holy men. Knowing love through Mary, Zossíma comes to know uncreated eros, to know the uncreated love which is God's love. He knows love in its fullness.

It's Parsifal.

Yes it is really. Whether I can do it or not I don't know. I would call it a liturgy of eros rather than an opera.

It's a liturgy of the erotic as necessary to the fulfilment of the spiritual.

Yes it is. I'm not sure whether it has to be a continent love or can be incontinent. I think it doesn't matter.

In that case maybe music doesn't have to end in silence. Maybe one can pray and yet go on composing.

Maybe.

12

Robin Holloway

Holloway lives in a college house in Cambridge which was decorated with exuberant fantasy in the thirties: he takes pleasure in sharing the elegant grotesquerie of his surroundings before we start. I remark that he ought to be writing Poulenc in such rooms. 'Some people think I do,' he replies. We tread back between piles of books, scores and records all over the floor, enough to make one feel that if the whole world were to be destroyed but for these rooms, then a large proportion of Western literary and musical culture would survive. Then we talk over sherry, but the atmosphere of a tutorial is rapidly reversed: he sits on a low chair, speaking quietly towards his shoes, and I feel myself put in the role of confessor. When I have to leave, he is concerned that I shall have nothing to eat before going on to a concert, and presses an apple into my hand. The recorded confession, however, is subjected to extensive revision – not in the interests of self-protection but rather of development and detailing – and what I receive back from him is a jigsaw of my typescript, his pencilled alterations and entirely new material typed on the reverses of photocopies of Webern songs.

Your rather large output suggests you were composing copiously from childhood. Is that right?

Yes, I think it began with the first piano lessons, when I was about 6: I remember the pleasure of altering the set pieces and making them take a different direction. Writing began a bit later, and was largely an affair of patterns on paper, more visual than aural.

What music impressed you as a child?

I was very excited by my parents' wind-up gramophone, to the extent that I'd run around the back garden in circles pretending to be a record. I remember vividly the complete *Blue Danube*, the *Italian Concerto* on the harpsichord (it must have been Landowska) and all the glockenspiely bits from *The Magic Flute*. Then from about 8 onwards I was a chorister at St Paul's Cathedral, and was saturated in church music all the way from Tallis to Howells.

Did you now write choral music?

No; I was learning the simpler Debussy piano pieces and writing pieces with pseudo-poetical titles. And there was an orchestral piece called *The Sea*! But the most ambitious effort, which I still have (all the rest was destroyed in a later self-conscious purge), was a three-act opera in full score on Hans Andersen's *Snow Queen*. My best friend at the choir school (he's now sub-organist at Westminster Abbey) wrote the words. Its musical value is negligible, of course; what I see now to have been typical was that I simply kept at it, though it was so big. This determination to see things through seems to me an important part of grown-up composing. And there was a real sense of fulfilling an expectation, because every morning before choir practice the organist would play and sing over what I'd illicitly written only a few hours before when I should have been asleep. This was already a sort of performance thrill, years before anything of mine was actually played.

You weren't having composition lessons at this stage?

No. I think that when I went on to public school they didn't know what to do with me, musically speaking. The director of music, John Carol Case, introduced me to John Carewe, and by special dispensation I was allowed to travel up to London to see him every fortnight, instead of corps. But they weren't real lessons: I showed him pieces, we talked about them a bit, and he loaded me up with scores of Schoenberg, Webern, recent Stravinsky, recent avant-garde music. In my early teens I would come back with piles of this stuff and pore over it: it was an escape hatch from the awfulness of school, whether academic, gregarious, or sporting.

After a time John Carewe sent me on to Iain Hamilton. This didn't work well, but another contact turned out to be extremely helpful. I often went to Dartington, and one year summoned up enough courage and money to take an hour with Nono, who told me with great suavity that what I was writing was dreadful but showed talent, and that I should go to the one composer in England whom it'd be worth studying with.

What sort of music were you writing?

Hopkins and Lawrence settings for voice and orchestra in an uneasy mix of Mahler and Vaughan Williams.

And who was the one composer?

Sandy Goehr, who was incredibly helpful to me in my late teens

Robin Holloway   *photo: Malcolm Crowthers*

and early twenties. Again it wasn't a case of lessons so much as wide-ranging conversations about music and lots of other things. I think this is what I needed most at that age, with all its problems, artistic and otherwise: the contact with a mature musical mind. But whenever he tried to formalize our sessions and make me do an exercise, it didn't work. I never did anything he asked: it always went off at a tangent. I must have been exasperating!

Presumably you were showing him pieces too?

Not at first, because I didn't write much in my late teens. Composers often get confused then: they're taking in so much so quickly, and it takes a long time to digest this mass of new and probably contradictory musical experience. I got writing again when I was an undergraduate at Cambridge. But I read English, not music. I was always trying to resist being musically educated; I felt music was too sacred, too private to be sullied by 'study'. But I'd go and see Sandy during the vacations and sometimes during termtime, and then show him pieces. I remember he wanted to make the music more irregular, break up phrases, sharpen, articulate, make more nervy. It began to emerge that I wasn't his kind of composer: he was very much more a Schoenbergian figure then than he now is. I piously carried my card for some years, and indeed was a convinced modernist. The different directions of later years were very slow, even reluctant, to reveal themselves.

Things were rather blank after I left Cambridge (where I'd finally given in and changed to music for the third year). I spent a period writing correspondence courses in English for African students, composing betweenwhiles and feeling generally frustrated. The music of this time is constructivist atonal Hindemith: strictly put together from little cells of four or five notes which come at you forwards, backwards, upside-down, augmented, and so on. It sounds dreary, and it *is* dreary.

Did you feel you weren't composing the music you wanted to compose?

Yes, I definitely felt that. It probably wasn't completely wasted, because it teaches one to care about notes, to see that they grow from each other, depend on each other, and that one thing can be turned into many guises of itself. But the result then was that these pieces are extremely stiff: it's as if they hadn't heard of the possibility of sounding agreeable, or lucid harmonically. And the orchestration was as grey as the pitches.

However, there was a flash in the pan, before all this and better;

when much later I began to give my pieces opus numbers I chose it as opus 1 because it seemed to be more along the right lines. It's a piece for nine players called *Garden Music*, written in 1962 after I'd been amazed and enchanted by the impact of *Oiseaux exotiques* at Dartington. This revelation that colour and freedom were compatible with tight organization was difficult to follow up, and it was after that that I got lost in the atonal All-Bran. The biggest piece of this kind, the First Concerto for Orchestra, sounds as if it's trying to break loose. It's a constructivist monster, violent, ugly and unremitting. After completing it I virtually seized up altogether.

Yet you still acknowledge that ugly monster?

I certainly do. I think it's authentic, though I can't say I love it very much. It is true to something – if only to how I felt at the time. I revised it a few years ago, with a curious sense of recovering something lost yet familiar.

How do you recognize those qualities of authenticity and truth when you're composing?

When one feels intensely excited, when everything one's got inside oneself is engaged and burnt up by the current preoccupation. That's certainly authentic, though it's no guarantee of quality or of interest to anyone else (one can imagine much highly charged bad music being written in just that state of mind). It's also rather an adolescent condition, and one can do things that are perfectly all right without feeling like that at all. But when I say it's adolescent, I hope I'll still feel it when I'm 80! I think one should follow such impulses. A warier sort of composer would say: don't trust it, send it another way, contradict it. I think that's where Sandy and I would now see things rather differently. I think of him as scrutinizing every move before making it, whereas I don't ask too many questions. When I've 'surged' like this I ask the questions afterwards. And of course composing isn't all surge: it can sometimes be painfully laborious.

How long after that First Concerto for Orchestra were the Schumann pieces?

About four years. The First Concerto was drafted very quickly indeed but only slowly realized in full score, between 1966 and 1969. After this I practically stopped composing. I was writing my thesis on Wagner and Debussy, and worrying about getting jobs and fellowships on the strength of this 'research'. And underneath I was very puzzled and depressed. I wondered if I was a composer at all – though not much good for anything else. 1968 is still a date to conjure with for many reasons: for me personally it merely evokes misery and frustration. I hated the *Zeitgeist* both in general and in music, but had nothing positive to put against it.

Even so, recourse to Schumann was pretty accidental. I'd been playing around with some of his songs, exploring their materials, with only the vaguest idea of writing something that grew out of them. And then suddenly, after no new composition for more than two years, I had to write a piece in a great hurry because the Cheltenham Festival announced a première, of the Concertino No. 2, the last dried-out gasp after the First Concerto for Orchestra. In fact it had already been performed, and they insisted on a première, so I thought I'd better oblige. I'm very glad I did, because all these latent possibilities from the Schumann suddenly fused, and I wrote *Scenes from Schumann* in a couple of months or so early in 1970.

What were your feelings in writing that? You must have had a strong sense of its authenticity, if you like, to dare go ahead.

Actually I didn't feel authentic at all! More like anxious, guilty and confused. And when the Festival people wanted to see a movement in advance, I posted it off with shame. I felt as if I'd committed some kind of crime. I think my feeling in the face of life at large was one of total embarrassment. I'd got a research fellowship at Caius for a mixture of academic and creative work. Recourse to the nineteenth century seemed to symbolize the conflict between the two, and the hollowness within; indeed it is only recently that some very loving performances have persuaded me that it *is* real composition – in fact a sort of second Opus 1.

Yet *Scenes from Schumann* didn't feel like finding terra firma after quagmire or truth after lies. It felt extremely tentative, the absolute opposite of a polemic or riposte. Before the first rehearsal I was absolutely terrified, and thought all the players would mock me, not only because of the well-loved tunes coming on solo trumpets but also because of mistakes in instrumental technique and overall orchestral balance. Remember, I'd only heard my own instrumentation in small groups playing grey pieces! It was an incredible relief when it all worked, and sounded so well so soon.

How did you then go on?

At first it was difficult to follow up *Scenes from Schumann* – indeed, I felt quite as puzzled as before, and hardly less guilty. But gradually more and more things opened out from this first apparently tentative move – not just the two further 'Schumann' works, but everything most loved and yet most prohibited by the *Zeitgeist*. All the favourite music that I'd spent my teens and early twenties taking in could now be exhaled. It's as if I'd held my breath till I was 26 and have been releasing it ever since. Somehow one takes in other music like food, water, air, sunlight: it becomes an inseparable part of one's consciousness and unconsciousness. All this, though simple enough, just wasn't allowed by the spirit of 1968. That was my problem with the time. Things were absolutely forbidden, and it was basically everything that I loved most: what seemed to me essential to the very nature of music, which was something that bubbled and flowed forth and gave simple pleasure.

Yet I remember very well being extremely excited at that time by what one was hearing from Boulez, Birtwistle, Maxwell Davies . . .

I'd been excited by the Glock regime at the BBC, hearing new music along with music from the beginning of the century; first contacts with the Schoenberg *Five Orchestral Pieces* or *Erwartung* are still red-letter days. But 1968 was the year of student revolt, and because one was just a few years older one saw how incredibly stupid that was. Perhaps it's not fair to associate this with the dogmatism of the musical world at large, or at any rate with the vociferous part of it that seemed to represent the spirit of the age. I can only say that for me personally it seemed like the spirit of denial. But my finding the times out of joint was obviously partly because I felt my own achievement to be so meagre. I was repelled by everything around me, but was painfully aware of the feebleness of the steps I was taking to get out of the impasse.

Did you go on feeling that after the first Schumann piece?

I still feel it sometimes.

Did you worry about being individual? Do you still?

Hugely then, but not much now. I trust to character to show itself willy-nilly, as it does when people talk, or walk, or act. The same goes for contemporaneity, or 'relevance' to use a favourite word of those days. These aren't things a composer should be concerned with.

Indeed, the times have changed. There's not the same drive to do things that have never been done before.

Well, I think I want to do things that haven't been done before, but

I also want to do things that *have* been done before, in my own way. Sometimes it almost seems as if I were a kind of shopping centre: I'd like to have a 'Delius' piece, a 'Rachmaninov' piece, a 'Xenakis', a 'Copland', and so on, among my wares. Of course, to write such pieces as part of a deliberate programme would be ridiculous; but something like this is what in effect happens as less and less is prohibited. One turns like a grateful plant towards all kinds of very contrasted composers who excite and please one, and pays them for what one takes in the form of a stylistic or technical homage.

There's a curious inversion, isn't there, that 1968 seemed the great dawn of freedom, and yet the unspoken censorship was severe, whereas since then one has been living in generally less liberal but artistically freer times.

Yes, so much so that it can be a real temptation to 'go modern' again, especially with all this soft-centred new tonal music that makes me scream and call for Xenakis.

Having felt yourself out of step in 1968, do you now feel that you belong more with other composers?

No. I don't like swimming with the tide; it feels uncomfortable. Although personally I'm soft-spoken and tractable, I think there's an inner stubbornness that flourishes on going counter. This is why I'm so appalled by the flood of easy, brightly coloured, tonally tinged music that's being written at the moment, which you might perhaps expect me to hail with delight as the antithesis of 1968. I don't delight in it as a movement (though I do in some particular composers). I want triadic and 'referential' music to be rigorous and strong, whether it's being craggy or whether it's being sweet. So there's a perversity here which I now see is connected with my strenuously resisting a proper musical education. I want the tonal means I use in articulating and expressing my musical ideas to be *my* way, untouched either by academic correctness or by this new *Zeitgeist*, though of course using either if they're needed.

It's like being contradicted by intelligent pupils. If you get them to agree, there's a petty triumph, which soon becomes tedious and eventually irritating. Whereas if there's dissension, if you disturb the calm water, something happens. I like that a lot, and not just in teaching! I'm always horrified when I'm claimed by old-style tonal composers who've kept chugging along through all the years that they disliked too, or by composers much younger than myself who've not gone through the grind of strong ambiguous feelings about what they're doing. I feel a shudder of dissociation: I don't want to fit.

And I think it's quite interesting that after the first flush of exuberance released by the Schumann, which lasted some six years, I then moved to much more constructivist, modern-sounding pieces, which resembled in technique the music I'd composed in the years that led to the impasse. But now, of course, this way of writing had something behind it, like harmony, direction, volatility of movement, a sense of instrumental colour.

How does a piece start?

The first idea may be any one of a number of things. For instance, the Second Concerto for Orchestra began as a vision of something enormous and distant but very defined. It was like seeing a huge cloud, but seeing it sonorously, with a strong sense of the kind of noise, and the kind of shapes, directions and movements the noises would make. But actually to find the *notes*, and from the notes the broader things, and thus the means to get ropes round this thing and haul it in . . . that was as difficult as the sonorous vision was effortless. I remember working on details and getting absolutely nowhere, until I'd simply have to leave it and go for a walk. Just thinking about this sonic cloud would bring it back again, distant and distinct, reminding me of what all the details were trying to make. I'd look at a real-life patch of seascape or beach, and look *through* them to get this mirage back into view. And then, recovering the sense of something palpable, I'd go back to putting one note against another, and gradually make it actual. So there can be a big discrepancy between the vision, which is so immediate, and the actual making, which is remote and abstract and *slow*.

What you've just been saying inevitably reminds one of Sea Surface Full of Clouds. *Did that come from looking at nature?*

Oh no, that came from the Wallace Stevens poem. It's a piece of virtuoso linguistic jugglery, perpetual variations within a set pattern: both the pattern and the variants are a gift to a composer. And I didn't think at all about natural appearances except in the sea interludes, where there weren't words to go on; and then indeed I did think of water and cloud-like shapes.

Sometimes the origin of a work can be very concrete: one is seized by an interval, or a chord, a kind of noise, some rhythmic pattern. I remember once being annoyed in a room where people were talking, relaxedly and casually except for one woman with a very nagging voice; as I drummed my fingers in irritation, it turned into a pattern, and became the nagging horn part that runs through the *Scherzo malincolico* in *Evening with Angels*.

Do you keep sketchbooks of these things?

Sketches tend to be scrawled on anything that lies to hand, like this agenda of a dutiful meeting. Then I try to use them as quickly as I can, catch them while they're hot. Quite soon they don't mean very much.

Or sometimes the stimulus can be, as it was with my schoolboy opera, the fact that someone's going to play it: that makes one salivate with immediate musical ideas. Someone telephoned last summer, while I was working on something quite different, and asked if there would be a chance of a bassoon concerto. I'd never imagined a bassoon concerto in my life, but while he was on the phone I was already thinking about the bassoon, that great long tube of bassoon noise that one sees and hears, and I wished he'd just shut up so that I could begin to write it down! I went back to where I was working and wrote an upbeat phrase, then couldn't let it alone, until a whole paragraph of bassoon line had been rapidly drafted. Every rational impulse says no, that one hasn't got time, that one's not really interested; but the saliva says yes.

So sometimes it's as if the work is already fully formed, and you just have to set it down, whereas at other times it has to be sought out, and with great difficulty you realize something that you know exists. And sometimes it's a surprise: you don't know that anything exists, but you follow where the music takes you, with pleasure, surprise and gratitude.

And perhaps sometimes the first idea would come from the text?

Songs used to be very immediate; quite often I wouldn't even read the poem through before beginning the setting (having, of course, decided already to set on the basis of previous reading). I could almost invent the song while I read the poem. But that's not true of the songs I've written more recently, which have been very difficult to do, and far less spontaneous. In fact I haven't written any songs for some time now, partly because I can't find texts that make me salivate, and partly because it just seems to have come to an end for the moment. On the other hand, the spontaneity can come straight out of an instrument, as I've described with the bassoon, and as I've recently found in writing within a few weeks a harp concerto that, again, hadn't even been imagined before the commissioning telephone call.

Once the impulse has started, does it always go to completion, or are there a lot of abandoned works?

I don't often abandon works. Once or twice bright ideas which have begun with a real impetus have just petered out. But I can't hold much in my head at the same time: I find it almost physically unbearable to have several things in mind at once, so I like to drive through and get to the end of something, then turn at once to its complement.

But weren't you composing other things while you were at work on your opera Clarissa?

Not really. I'd thought about *Clarissa* over some years, of course, had written fragments, and indeed had several bosh shots at starting the whole. But eventually it was written in one go, uninterrupted by anything else. And that's been true of all my largest pieces: they've been written in one breath, as it were. I'll turn for relief to the complementary songs or small piece only when the big haul has been safely netted.

Clarissa *was exceedingly unusual, not only for you but generally, in having been written without a commission.*

Well, I'd better say what I really feel, which is that what I most want to do, and what I believe I can do best, is write big pieces – not necessarily operas or ballets, but mixed-genre pieces that tell a story, like the Berlioz *Damnation of Faust*, pieces that are a whole evening, a whole event, a whole world. I have three or four visions of such works, which in the concert hall can bring many things before the audience's eyes in a fantastical way impossible in the theatre. Since these are never likely to be commissioned, I've just got to write them anyway, preferably while still youngish and full of juice, without waiting around for commissions that won't come. It's the strongest urge I've got, so much so that it's as if my other pieces had only been written at half-cock. But this might always be self-delusion!

What are your stories?

The first two are both after Ibsen: *Brand* and *Peer Gynt*. The idea of either of these as straight opera seems to me either impossible or crashingly obvious. Instead I've melted down the original poetic dramas and completely recast them. *Brand*, already composed, is a choral ballad that tells its story in narrative rather than showing it in action, and *Peer* will become I don't know what! Again the concert hall is the place, and the medium that of soloists, chorus and orchestra, for a story that is part ballet, part play, part travel film, part opera, as well as being song, cantata and symphonic poem. The chief influence, I suppose, is from the incredibly close correspondence that can be achieved between music and setting, music and human gesture, when opera is filmed or televised.

And later?

The others would be less story-oriented, more like explorations of an area of subject matter and experience, like Tippett's *Mask of Time*.

Do you make efforts to get these pieces performed?

Not strenuous efforts; these days the egotistical sublime tends to be impractically expensive to realize, and I'm resigned to probably never hearing these great white elephants. Which is not to say that they're private or closet pieces; they're certainly meant to speak. But the truth is that commissions are on the whole going to be for modest, useful pieces – like bassoon concertos.

13

Nigel Osborne

The interview with Osborne takes place slightly furtively against the screen of chatter in the crypt of St John's, Smith Square, before a London Sinfonietta concert. He seems like the leader of a small anarchist cadre stating his plans, quietly but quickly and excitedly. My digest of the proceedings I begin to fear has been swallowed, but it comes back at the last minute via one of his fellow lecturers at Nottingham and my editor at Faber's.

In your introduction to the first issue of Contemporary Music Review *you remarked how young composers in the 1950s seemed very single-minded whereas now the situation is much more diffuse. Could you say how you were affected by the music associated with Darmstadt?*

Well, first I should qualify that statement to say that obviously in retrospect the situation can always look more coherent, and maybe eventually the eighties will appear more coherent than they do at the moment. But the main point is that there was a group of composers who were forging a bridgehead and inventing an aesthetic. I don't know whether or not one can do that in such a contrived way, but they were making a conscious stand which one has not had since then so concertedly.

The answer to its influence is that it was very profound, in the mid-1960s when it began to filter through. I got to know the Stockhausen *Klavierstücke* quite well, and the major early Boulez works: *Le marteau* and later *Pli selon pli*. That was the music I got excited by: it was a fascination for that which shines and dazzles. At Oxford Wellesz was carrying the torch of the second Viennese school, but this new music one discovered on one's own, and that was when my music really took off. It was the one time I've taken a jump and suddenly started composing in a different way. Everything that has followed on from that has either been a measurable reaction or a measurable continuation.

Were you having pieces performed at Oxford?

Not very much. There had been a phase before when I had heard things done at local performances, but most of the music I heard performed in Oxford was for the theatre: incidental scores and revue. That very lively theatre world at Oxford did generate the chance for creative composition, with a lot of very specific demands that made it a good apprenticeship. So I was living a schizophrenic compositional existence, in that the more serious works weren't getting much of an airing.

Then after Oxford you went to study in Poland?

Yes. I think the decision to go there was the beginning of encountering the limitations of what had fascinated me. Darmstadt is young man's music, in its bravery and in the way it engages one: it's something one's very receptive to at a certain age, as I see in my own students now. But by the time I went to Poland I was beginning to find it avoided certain questions that became of increasing importance to me: aspects of directness, to put it very bluntly, but also the fact that it had a strange emotional life in not always seeming conscious of what it was. Once one had entered into the Darmstadt world, about which we're generalizing very brutally of course, one had taken on board a whole area of surface language which operates very strongly in an emotional and aesthetic way, and that bothered me. I wanted to cut away what sometimes was over-elaboration, was too clever. I started to be interested in taking ideas and smelting them down to what one imagines their essence to be – even sometimes to their annihilation: it's a dangerous process, and one can put too much attention on refining one's musical objects until they melt into amorphous globules. I think I tend to do that.

But whether rightly or wrongly, the Polish school as it existed in the 1960s seemed to offer an alternative to Darmstadt, and also I was fascinated by the society. Polish music seemed to offer, too, performer engagement. I was very interested in putting the performer in a position where through his own creativity, his physical and intellectual involvement, he could arrive at the compositional result. And I found traces of that in, say, the way Penderecki was influenced by Xenakis and found physical, muscular, motoric methods of creating a random cloud which in Xenakis had been put together in a very determined way.

Who did you study with in Poland?

Witold Rudziński. He's an opera composer, and not, for a number

Nigel Osborne   *photo: Malcolm Crowthers*

of complex reasons, one who was ever promoted in the way that some composers of the Polish school were. He was a tremendous renaissance man, and so we had a lot of fun talking about philology as much as we talked about composition. He was also a very acute teacher, and I think I got a lot from him.

Also I worked at the radio experimental studio. That was my first real experience of electronic music, but a lot of pieces weren't finished, because there were tremendous problems in getting enough time. I'd played with tape recorders before, but that was a crucial musical and aesthetic awakening: to be able to break into sounds, become more acoustically sensitized, which brings you back to instruments refreshed. One can see this danger of the ugly, un-alluring electronic medium as compared with the live world of instruments, but I really think that when you go into the studio you are in touch with a twentieth-century instrument. And you know that: you feel the exhilaration of that. Obviously I love traditional instruments, even though, because of this strange time warp we're in, they've remained frozen for a hundred years or so: their sounds still have a vibrancy, an attraction, a potential that one wants to use. The studio is really very important in leading one to hear traditional instruments in a different way – I'm not romanticizing here: it's a very concrete thing. And there's an excitement in being able to develop that in the way that composers of the eighteenth century helped to develop the flute and the clarinet through a process of compositional aspiration.

Yet you haven't done much electronic music since, except recently at IRCAM.

I did go back to the Polish studio in 1978, and I've done a lot of live electronic music: that began in Poland, where we had a live electronic improvisation group, which was very formative for me as well. And that continued during the 1970s, when I performed a lot of live electronic music, though not in exposed concert situations. Improvisation is very important. It belongs obviously with the attitudes and ideas of the late sixties, and like them it perhaps suffers from *naïveté* and a lack of self-examination at one level, while at the same time being a very powerful and intellectually generous jump.

Did you have any lessons with Lutosławski while you were in Poland?

One doesn't study with Lutosławski: one has consultations. But I never had the guts. That was one of the things I'd gone for: I really did want to study with Lutosławski, but when it came to knocking on the door I couldn't do it.

Was it in Poland that you wrote the first works you now acknowledge?

I think the first was probably the cantata *Seven Words*, which I began in Oxford, worked on in Poland, and finished when I got back.

Did you feel in that work that you'd found the music you'd been wanting to write?

I think there are probably a series of such moments, and then a lot of steps backwards as well. There is an intuition in the act of composition of authenticity: there are times when you know you're writing in a way that is totally as it should be, and is realizing itself to a maximum. The first of those exhilarating, potent experiences was around that time, but it only gets knocked down by crippling self-doubt.

The rate at which you compose doesn't suggest you have crippling self-doubt.

I think I do. I have terrible psychic battlefields in which pieces happen.

Do they ever get abandoned?

Not as a rule. I'm rather ruthless with myself about that: I think it's important to see things through even if they're not going to be what you hoped sometimes. And sometimes things are meant to be not what you wanted them to be. Another law takes over, and the act of composition can be making oneself vulnerable to things that are going to change direction.

Composition can be embarking on a wave of energy, if that isn't too metaphysical, a wave that will begin and will expand itself: that will be the process of composition, and that will be the composition, the articulation of that energy.

How does that energy first present itself?

In various ways. I suppose these days it comes far more as a feeling of the whole, hearing what it is – but it's a funny kind of hearing, in a very inner ear, that almost feels as much as hears. So it presents itself as a sound world, an energy world, and then one begins a kind of analysis.

I'm disturbed by the fact that I don't very much compose from individual ideas, from what Asafyev called 'intonations', from the utterance, the *énoncé*, because I value the utterance very much: it comes back to my smelting metaphor of earlier on. I think that music's existence for us is very much centred on the utterance.

Is that something that would take a line through a piece?

It might be an element of it. One of the areas of my interest in ethnic music is in the construction of an utterance from an archetypal base: utterances very often are archetypal elements, in that an archetype is the template against which utterances exist. My instincts have been leading me towards creating the musical utterance in the context of something that has already been assimilated in society's ear.

A lot of our problems do arise obviously from this question of assimilation: we have this over-assimilated tonal language, and we tried somehow to replace it with systems which do not have that depth of assimilation. Instinctively – this isn't at all an intellectual thing – I've been interested in ethnic music and in archetypes as one way of striking a level of assimilation, so that the idea has a reality, a real significance in the composition.

Does this mean that you would analyse a piece of ethnic music you were interested in?

Yes I would, but very often it's a kind of magnetism. I know where I have to look now for the kinds of intuitions I've felt about the sorts of deep structures that I'm aspiring towards: there's an appetite for such deep structures, and then I find them. I'm sure it's very temporary: I don't hold this up as any kind of salvation for anybody. But one of the virtues of the present situation for composition is its temporariness. I don't think we'll produce the masterworks, now or for some time: the culture is not in that state. It's in the state for something almost higher, for the uninhibited, intellectually generous, vulnerable utterance.

Are you saying that works of today are going to be immediate, not lasting in their importance?

I don't write for posterity . . .

But what about your own viewpoint? How do you react to works you wrote maybe fifteen years ago?

I'm very grateful for their traces of my existence; I'm very touched by them. But I'm talking about the musical language rather than about particular works. There are composers who are attempting to find various ways to reinvent the building blocks for works that have the integrity and all the other qualities we associate with masterpieces of the past. I think that's a very worthy direction, but I also think this may be the time for a temporary utterance, a kind of exploration, something that may not be built on a consciously contrived system of technique but may represent a very temporary phase in the grappling of our consciousnesses with what music could and may be.

I suppose it's tied up with my belief that the music which is meant to be is there already. There's a sense in which the composer has to be definitive, not caring whether what he writes is in anybody else's head or not. But in this strange dislocated world we live in there is, I suspect, a frustrated musical subconscious, and the more temporary products of our culture may be an expression of that, which is why I said they might be higher in their attainment than the perfected masterwork.

It's just a personal thing: in my own case I feel that when the energy of a work is completed, that is it. I would be very happy, almost pleased for the music I write to disappear into thin air – though I'm very glad too for its existence. I don't like the idea of compositions as commodities. Composition should be an open field, something which must be in a way evanescent and disappearing.

But we live in a world where pieces are going to be published, recorded and broadcast, and so given a concrete existence.

Yes, but I wonder whether the spread of information technology won't produce a much greater flow, so that the importance of the individual work of art recedes.

In a sense we're there already, in that there are so many composers writing today that it's impossible for anyone to keep pace.

Which is the unfortunate side of it. But I think the composer is a representative of the human race's creativity, and it's very encouraging that it spreads.

Don't you, though, see your own music as the expression of a very individual sensibility?

Yes, I think so, but I only see that sensibility in terms of something broader. If there's any proselytizing thrust, it's not saying, 'Here is me', but rather 'Here is a way of being.'

Often that way of being has involved the use of poetry, in various languages. How do you choose texts?

Usually they announce themselves, either because one is immediately musically turned on by the words (and that's probably the more dangerous kind of inspiration), or else because one is just excited, and then the turning of that into compositional energy is rather more interesting. That happens, for instance, in my work with Craig Raine, which also raises a lot of problems of vocabulary and so on, problems which I'm interested in trying to work out. Because I think we have to set contemporary poetry: it's something that hasn't been done enough, and it requires us to face up to ourselves.

What about opera, which suddenly you're embarking on in two different ways, for Glyndebourne and for Opera Factory?

Actually the interest in music theatre has been there for a long time: I believe one of the futures for theatre is music theatre, for the moment. Also I'm aware of a dramatic element in the way that I write, and so it's almost inevitable that I would want to tackle that medium.

Yet it seems to me there's a central difficulty, if one's dealing with narrative, in creating music that can cope with continuity in something other than a diatonic way.

Yes indeed: I shall be interested to see how I solve that. I think I know how I'm going to do it, I hope by means of a harmonic-acoustic consistency, because in my work harmony and acoustics are very tied up together. My harmonic practice is derived from acoustics – again not intellectually but rather from this process that began in the studio of hearing inside sounds. I agree very much with Varèse when he speaks of music being the intelligence that's inside sounds: I think what he meant was that much of our harmony is an externalization of intuitions about the internal structure of sounds. For example, I've often found that the harmony I wanted to hear was attributable to frequency modulation, which in turn may be associated with inharmonic sounds: that happens in *Zansa*. And similarly when I dissolved the human voice in the piece I did at IRCAM, the harmonic logic related to the formants in the spectrum, and met an intuition that I'd been working towards for some time. I think the music I'm writing is a decoding of the interior behaviour of sounds, in the sense that the triad is a decoding of harmonic sounds.

14

Tim Souster

Souster greets me at his Cambridge semi, makes me a colossal mug of tea in the kitchen, and then leads me out into the garden, where he has established himself in a long brick shed. One half of this is peopled by a circle of hi-tech electronic instruments and consoles; for the rest, there is a sofa and a chair, an upright piano, and a bookcase groaning with scores and an opened packet of Jaffa Cakes. The tea is gradually consumed during our conversation, Souster afterwards makes little comment about his script, except to suggest that it says more about Stockhausen than about his recent music. I endeavour to set his mind at rest.

Did you begin composing with an interest in electronics, or did that develop?

No, I came to electronics very late. I suppose I first became aware of it at Stockhausen's courses at Darmstadt, and through a recording of *Kontakte*, which I really got obsessed by during my last year at Oxford, in 1964. I'd been to Darmstadt in 1963, and attended Stockhausen's courses on *Gruppen* and *Carré*, and I went again in 1970.

But my first electronic equipment was primitive in the extreme. I got Hugh Davies to build me a ring modulator in a cardboard box, which I've still got, and I started putting discs through that, and bought an old oscillator from an army-surplus shop and an old guitar amplifier: it was really Heath Robinson. At the same time I started getting interested in the more experimental rock music that was coming along in the mid-sixties. Then through working at the BBC as a producer I got to know about recording techniques, and that was all very valuable. But it was ages before I was able to do anything at a full-blown electronic music studio: that wasn't until 1973–4, when I worked at the West German Radio station in Cologne on *World Music*.

Though before that you'd been playing live electronic music with the group Intermodulation.

Certainly. There were various reasons why Intermodulation started up. In the first place, there were all these pieces that Stockhausen was writing for his own group, and we wanted to do our own versions, to do them differently: some of the pieces we did very differently. So Roger Smalley and I got together and formed this group, and we got a grant for some equipment. That was when the VCS 3 synthesizer came out: it was an extraordinarily forward-looking, clever device, that you could signal things into, rather than just using it as a keyboard. Nowadays 90 per cent of the machinery is oriented towards the production of pop music, which is a terrible reduction.

So in my present situation I tend to buy things that have been made for a different kind of music and then undo them a bit, and put them together in different ways: you can do a lot like that. It's an interesting parallel with the way electronic music started off in the first place. You have to misuse the equipment creatively in order to get really interesting results out of it.

Why was it that you went to Darmstadt in 1963? Presumably you were already familiar with Stockhausen's music.

Oh yes, I'd got the old 10-inch record of *Gesang der Jünglinge* while I was still at school, and I'd always been fascinated by that piece and by the two *Electronic Studies*. Also I'd studied German at school and been to the youth courses at Bayreuth, playing the viola in the orchestra: Darmstadt was just a more avant-garde version of that study-trip idea. And I'm very glad I went, because it was only then that the whole idiom of Stockhausen and his contemporaries fell into place for me.

Before that I hadn't really been able to understand it. I remember I heard Boulez play his Third Sonata in Freiburg in 1959, and I couldn't make head or tail of it. But then in the middle of a lecture by Stockhausen on *Carré*, at Darmstadt in 1963, it suddenly all began to make sense. So I was motivated to study the way in which the music had been put together, the methods associated with Stockhausen's music of that time: group structure, moment form, the interrelationship of the micro and the macro, and so on. That taught me a lot, and even in my recent music, where I'm using intentionally banal material or referring to pre-existing styles, the way I try to make something of it *does* relate to Stockhausen's use of 'found materials' in pieces like *Hymnen* and *Telemusik*.

Before you went to Darmstadt, then, had you been writing in some quite other style?

Tim Souster   *photo: Mark Warner*

I didn't really feel that I'd started writing at all seriously until well *after* that. After I left Oxford I went to London and had a few sessions with Richard Rodney Bennett, and it was only then that I properly started to compose. That was still instrumental music: it wasn't until even later that I got to grips with electronics. I think I got the famous ring modulator in 1968, and my first electronic piece was *Titus Groan Music* in 1969, which has been withdrawn because we couldn't get the equipment it needed: that was for wind quintet and electronics.

So it was quite late that I came to electronics, and it's always gone in parallel with writing for purely acoustic media. I happen to have specialized quite a bit in electronics, but I've never regarded myself as a purely electronic composer.

Though there was quite a period from 1969 up to the late seventies when nearly all your music was electronic.

Yes, but that was because I was working with electronic groups: Intermodulation and then OdB. And there's a tremendous disadvantage to that approach, because you end up with a lot of pieces that nobody else can play. I think that must have been Stockhausen's experience: now that he no longer has his regular group, nobody does pieces like *Kurzwellen*. And to take another example, the climax of my work with Intermodulation was *World Music*, which is a big piece lasting seventy-three minutes, where I wrote a part for Robin Thompson in which he has to double on soprano saxophone, bassoon, electric piano and electric guitar. Now the number of people who are going to be able to play that part . . . well, I think it's still just Robin, and he lives in Okinawa.

But perhaps obsolescence is natural to electronic music. You mention Kurzwellen, *which exists on record and so in a sense it gets played all the time. It's like rock music: one could say nobody plays* Sergeant Pepper *any more, but that's not really the point.*

Yes, but the difference is that *Sergeant Pepper* was entirely a studio product, whereas *Kurzwellen* is essentially a live process, which has to be quite radically recreated each time. Though it's true that even *Sergeant Pepper* now sounds entirely different from how it did when it was new: I keep hearing it now because my daughters and their friends seem to be reliving the whole sixties development of rock music, and playing the Beatles, the Rolling Stones, Simon and Garfunkel, the Beach Boys, the Doors.

But I still think there has to be a live element, because the really exciting thing is in the interaction between the live elements and the technology. For it all to be fixed, in no matter how perfect a version, is a lot less interesting. And we experienced that at the recent Stockhausen festival in London: it was marvellous to hear pieces like *Kontakte* done live again.

Is it still the Stockhausen works of that period that particularly interest you?

Oh yes. I parted company with him quite early on. I was his teaching assistant in Cologne only until 1973, and the last practical collaboration was when Intermodulation took part in the recording of *Sternklang* in 1975. Since then I haven't followed the development of his music so closely. I suppose a reaction sets in: I'd been intensively engaged in it, doing seminars all day long on works like *Mantra*. After that I wanted to break away and interest myself in my own areas, which stylistically are very far away from Stockhausen.

Has that sort of distancing happened also in your relationship with rock music, where there was a very fertile interaction in the late sixties and early seventies?

I had Stockhausenesque ideas of integration, and I think, yes, since then a reaction to that has also set in. Paradoxically, though, I'm now doing more rock-type music occasionally for practical reasons. Previously I was dreaming of an integration but not actually doing rock music myself; nowadays I do it, but keep it separate from my concert music. Because I think both kinds of music are better if they are more concentratedly themselves.

Also surely rock music is a lot less interesting now than it was in the sixties?

Certainly it's lost its fluidity, become more organized, more packaged. And certainly the most interesting rock bands I've ever heard were the Soft Machine and The Who around 1966–8. But you can't turn the clock back, and nowadays some of the commercial stuff is wonderfully done: people like Bucks Fizz are very skilfully produced. I'm still influenced by that to an extent as recording technique, but I would want to keep the different kinds of music separate. Everything tends to get overrun with influence from everything else, and it's wonderful to find something that isn't influenced from outside.

Are your working methods different in the two media, electronic and live?

Yes. Because I have my own electronic set-up, I tend to write more pragmatically and experimentally on that side. Where I might start an instrumental piece by working with intervals and harmonic structures, an electronic piece would begin from a more technical, acoustical angle. For instance, with *The Transistor Radio of St Narcissus*, which is for flugelhorn and tape, the first process was just to record a lot of flugelhorn tones and analyse the spectra. Then out of that came a means of organization. I recorded a lot of sweeps, lip glissandos, on all the fundamental notes going down to the bottom B flat. I laid out all the pitches produced by these lip glissandos in a kind of table: I think there were seven spectra. Then I traced out wave forms through the table, and produced artificial spectra which were combinations of the ones I'd recorded. So acoustical analysis produces a musical system out of which you then build the piece. It gave me a way of mediating between the very noisy beginning, which uses all the upper areas of the spectra, and the very simple harmonic relationships at the end. The piece ends with almost tonal harmony, though it's got nothing to do with tonality in the traditional sense: it's simply using the intervals that come at the bottom of the sound spectra. The artificial spectra gave me a way of going very coherently from noise to simple harmony, without bunging in tonal chords for nostalgic reasons.

How do you see your use of tonality in the instrumental pieces, like the Sonata?

That's rather comparable, in that what I found most unsatisfactory about the serial language was that it precluded the use of consonant intervals. It seemed rather outdated to have taboos of this kind. But the problem was how to make coherent use of the simple ratios, and relate them to the more dissonant intervals. In another 200 years it may appear that pieces like the Sonata *are* just late examples of tonality, but I don't think of them myself in those terms: I think of them more in terms of serial music and acoustics. There is a cadence structure which keeps recurring in the last movement, which is just based on a series of eight chords; but the fact that the second chord in each pair is diatonic is almost coincidental. The blocks are animated as *sound*, rather than with reference to a tonal structure: the same hugely elaborated dominant chord comes four times, and it's resolved in four different ways, towards different keys. But I was using the chords essentially as sonorities, sustaining different notes and getting all sorts of other chords out of them.

But they're sonorities one wouldn't have found in one of the early Stockhausen Klavierstücke.

Exactly. But the way they're layered and patterned out is very much a post-electronic kind of instrumental writing. That movement is certainly very post-Riley and Reich: I didn't write it in imitation of those styles, but that must be the influence. It's tonal harmony, but after a certain point the exact nature of the chord becomes irrelevant, because one's listening to it as a sound object. The interest is in the constant variation, and in hearing all the detail.

And I didn't mean the title 'Sonata' to suggest that it was a traditional piece: I feel I've rather grown away from the whole central European tradition. Even so, I started writing it as a sonata for cello and piano with accompanying instruments, like the Berg Chamber Concerto, and that was for personal reasons partly, because as a student I'd spent a lot of time playing Beethoven cello sonatas with Christopher van Kampen. Then, as often happens, in the writing it became something else: it became a sonata for cello, and the piano joined the ensemble. Moreover, the pre-classical concept of the sonata was in my mind as well.

Did you start that piece with an idea of the whole form?

No, it's rather large, and it tended to grow in the composition. It started off with the harmonic progression of the last movement, and it was much later that I wrote the theme for the first movement. I was trying to get away from taboos, and I kept coming up with material: I wrote the first movement in California, and I was playing it on a Wurlitzer electric piano, which has a very fine Beach Boys pedigree. It's very difficult to believe in any kind of musical taboo under those circumstances. I kept coming up with ideas that I couldn't account for, and for that very reason I tended to include them: it was like going against all the principles I'd learned of organization, rigour and conscious derivation.

I like to do that, to take material almost at random and then bind it together afterwards: it might be a found object, which one then analyses and makes something of, using rules that are proper to that piece of material rather than imposed. *Spectral* was a case in point. I was attracted to the sound of the humpback-whale song, and I transcribed it from a record as accurately as I could. Then I analysed the pitch structure and derived the harmonic structure of the piece from that. The opening is an actual bit of whale song transcribed on to the viola, but then it goes away from that and develops into something else. It's the same in the soprano saxophone piece *Zorna*, which starts out as a transcription of a piece of Turkish oboe music.

That kind of working leads to a very heterogeneous output.

I think there *are* links, but I do have a tendency to want always to do something completely *different* from last time. I am hopelessly eclectic.

15

Stephen Oliver

Oliver trumps all his colleagues by his choice of rendezvous: he suggests an assignation by the Bronzino allegory in the National Gallery. Having thus assured himself an invincible lead in the game of interviewmanship, he is thoroughly relaxed for the remainder of the afternoon. I rescue my cassette recorder from the left-luggage counter where I had been obliged to leave it (no unauthorized recording of the collection), and we talk over tea in the gallery café. He is at once affable and arrogant, open and sardonic; it is a delightful performance. Some weeks later he returns the script, not scrawled as usual with changes but beautifully retyped by his secretary, and accompanied by similarly pristine lists of works and recordings.

How did it come about that you were already writing operas at a phenomenal rate when you were still a boy?

Phenomenal? Would you say so? I think perhaps children are naturally fertile and find it quite easy to make things.

But why operas, rather than mud pies or sandcastles?

Well, thinking you might ask me that, I've been trying to work it out myself: but really from this distance it looks an inevitable thing, like one of those not-to-be-avoided dooms that fall on people in Greek plays.

For one thing, my father was an amateur actor. Twice a year his company would put on plays with titles like *Plaintiff in a Pretty Hat* or *Dear Charles*; faintly risqué comedies of the 1950s. I loved them. There were plays like that all over the house, and I read them all. Indeed it was only in search of similar scenes that I opened other books. Boswell, for instance – I came upon him when I was about 13, and I can still remember the glow of pleasure with which I discovered Wilkes and Johnson meeting at dinner. That's a perfectly structured scene – a surface of elegant, even beautiful, cadences, and all sorts of tensions stretched beneath them.

And then, there's a tiny group of children in this country who spend day after day pouring out in public the most impassioned and

Stephen Oliver   *photo: John Goldblatt*

profound utterances of the human spirit, couched in a heart-searchingly personal rhetoric – the Book of Psalms. These children are choirboys; and I was one of them, at St Paul's Cathedral. After that, what can you write but operas?

I didn't actually see an opera, by the way, until I was about 17, by which time I suppose I'd made up about half-a-dozen myself. And then I rather took against the whole thing. The style of singing puzzled me, for instance. I didn't see why the singers swooped from note to note, or took to my mind impermissible liberties with the rhythms. And the freedom of pulse in very rhetorical composers like Puccini foxed me completely – I couldn't hear where the beat was or how the music was shaped.

What was your first opera about? How old were you, 12? What does a 12-year-old think is a good idea for an opera?

Well, I'm afraid in my case it was the story of St Paul blinding Elymas. I never finished the music; partly no doubt because of the distractions of childhood, but partly because the more I thought about it the nastier the incident seemed to be. So my second one, which I did finish, was a pleasanter tale about two ghosts in the

Tower of London whose heads have been chopped off. Of course, neither of them was performed: it's not that easy to find singers willing to be blinded or lacking a head.

So when did you start writing operas that you did *want performed – or indeed that you* do *want performed?*

Or ones that, once you've seen them performed, you want performed again. Yes, when I was at Oxford, I suppose. I went up to Oxford with a little one-acter, *All the Tea in China*, which I took to my tutor, Kenneth Leighton, who played it through from the full score – that really impressed me – and said it was OK. So we put it on: Nicholas Cleobury conducted it, and I directed, and David Pountney, who was at Cambridge at the time, took the trouble to come and see it. It was an entirely trivial occasion, but it did give me the impulse to go on and write some more.

So I did; and a couple of operas later came up with *The Duchess of Malfi*. We did that at the university theatre, the Playhouse. Andrew Porter was very generous about it in the papers; and Colin Graham came to see it: and thus I got to write *Tom Jones* for his company. You yourself weren't so kind about that one, I remember. And you know the really frustrating thing about a bad review is not what it says but when it says it. It comes out after the first night, by which time it's really a bit late to alter things; and it's mortifying to have some idiocy pointed out to you then that you ought to have foreseen.

That's one of the advantages of writing incidental music for the theatre, or for TV or films: there's a minutely observant critic built into the system. He's the director. He's on your side – he wants the thing to work; but at the same time he won't let anything pass that doesn't convince him.

Though some directors must be more musically responsive than others.

I've never worked with a director who hasn't had at least a sense of musical atmosphere: knowing what sort of music he needs, and able to judge whether what he gets is what he wants.

Can we take an example? For instance, Elijah Moshinsky's production of Love's Labour's Lost *for BBC TV. Now presumably you did that in Mozartian style because he wanted it so.*

Yes, that's right.

Did he decide where he wanted music?

To a large degree, yes: though music itself is curious stuff, rather like experimental medicine. You can't anticipate all its effects. Sometimes what you write for one place turns out better in another; sometimes what you've written changes the emphasis of a scene too much, and so on. I think the thing is to avoid decisions as long as possible. For instance, I did three settings of the song in *Love's Labour's Lost* before both Elijah and I were satisfied. I liked the first one, but he didn't: it was a slow serene Mozartian thing. Then I came up with a very light folky tune which he preferred, but I rather took against. In the light of this, we tried to home in on to exactly what it was he was thinking of, and it turned out to be that little duet in the Act III finale of *Figaro*. So I wrote something on those lines.

But in the Russian masque scene he very sweetly left a lot of time for the music to do the work, and cut in the actors at more or less arbitrary points: so I was able to expand myself a bit.

Do you like writing absolute music, away from those constraints?

I've written a symphony and been asked for a second, but it's very difficult nowadays to think of a reason why you should write a symphony. But I like writing chamber music, because it's very good to do something where you don't have to give the note to the singer or worry about when the curtain's coming down.

Yet you haven't written much chamber music.

I suppose I'm really quite passive; I write what I'm asked to. There are several reasons why people write tunes, and one of the most fundamental is that someone else wants them to. That's extremely gratifying for a composer, and a perfectly good motive for writing.

But don't you ever bend the commission towards what you want to write?

I have done that, yes. I was asked to write a mass for a festival in the Midlands, and I turned it into a highly secular, rather satirical piece.

But I don't have any sort of master plan about writing. I remember a friend of mine who is a dancer saying something like, 'Well, I'll do a couple of seasons as a soloist, then I should be OK for principal roles, and in about five years' time . . .' and so on. I've never thought remotely like that. Getting through the day is quite enough future for me.

Are you saying really that you only write because people pay you to?

Oh no, no, not at all. I wrote long before I had an economic motive for it; and no man proposes to earn a living in the 1980s by writing operas. I write theatre and TV and film music primarily for the fun of it – I like to do it, and I like to work with the people who do it – but also so that I can put money into operas – my own or other people's.

And then odd things crop up. I played Richter in Tony Palmer's Wagner film, thus getting to conduct a bit of *The Ring* at Bayreuth – a thing nobody else is likely to ask me to do. And I got a sizeable amount of largesse for that, which went straight into an opera company that wasn't even doing one of my operas.

Though it's also important to me that I pay my way. Of course, it doesn't matter to anyone else, but apart from a year immediately after Oxford I've never had a salaried job; I've lived wholly off writing music. It's a comfort to me that I've been able to do that; and perhaps a compensation for those times when you're told your music is the worst thing about a show.

What's likely to be the next show?

Well, I'm translating my *Beauty and the Beast* for London at the moment (it was written in Italian, and opened last year at Adam Pollock's festival in Batignano). And then ENO have discussed with five of us the possibility of writing operas which, as the management rather charmingly puts it, aren't worth cancelling: no chorus, probably no singers if we can help it. I've got an idea for an opera about the girls in the harem in Constantinople. After the sultan was deposed in the 1920s, a few girls lingered on in the palace while the whole of the world around them changed: they must have lived through extraordinary times: revolutions, wars, the face of Europe changing: and there they are, living forgotten in an old palace. Great. It might suit ENO: or it might fit into another idea I have, for a quartet of operas for four women: three one-acters before the interval and a longer piece after. There are, after all, far more women in the opera world than men, yet infinitely fewer parts for them to play.

How do you go about the business of composing? How do you decide whether an idea's right or not?

By thinking. The best thing I ever read about my music was in Hugo Cole's review of the unrevised *Duchess of Malfi*, thirteen years ago now, when he said there were moments when I knew what music should be written but I hadn't actually written it: in other words, I'd made the gesture, but I hadn't informed it with music. So now I ask myself: have you really written the music there, or is it just rumbling along? That's something you have to think about in a second draft. You can't in the first draft, because then you're just getting the shape right, sorting it out; but in the second you have to ask: are you really saying something useful or beautiful by putting that note there? So in that sense I do think of style.

But it's different when you're writing in the style of Mozart for *Love's Labour's Lost*, or in Victorian style for *Nicholas Nickleby*, or in Edwardian style for *Peter Pan*, or – as I am now – writing Tudor music for a film about Lady Jane Grey. Then the criterion is: is the moment more effective because I've used divided violas, or are they getting in the way?

Do you feel, then, that there's an Oliver style for the operas and a pastiche technique for the other things?

Well, they're different things, so clearly yes. It's a two-way traffic, though; there's pastiche in the operas and there's modern music in the television scores particularly. It depends what the style of the production is: I did a score for *Pericles* which was entirely in a modern idiom, because the production wasn't based in any particular century. But when the music is there in an auxiliary role, then it's your business to provide the music that's required. And not only business but pleasure too: I feel that particularly with Shakespeare. I came to Shakespeare very early: he was a home to me before I ever thought of being involved in putting the plays on the stage. So to assist in the performance of the greatest writer in the Western world, and one whom I loved since childhood, is to me a privilege. I can't play the viola in a Beethoven symphony, but I can at least provide Shakespeare with something he needs in order to live.

Might you write a Shakespeare opera?

There's one play of which he did only a draft, at the very greatest period of his life, and it's a bit like *King Lear* and a bit like *Measure for Measure*, but it doesn't work at all, because really it's an opera libretto; and it's called *Timon of Athens*. One day I'm going to destroy a city and perform *Timon of Athens*. Actually it was commissioned by Scottish Opera, but it got dropped. It would be a very self-indulgent opera to write, because it's an awkward cast. There would be no women, and it's just got to have a big chorus; the thing about Timon is that he's set against the whole of humanity. It would suit the Coliseum admirably, and indeed I did a draft vocal score a couple of years ago, but they can hardly afford to rehearse the chorus for a modern opera.

So you know how it's going to sound?

Oh no. If I were commissioned to write it now, I'd start again; it would be completely different. Though I would keep one whole element that I added to the second half, in which Timon in the play has hardly more than a series of dialogues, after which he kills himself. In the opera, he gets religion before his death; his situation merged in my mind with the story of that lady who was a director of Benson & Hedges or whatever, and who went out one day and set fire to herself. That seems to me an absolutely plausible human act, and it's no doubt what happened to Timon. He views human life from a completely different perspective in Act II; the eternal suddenly becomes real to him.

You must understand that having been brought up in a wholly religious atmosphere like St Paul's I'm very moved by sacred music. For instance I think Jonathan Harvey a wonderful composer not just because the notes he writes are good but because of the things he writes about.

Yet you don't write religious music yourself: you mentioned a mass that you turned into a secular piece.

Well, they had asked for a mass to feature in a concert, and I didn't see the point of that. I wouldn't feel easy about writing a mass which wasn't being used directly for worship; the words mean something, after all. In fact a couple of years later I was asked to write one for liturgical use in Norwich Cathedral, and did so with enormous pleasure. And now whenever I catch it it's a big thing for me, because the people who perform it aren't doing it for my benefit; they're performing *ad majorem Dei gloriam*. You're listening to people doing something they think far more important than putting on a concert.

Where do you do your composing? Do you try to keep regular hours?

When I'm in London I try to work for some hours in the morning, before the phone rings; then the rest of the day is generally taken up with business and rehearsals, But I write the operas in a little cottage I rent in the country, where I can work a ten-hour day without doing anything else: I go for walks, cook my food and don't speak to anyone for six weeks or so.

You don't work with a librettist when you're writing an opera?

No, I don't. Though I get sent several libretti every year, which is surely a very odd thing. Who writes an opera libretto on impulse? In fact, a number of them are simply mad; and curiously enough you can distinguish them immediately: the stage directions are invariably typed in red.

Actually I did work with David Pountney on two operas for Scottish Opera's educational scheme, but that was really like writing elaborate incidental music. Then with *Blondel* I wrote the music first, and Tim Rice worked out the words afterwards. The songs were easy enough; the tricky bits were the scenes where the narrative goes forward. There's a big court scene, for instance, where people present petitions and have them dismissed, and the heroine has a fight with the prince. That was somewhat difficult to write without words.

But normally you write your own words, or adapt an existing play?

Yes, but that's really a distinction without a difference. If somebody asks you for an opera, you recover from the shock, and then you take along maybe ten ideas: five of them might be your own ideas, and five of them might be famous books. Of course, the managements take the latter, because they're sellable, and because they think they know the sort of things they'll be – although you may not. For instance, I was commissioned to write an opera for the Banff Music Centre, and I based it on a play by Ostrovsky. I went away to write it, and came back with something quite different: in the opera only two lines of Ostrovsky remain.

It's fatal to get too clear an idea of what's going to happen. Like with this Turkish idea: I could start tomorrow without knowing any more than that there are four or five women stuck alone in a palace around which great events are happening. The rest I'll work out as I go along. But I can't tell a management that.

16

Gavin Bryars

Bryars receives me in his spacious, light, sober but very trim London flat. This is one of the last interviews to be recorded, but I am still uneasy about what to say before starting to ask questions. A tray of Lego on the kitchen table – and sundry other toys stationed about the place – suggest a light comment about children, and yet I fear this may show a want of subtlety: after all, these carefully placed objects could be part of the décor, like the many large, flat, exemplary paintings of farm animals on the walls. He offers coffee, and we sit across the Lego-laden pine, he with shirt sleeves rolled up and elbows placed workmanlike on the table, as if he were a baker discussing his trade between batches.

You studied philosophy at Sheffield: were you already writing music then?

I think I started writing music when I was 16, writing something which was grandly called *A Life Suite*, in the style of Ravel. I wrote about three bars. But I was most involved in playing jazz before I went to Sheffield, with a small group of friends in Goole. I went to Sheffield to study music, but at that time you could only do music as a dual honours with a modern language. I had good results in French, but I'd rather had enough of French, and so I studied philosophy while carrying on studying music privately with people related to the university, especially George Linstead, who was the cathedral organist and much the best musician on the staff. He was quite an eccentric man (he listed his recreation in *Who's Who* as 'standing and staring'), but he was a very good teacher, very strict. He wasn't interested in seeing any original work: we just did stylistic exercises.

Also I taught myself to play bass at Sheffield: I'd always wanted to play the bass but never had an instrument. That was mostly as a jazz activity, but I also played in the university orchestra. And before I left Sheffield I was already working as a jazz bass player in night clubs, so I wasn't really a very diligent student.

Were you writing things at that time?

Gavin Bryars   *photo: Leicester Polytechnic*

Not really. I started writing towards the end of my time as a full-time jazz musician: I started writing things for the ensemble I was in with improvisers like Derek Bailey and Tony Oxley. We were all working together quite closely until about 1966. Little by little, partly to codify the free improvisation we were beginning to do, I started writing pieces that were controlled improvisation. I also suggested other ways of approaching improvisation, even within a conventional jazz sphere. For example, normally one improvises on the harmonic base of the tune, but I suggested one should play the tune and improvise on the chord ahead, or the one behind, or try and stay uniformally in a key a fixed distance away, or freeze and improvise on a single chord.

So most of the influences on you were coming from jazz?

Yes, except that I was buying a lot of Cage scores with the earnings I got from playing in cabaret clubs. I also bought *Silence* and the 1958 retrospective-concert record.

How had you heard of Cage?

Oddly enough, through my grammar-school teacher, who told me about the prepared piano and about *4′ 33″*. And Linstead too was sympathetic to Cage, which was unusual for someone who was a cathedral organist and wrote the programme notes for the Halle. Then I read Calvin Tomkins's *The Bride and the Bachelors* (later published as *Ahead of the Game*), which included portraits he'd written for the *New Yorker* of Rauschenberg, Duchamp, Tingley and Cage; a later edition added Merce Cunningham.

So I used most of my earnings to buy Cage, and also Feldman, Christian Wolff, Stockhausen and Messiaen. I remember writing to Messiaen in about 1963 or 1964, and I got a pleasant letter back: I'd asked a question about modes, and he suggested I should buy his book, so I did. Little by little I began to write things for the group in that kind of idiom: I did an arrangement of the last movement of *L'Ascension* for jazz piano trio, and some Cage-ish pieces for the same group.

I began to find that I was not enjoying improvising, that I was only bringing to improvisation what I already knew beforehand, and it was just coming out in different permutations. I felt that this wasn't only my problem but that it was a limitation in improvisation itself, so I stopped playing the bass altogether in 1966 and didn't touch it again until two years ago.

You didn't then start improvising again?

I did actually, and continue to, but I keep fairly quiet about it, having made a public renunciation before. So jazz and other forms of improvisation were very important activities for me up to 1966, and then it stopped.

And then what happened?

I went into teaching. I took a job teaching liberal studies in a technical college, but I didn't find that very rewarding: talking about music to day-release welders and bricklayers, I didn't get much feedback. Then I did some playing for dance classes in London.

Were you composing?

Yes. It was almost entirely rubbish, in retrospect, but I wrote some pieces for dancers. One of them was on a master's programme at the University of Illinois and asked me to go out to rehearse, so I went, in 1968. As it happened, that was where Cage was working on *HPSCHD* with Lejaren Hiller. I'd met Cage when he came to the Saville Theatre in 1966 with Merce Cunningham, and he'd taken a couple of scores for his notation project. He remembered me, and he gave me some work on *HPSCHD*, and I ended up staying for about six months. It was a very lively place: apart from Cage and Hiller, Herbert Brün was there, Salvatore Martirano, Kenneth Gaburo and a lot of good student composers. I was doing lots of playing, and also getting things played. It was very helpful. Then I came back to England and started working with John Tilbury in duo performances for about a year and a half.

Had you met Tilbury and Cardew before you left for America?

I knew Tilbury: he'd helped me in recording the piece I took to Illinois (it was for two pianos six hands). And I'd seen Cardew performing in 1967 but hadn't met him. I'd sent him some scores to get his opinion, and then I arranged to pick them up when I got back and we became quite friendly. His wife Stella remembers the occasion, because I had a terrible book called *Loves of the Great Composers* by Kobbé, and I read bits out of it to them. Cornelius was quite encouraging. He didn't say much about the stuff I'd sent, just that I was on the right track. I was never quite sure what that meant.

Was it when you came back from America that you started teaching at Portsmouth?

Yes, I started in January 1969, in the fine-art department, and I was there for a year and two terms, though the Portsmouth Sinfonia had an existence after that. It was formed in May 1970, but before that I'd worked with a lot of the fine-art students on performance material by Cage, Ichiyanagi, Kosugi, George Brecht – in that Fluxus territory between fine art and music. Then the Portsmouth

Sinfonia was formed as a summer event. Most of the members had little ability on any instrument; they simply had the will to play. There was no question of fooling about: they were doing the best they could with very limited abilities, and I think one of the interesting things about the Sinfonia was the gap between the effort they were putting in and the results that were coming out. There was this gap between aim and achievement that was sometimes quite moving, though often it was quite hilarious as well.

Things would go disastrously wrong. I remember one of the last concerts we did was in the Albert Hall, and we were doing the *1812* overture. We could only afford six cannon, so we used just one in rehearsal, and it was phenomenally loud. When it came to the performance, the conductor – he was one of the people who knew least about music, but he looked the part: he had a very good profile, and the hair was right – suddenly remembered that his grandmother had come to the performance, and he was worried that the cannon might actually cause her a heart attack, so he started waving to the man as a signal not to do the cannon. And of course that was taken as a signal to start, so all five cannon were let loose at completely the wrong moment. That kind of thing happened all the time, but the intentions were pretty straight, even noble.

What about the intentions in the pieces you were writing?

A few of the pieces fed off the fine-art tradition: working in an art college, the climate was different from what it would have been if I'd been working in a musical environment. At Portsmouth there was a strong element of the 'systems' group, people working with mathematical permutations and elements of repetition – this was before composers like Steve Reich and Phil Glass were known over here.

Had you come across their work in America?

No, I met them for the first time when they came over here in 1970, and Reich came to my flat to play tapes to a group of English composers: there was that kind of exchange then. He played us *Four Organs*, and I played him a Sinfonia tape, which changed the atmosphere a little. They also had a relationship with the fine-art tradition, and in particular with minimalist painters like Sol LeWit. Similarly here there was a much freer atmosphere in art colleges: I was teaching at Portsmouth, John Tilbury was at Kingston, Cornelius Cardew at Maidstone, Victor Schonfield at Walthamstow, Tom Phillips was the academic librarian at Wolverhampton . . .

There was a network of people working in fine-art departments, which tended to develop a rapport with what was going on in those departments, and to encourage the use of untrained performers.

Did you feel that you were working in a different way from other contemporaries, that there was a division, as Michael Nyman remarked in his book, between 'experimental' and 'avant-garde' music?

There wasn't that polarity in my mind at the time. For example, I did the first broadcast performance of Stockhausen's *Plus-Minus* in 1969 with John Tilbury and Tim Souster, and I was certainly as interested in Stockhausen until the late sixties as I was in a lot of other music. Also, I've continued to be interested in Messiaen's music, which isn't experimental at all. But an interest in Cage does point eventually to a difference from the European avant-garde: it's less a musical than a philosophical difference, a matter of approach.

What is the philosophical difference?

I think it's one of control, of how much material you want to control and how much you're prepared to let go. Even if the musical ends sound remarkably similar – some of Cage's music from the early fifties can sound like Pousseur – the intentions are very different, and the kinds of compositional activity that produce those results are very different. It was that area that I found interesting: to find compositional means which may lead to things that sound like something else, but through a different approach, with a different intention and therefore a different meaning.

Do you mean you were more interested in the compositional process than in the sounds?

Certainly in the early seventies that was true. For instance, *The Sinking of the Titanic* was an attempt to consider what sort of music might be 'conceptual', in the way that some art of that time was termed 'conceptual'. I tend to view performance of that piece as not absolutely essential: what interested me most was the whole network of things capable of becoming compositional material.

That puts you in rather a strange relationship with your audience, doesn't it, in that they may not be aware of the rationale?

The processes aren't obvious, but I think they can be deduced. And that harks back to my philosophical training: from the data you can work out what the structure is, even if you don't have the whole picture. And I've tended to write rather lengthy programme notes, giving the flavour, the background, the thoughts that have gone into a piece. I certainly don't believe in concealing things from an audience, though there can be a problem where if you say something specific about a piece, that becomes what the piece means for the audience.

With the *Titanic* piece, I published forty pages of research notes in the American magazine *Soundings*, and for me that serves as the notation.

Do you feel, though, that you were writing for performance conditions that don't exist any longer?

I don't mind people doing the *Titanic* piece now, though I didn't particularly want to do it when I was asked to put it on at the Riverside Studios a couple of years ago: I had the feeling that I'd been in that territory before and that it was quite a long time ago. It's all right for other performers to do it, but as a composer-performer one should perhaps do things that are more of one's immediate environment, unless one's giving a retrospective concert. Then one changes perspective gradually during the performance. You wouldn't be the same kind of performer in the first piece as you would be in the last.

But you're still a performer in the 1980s and not in 1969. It's very difficult to get back to performance styles of the past, and if there's very little notation, then the music's gone forever.

In that case, though, one can relate it back to the context in which it was written, and it does become like a slice of the past. In the case of the *Titanic*, because it's open-ended, it can be reinterpreted in the light of anything that happens subsequently. I have done the piece on a couple of occasions with sound materials that are nothing like those on the recording, On one occasion it was very short, lasting only about eight minutes, and it had no strings, no tapes: it was a very minimal piece for a couple of woodblocks, a reed organ, a tuba and a cello. It was still the same composition: I simply extracted different kinds of data from the material.

You mentioned that you'd got into minimalism through visual art, but when you got to know Reich and Glass did they have an effect on you?

A negative one: I started writing something else. That was when I started doing conceptual pieces. I like their work, but I'd no intention of mimicking them.

Then in 1972 you stopped altogether: how was that?

Composing didn't seem to be the activity I should be doing at that time. I was working in an art department again, at Leicester Polytechnic, and I spent a lot of time on art history, mostly on Duchamp.

Also, I think a lot of composers are by nature lazy, and need something to get them going. Until 1972 I was working in an artistic climate in which many things were being produced, and then that stopped: for example, John Tilbury was in the Scratch Orchestra, which at that time moved into political debate.

You were never tempted to be part of that?

Not really. I could sympathize politically, but I thought that the combination of politics and artistic activity was what in philosophy one would call a 'category mistake'. The criteria for evaluating excellence in each were different, and therefore to apply criteria from one to the other seemed to me inappropriate. I still find it hard to equate political thought and artistic activity, though I admire people who can: I think a lot of Frederic Rzewski's music is very well done.

In 1972 there was a clear divide, and the people who were working politically were repudiating some of those who weren't. It didn't produce any personal hostilities: John Tilbury and I continued to go to Queen's Park Rangers on Saturday afternoons together for fifteen years. But in terms of work one was thrown back on one's own resources.

Then when I was eventually asked to do something, in 1975, I did. That was when I made the version of the *Titanic* for John White, Chris Hobbs and myself that I mentioned, and I also did a little piece called *Ponukelian Melody*. I'd spent a lot of time examining Satie's notebooks from the Rose Croix period, and I'd been reading a lot of Raymond Roussel through my Duchamp work. The piece was completely notated in an implacable crotchet = 60 (I did that so that I'd know it would last for exactly ten minutes: it was very strict), and it was modelled on Satie's *Les pantins dansent*.

Had you got into Satie through Duchamp or into Duchamp through Satie?

Independently, I think. I'd certainly known Satie at university, but only the better-known things. Later I got to know the Rose Croix period, which still I think is interesting, as well as *Socrate* and the late nocturnes.

The problem I always have with Satie is not knowing what's technical limitation and what's intention.

That's something I almost admire. Satie was essentially self-taught, and what you find in the notebooks is the endearing quality of working out a systematic music theory for himself: how to harmonize a step of a major second, or imposing deliberate limits like choosing to write a piece entirely as a sequence of triads in which the bass and treble go in contrary motion. Certainly he was technically limited, but what one has to measure is how much he succeeded within his own terms. In many cases his achievement was quite remarkable.

But it's difficult to know what he was trying to achieve. Is the orchestration of Socrate, *for instance, meant to sound so plain wrong?*

You do get instruments given things to play that would be better given to other instruments, but I think that's quite a conscious choice. The melodic line is almost anonymous, and the orchestration is very pale, because his main intention was to draw attention to the beauty of the text. It was rather like, say, Grainger or Britten setting a folk song: the important thing was to find a framework that wouldn't draw attention to itself, but rather highlight the object that was being set.

Did the relationship with Satie continue after that 1975 piece?

On and off. I didn't write conceptual pieces any more, except for one piece based on detective fiction, which wasn't very successful.

I got involved with the College of 'Pataphysics in 1974, and through that I became interested in all kinds of technical processes for writing literature: different ways of putting texts together, often by highly elaborate and artificial means. There was a sub-group within the college concerned with how to write and analyse detective fiction, and I became very interested in that; I still am. And some of that interest carried over into the music I wrote in the later 1970s, where there were internal references that weren't particularly important to what was going on – except that an attentive listener might notice, for example, that it's rather odd to have a piece otherwise in 12/8 beginning with a bar of 19/4 time, and then half-way through to have a bar of 19/32 time, and he might work out that those might be years rather than just metres.

Though without a score you might not realize that 19/32 time was going on.

You'd certainly notice it in the middle of 12/8.

But you might not be able to count the nineteen beats.

No, but you'd notice it was odd, and that's enough. Then if you want to find out why, you can take it further and find out more about the mystery, just like the detective; but unless you're curious you won't do it. That seems to me fair.

You mentioned that you started writing again in 1975 because you were asked. Is that how pieces normally start?

Yes. For instance, I wouldn't write an orchestra piece and then hope somebody would pick it up.

But might you have an idea for an orchestra piece, or do the ideas only come when you've been asked?

Only when the possibility's there. All the time I have ideas for pieces, and I write them down in notebooks, but they always relate to practicality – or if they don't, then they become conceptual pieces.

How do those original ideas come? What might you be putting down in your notebook?

The best thing would be to give you an example of something that hasn't materialized into a piece. There was a detective story I was reading about Prince Zaleski, who solves crimes by staying in his room: he does it all by pure mental activity. And to stimulate himself into activity he fingers an Egyptian scarab, smokes hashish and plays an air from *Lakmé* on a harmonium. I thought that was striking, and made a note of it. Then a little bit later I came across an Ellery Queen story which also involved an air from *Lakmé* at a critical point in the solution of the mystery, and I thought something might be made of that; but it hasn't yet.

Clearly, none of that relates to whether it's going to be for orchestra, a theatre piece, an opera, a ballet, a piece for solo piano or what. It's just that there is some kind of material.

But conceptual material, not sound material.

Is there a difference?

Well, let's say you wouldn't think of a tune and decide you might make a piano concerto out of it.

No, I don't think I'd do that. A harmonium concerto maybe . . .

How do you relate to what one's brought up to regard as the tradition?

What do you mean by 'the tradition'?

Haydn, Mozart, Beethoven, Brahms . . .

I take those composers seriously. I'm not dismissive. But there are many composers who have an uneasy relationship with that tradition: Busoni interests me a lot, so do Liszt and Rossini, especially late Rossini. Maybe I find heretics more interesting. I don't view myself as an heir to Mozart, Beethoven and Brahms, that's true. But there are composers from the past to whom I relate quite strongly, like Berlioz, Liszt, Schubert, Mahler, Busoni and a whole area of composers from around the turn of the century, like Reger, Karg-Elert, Skryabin, Szymanowski, Satie. Some Haydn I like a lot: the Symphony No. 22, especially the first movement, or the *Seven Last Words*. A lot of Mozart I enjoy very much: certainly most of the operas.

That's not heretical at all.

Perhaps that's a heresy within a heretical position. In the recent past I've been very involved with opera, and looking at opera, which tends not to contain very much musical heresy: I've spent a lot of time listening to Strauss, and also to Busoni's operas – *Doktor Faust* is a masterpiece.

Was that a deliberate preparation before writing your own Medea?

Oh yes, because I knew very little opera in any practical way before I started, which was in August 1981.

Had you worked with your collaborator Robert Wilson before?

No, we were put together by mutual friends in France. He'd envisaged the *Medea* as a play with incidental music, and we talked about the possibility of sections being sung, and little by little the thing became an opera with a few bits of speech left in it.

What did you learn from your study of Strauss and others? Was it helpful?

Oh immensely. One of the first things I wanted to do was look at orchestration, and so I spent a lot of time with composers who, as well as being good composers, were also first-rate orchestrators: Berlioz, Rimsky-Korsakov, Strauss, Mahler, Busoni, and quite importantly Grainger. I made some decisions which were perhaps not particularly practical in terms of the reality of opera production. For instance, there are no violins in the orchestra, and originally I wanted a chorus just of altos and tenors. That produces the problem of what the others are to do while this opera is being put on, and so I had to make compromises: I didn't compromise on the violins, but I did take mezzos and baritones. Also I used saxophones instead of oboes, because the saxophone relates very strongly to the human voice in terms of its divisions into soprano, alto, tenor and baritone, and also because it has such a wide expressive range. I used a very large tuned percussion section (something I enjoy in Grainger and Messiaen), which in a way becomes like the first violins: the timpanist is in a sense the leader of the orchestra, or at least the anchor.

I think I learned a lot from other opera composers in seeing how they handled the orchestra in relation to the voice. Rimsky-Korsakov even made some specific recommendations, for example that soprano arias should never be accompanied by double-basses. I didn't believe it, and so I chose to ignore it, but at least I was doing that as a conscious opposition to what had been theoretically permissible.

Were you writing for particular singers?

Not originally, but then I worked with the cast for the projected 1982 production in New York in February that year. As a result of that I made one or two little changes. For example, the part of the Nurse, originally for Caroline James, goes down frequently to low E natural; and she could do it (she says she can go lower: she just has to have brandy and cigars the night before). But keeping the voice constantly in that low octave and a half became uninteresting, and so I gave her some higher transpositions. That was something I got from physically hearing the voice do it as distinct from playing it on the piano.

Are you going to write another opera?

Yes, there are two under discussion at the moment. One, which I'd like to do in German, is based on De Quincey's *The Last Days of Immanuel Kant*. It's a curious piece of writing, because it's some-times hard to know what is De Quincey and what is the source that he's using – like a Duchamp piece where you're not sure what is Duchamp and what is the readymade. The other idea is to do something from Flaubert's *Bouvard et Pécuchet*, because my sym-pathies are with France, and I find setting French texts very easy. English texts I find hard, because one always has the spectre of the voice sounding like Britten, and there are certain 'English' sounds in music that I simply don't like.

In Leicester you're still working in a fine-art department?

No, since 1978 there's been a new degree in performing arts, and I'm head of the music department. Maybe that's one reason why I'm now working more purely musically, doing things like operas. The climate has changed.

17

Dominic Muldowney

We meet at his place of work, the National Theatre, and talk across a kettle drum in the music studio: a crammed cube of instruments and music stands. Since the transcript I later send is not returned, what follows is a pretty much unamended version of what is said. It is the only time a composer actually starts the questioning.

How much of my music do you know, actually?

Well, of the most recent things, the Saxophone Concerto, the Piano Concerto, a couple of Brecht song-cycles . . .

You see, what's happened since I came here to the National Theatre, which was in 1975, is that the exposure of my music has tended to be in the theatre rather than in the concert hall. And increasingly it's been in films and television too.

Has that just been for financial reasons, or because you wanted to work in those areas?

I can't believe people when they say they always wanted to write film music, because it is, after all, extremely well paid, and because it can be a nightmare working with directors. You can go right through the whole experience and not really feel you've been creative at all: in fact, you feel drained of creativity.

What about writing music for the theatre?

That depends on the director. With the right director – like Harold Pinter for me – there's a degree of trust, and you're left to yourself, though with the proviso that you *are* working in the theatre. What the theatre seems to have done for me is to remind me of the audience, and the thing about the theatre audience is that they're more intellectual and more aware. They're more receptive to those aspects of the new that still cling to sense, or to grammar, or to structure. You can't really get away with non-sense in the theatre, and I'm glad that that has affected my music, because it's made me

Dominic Muldowney   *photo: Malcolm Crowthers*

more and more simple structurally, but with more and more complex musical ideas.

People argue that I'm worrying about the audience when I ought to be worrying about the dots, but worrying about the audience changes the dots: you're immediately making decisions about music. It's probably why I'm less and less interested in new sounds. For instance, I've been working with Harry Birtwistle now for ten years, and what's rubbed off is not the sound of his music but a much more abstract and simple thing: how gestural it is, and how simple those gestures are. It's a matter of how things are presented, which involves textures and harmonies and orchestrations but is also more general. It might just be about how much information one has in half a minute.

Might it also be a matter of presenting the music as if on a stage? I'm thinking of your Second Quartet – which is another piece I've heard – where you take characters out of Stravinsky.

Yes, and another influence from the theatre has been Brecht. I'd always been, if you like, left-wing: my father's a Stalinist and was intensely active in politics, so I grew up with it. All through my youth there was just politics, no music. And I guess I reacted to that, in that my father felt that the new in art must be revolutionary and wonderful. I disagreed with him later, and I now feel musically that I don't want to be 'new'. I'm looking for what we all are: some kind of truth about oneself and the music.

It's got nothing to do with 'Neo-Romanticism' or 'New Tonality'. To me, it's a highly personal, quirky reworking of what Stravinsky was doing, and it's not nostalgic at all: it's come out of all the things that I've studied. I'm so desperate to make the structure clear that it may give the impression of a return to tonality, but I think of it as an extension. It never occurred to me that I was nostalgic.

No, it always seems to me in your music that the stance is very ironic.

Though that too can be dangerous. I remember one reviewer said of the Brecht cycle *The Duration of Exile* that it parodied Brahms, Ravel and so on, whereas I'd just started out from the poems. One of them is very simple, like a haiku, and I wanted to scoop it up and present it, rather sculpturally, on a pedestal, not give it a 'setting', which would immediately soften it. Also, I wanted to be completely unequivocal about the sense and the grammar. So, for instance, you can't have melisma, and it's better not to have musical illustration. In that very simple poem there's a line about smoke rising, and the music goes up a minor third: that's always worried me, because I think it should have stayed on the same note.

I usually write the music very quickly, taking perhaps a day per song, and I couldn't have done that ten years ago. I couldn't have done it even in the two earlier Brecht cycles, which some people might think have more musical interest. But in *The Duration of Exile*, except for one song, I got for the first time to the music I wanted to write. It's only in these last three or four pieces that I've felt I'm really in control. I suppose it's a question of technique, but that technique has come through very boring, practical, everyday work here, which makes me feel very isolated from the musical world, but very much included in the theatre world.

So opera might be very natural for me, and I've been discussing it with the ENO. But if I did write an opera, it would be very strange, not for strangeness's sake, but because I'd want to include everything from speaking to vocalise. The thing it would discuss would be: why sing?

You mentioned Brecht just now, and then went on to talk about politics, but in fact you haven't chosen political poems by Brecht in your song-cycles.

I think if one set the more overtly political poetry one could be accused of nostalgia. You can't pretend we're living in the thirties – even if we are: in fact, we're living in a much more serious time than the thirties, both in the way one can be protected from reality, and because of the nuclear thing. I'm desperately looking for a poet who's doing what Brecht was doing then, but I can't find one. Even Tony Harrison, who's the nearest thing to a voice like Brecht's, is still more poetic, more complex.

Composers have tended to hide themselves from the political situation in one of two ways: through mythologies, or through complexity. I really think the new complexity of composers like Ferneyhough and Finnissy is a desperate kind of intellectual game, not unlike the music of the late fourteenth century in France: very decadent. It doesn't worry me: I'm just very curious about it. I feel that now, with all the madness that there is, one must harness everything one can summon up in order to present a case for sense.

How do you know when you're making sense?

This is going to sound a bit Zen, but you only know when you know.

Do you ever try and analyse it?

Well, in a bar of music there might be ten decisions –

It depends whose bar.

Only ten in a bar of mine, and I still think it's far too many. But all those decisions are filtered through an intellectual mesh that I've been sewing since 1976, when I felt there was a freshness in my mind about what I was doing. I suppose you know when it's worked because then you feel you can almost cope with a bad review. You never actually can, but you may have the conviction that you've done the right thing, and it doesn't matter what people say. That's when you know you've reached the truthfulness.

How do you arrive at that point, and how do you set it down?

I work at the piano. What tends to happen is that there is a very quickly written first draft, and then –

But what happens before that draft?

Let's take the opening movement of the Saxophone Concerto, which was the last movement of the three to be written. I wanted to write something in continuous semiquavers, to give the illusion of a first movement in a concerto grosso. And I remembered doing that before, but the semiquavers hadn't sounded continuous, because what's important is that there should be a certain continuity in the harmonic rhythm. So I sat around for a day, looking at old scores, looking at old mistakes, looking at other composers, listening to Oliver Knussen's music, to Birtwistle's, to Bach's. And then I put everything away: after that day of preparation I don't have any more music out. It might just happen that something from all that music stays with you, tugs you in: in fact, it gives you the start sometimes.

The only thing that's of interest in that movement is something Oliver Knussen pointed out, that it's all C major, F sharp major and so on, but none of them work like that. It's just an exercise going up in whole-tone steps from C to F sharp and then coming back again. It's ever so simple.

Then the process of composition is very immediate. I sit at the piano, and I shape, and then I go away – which is why I can work on several things at once. I can be doing something here, and then go home and do a bit on a piece. The analogy's with the way a painter works: somebody who's got immediate access to the thing that's growing. You see, I'd never write anything without checking absolutely every vertical at the piano. What you're asking is: when I check it, what are my criteria? And I think my criteria are entirely my ears.

I deliberately started and ended that movement with F sharp major and C, with the C rolled in the manner of a nineteenth-century piano piece, so that I was saying: this isn't just C, but it's *intended* to be C. It's not C so that you weep with joy at hearing a consonance, but because there's been a whole story – a musical story – about finding that chord from its opposite axis. So it's a very musical reason why I sometimes end up with very simple results. I try to get rid of as much as possible that I don't need, and that has certainly affected my orchestration. You have to be very careful, because you run the risk of alluding to a kind of orchestration that's not yours: there's a sort of Satie-esque style that isn't simple but is actually naive. I loathe that.

More and more, during the course of the picture that I'm creating, all the pre-compositional decisions disappear. If you're really being truthful, then you have the confidence to get rid of those things, because you only need them to get you working – and that can be the hardest thing in the world for a composer: just to start. It was working here in the theatre that allowed me to find those emotions which I had thought one wasn't allowed to use. And obviously the first thing that's going to come back is the thing that one's always been surrounded by, which is the whole world of simple pitch relationships often known as tonality – and not so simple either. I think there's something very unsettling about my harmony, particularly when it appears to be behaving itself.

So I feel I'm more and more able to be clearly emotional: the old expression is 'to be in touch with your emotions'. But make no mistake about it, as Arthur Scargill would say, even music in touch with its simplest emotions is still going to be quite an esoteric, middle-class pursuit. I just think it might be handy to know why that situation isn't going to continue.

What's going to happen?

The musical world we're involved in has traditionally buried its head, and it has done so most drastically since the war. But I don't think that's going to carry on being possible.

18

Nicholas Maw

Crossed transatlantic post means that I miss Maw during his one visit to England in the early months of 1985: he suggests, therefore, that I send to him in Washington some questions that he might answer on tape. It seems a good plan, until, very near the deadline for this book, two ninety-minute cassettes drop through the letterbox. Maw in speech, though, is slow and deliberate, so that what follows is, I trust, not too disfigured an account.

When did you start composing and why? Was there any trigger that you can identify? Was your family musical? Were you studying an instrument?

I first started composing at the age of 15 or 16 at school, under the encouragement of a rather enlightened music mistress, writing small pieces for piano, settings of Walter de la Mare, pieces for solo instrument, etc. I was encouraged by her, and also by the school, by having these pieces performed. As for any trigger, that's rather more difficult. I can recall lying in bed at night and beginning to hear things, and at some stage, I suppose, there began to be the idea of putting these things down on paper. I had one or two attempts, and of course at first they were failures, because, as is so often the case, one might have an idea but have very little conception of how to elaborate it into any kind of piece. Shortly thereafter I began imitating short pieces I'd heard played by my friends at school.

My family was musical. My father was a very good pianist, and if he'd been born later he would certainly have become a professional musician. But he went into the music business, and that was a great sadness in his life; so I became the repository for all his blighted hopes in that direction. I started off playing the piano, but that was hopeless, because I could never practise in the house without him interfering, so I took up the clarinet, and I got on rather well. But of course the clarinet is not really a very good instrument for a composer to play: it has a very limited repertoire until the twentieth century, and as a beginner one is not up to the technical standard they require (though I recall I did play the Hindemith Sonata as a schoolboy).

Nicholas Maw *photo: Misha Donat*

I ought to add that my father's hopes were that I should become a professional pianist or teacher. That was a cause of very considerable friction between us, and it wasn't resolved until much later. Only when I won a scholarship to go to Paris to study with Nadia Boulanger did he begin to realize that my hopes were not founded on absolutely nothing. And later on he became an avid fan.

The result of the situation with my father was that I wound up not playing any instrument properly. I had to sell my clarinets when I came back from Paris because I was desperately in need of money. And I don't play the piano well: I use the piano quite a lot when I'm composing, but I certainly wouldn't play it in public. This is a nuisance when one's teaching, and also it would be very nice to give performances of one's own music.

Bayan Northcott in New Grove *suggests that you met 'contemporary' music only when you came to London. What music was this? Was there a decisive turning point?*

That's substantially correct. The music I'd heard before was, first of all, Ravel and Debussy, Bartók, Stravinsky, and quite a lot of English music: Vaughan Williams, Walton, Britten (not much

Tippett). When I got to the RAM I came across the second Viennese school with a bang, as it were. Not only that, there were other things that were a big shock to me. I was the archetypal provincial boy coming up to the big city. I was very ignorant of many things, including the extraordinarily high musical standard of some of my contemporaries: I remember to this day my utter astonishment in my first week at hearing someone play the whole of Ravel's *Gaspard de la nuit*. Also, I heard compositions by Cornelius Cardew or Richard Rodney Bennett that were technically streets ahead of anything I could achieve at that period.

The result was that I became extremely depressed. I felt uncouth, gauche, ignorant. So the music I had to come to terms with when I went to the RAM was that of Schoenberg, Berg and Webern; a bit later on, of course, it was much more up-to-date figures, those composers of the 1950s who loomed extremely large in our lives: Boulez, Stockhausen, etc. As for there being a decisive turning point, I'm not so sure. Because of my background, I didn't plunge into the ferment of post-Viennese school activity. I've subsequently come to regard this as a very great advantage, that I was able to stand apart and not get swallowed up, although at the time it caused me extreme anguish, because I felt that I ought to be keeping up, even though I didn't feel at one with what was happening. I realized as a very young man, I suppose, that if I was going to do anything I would just have to find my own way. I simply did not hear music in the way it was organized at that time.

Why did you want to study in Paris? Did you have any contact with Messiaen or Boulez?

It was really *faute de mieux*. I didn't want to go to Germany: I was very clear that I didn't want to sit at the feet of the gods of Darmstadt. Nor did I wish to go to Italy. Several of my friends had gone to Paris, including Susan Bradshaw and Richard Rodney Bennett, and my teacher Lennox Berkeley had been a pupil of Nadia Boulanger. He suggested I go and study with her; I was rather ambivalent about the idea, because I realized she was a figure of the past. And when I got there, these doubts were soon borne out, because she enquired whether I had made a study of *solfège*; when I said no she said we would begin immediately. I'm amazed now at my own chutzpah, but I jibbed at that: I said I'd only got five or six months to study at this kind of level with anyone abroad, and I didn't want to spend the time studying *solfège*. At first she was outraged, but she asked me to leave the compositions

I'd brought with me on the piano. I then heard nothing for about a month, which plunged me into a state of intense depression, but she asked me to come to see her again and was quite changed in her attitude, and thereafter we had a very amicable relationship which was based largely on our not talking about music. I used to ply her with questions about people she'd known – Eluard, Cocteau, Diaghilev, Stravinsky – and she was very happy to answer. She also performed great kindnesses to me. I was very ill with an ulcer, and she sent me off to a farm in Normandy for two or three weeks. And she made it possible for me to receive the Lili Boulanger Award, which enabled me to stay in Paris for another six months. Alas I became a bit of a turncoat, because I then attended the classes of Max Deutsch, and very enlightening I found them too.

I didn't have any contact with either Messiaen or Boulez. For some reason I found Messiaen not only forbidding but also a rather distasteful figure. I can recall hearing the first broadcast performance of the *Turangalîla-symphonie* with my father, and I was attracted to it but also found it oddly repulsive. I'm rather glad I didn't go to Messiaen, because I don't think he was the kind of personality who could have given me what I needed at that stage. As for Boulez, there was no question of going to him: what I was doing would simply not have been of any interest to him. And I had a rather ambivalent attitude towards his music, as with Messiaen. Later I got to know several things very well, including *Le marteau sans maître*, which I came to have a very high regard for.

Did you ever, or do you now, see any alternative for yourself to tonal harmony of some sort? If not, how did you react to the music of Boulez, Stockhausen and others that must have seemed almost inescapable in the early sixties?

I think probably all twentieth-century composers have to define their relationship to tonality: since about 1914 it's been impossible just to accept tonality as the effective language. Though one has to be a little careful here. The term 'tonality' is bandied around as if it were a fixed definable object: I don't think that's the case at all. There are and always have been many different types of tonality, very often affected by modal inflections from folk influence. In my own case, as a young man, I don't think there was any question of deciding which way one was going to go. Because a work of art is accomplished and fulfils what it set out to do, that doesn't mean the aims were all clearly defined beforehand. When you sit down to do something, you're searching around in a fog: you have to define your terms of reference anew each time. And when you're young that's very much more so the case. One result is that a young composer will wholeheartedly embrace some prevailing style in order, hopefully, to find his own style. And with this concentration on style comes the cursed onset of self-consciousness, which is the characteristic of culture in a silver age – or, some might say, in a period of decline.

The particular style that prevailed when I was beginning in the 1950s – the Darmstadt version of the post-Viennese school – was one that rejected too much of the past for my temperament. One result was that I rejected the whole notion of style as an operating principle, so the question of tonality wasn't uppermost in my mind. I finally found my feet when I simply tried to put down what I heard, and this turned out to be related to tonality in some way which I hope was and is personal. I put down my roots in the place where I felt they needed to be put down: in the music of before the First World War. Nevertheless, I think it's quite clear in my music of the 1960s that it was written against the background of recent developments. I think what I did was like what Stravinsky did – though less consciously than he did it – when in his so-called 'neo-classical' works he put down roots at particular points in musical history, enabling him to renew his language. Stravinsky realized that in the twentieth century the whole of musical history is available to us: we can hear it all in extraordinary profusion. We can plug in anywhere we like in order to nourish our own music: in my own case it was somewhere between about 1860 and 1914.

Nowadays my attitude to tonality is defined by my feelings about the flexibility of language. The fixed point gives one the great advantage that one can move away from it and then come back: that is, it's possible to do two things. If you have no fixed point, it's very difficult to do more than one thing. It's also very difficult to define the tempo: music has become either very fast or very slow; the whole middle range has been lost. That seems to me a loss so central that it has to be recovered. In my own case, I've made continual attempts to write really fast music and which can be slowed down to another clearly defined speed.

My version of tonality is of course not tonality in the old sense at all: it's much more loosely defined. Sometimes, for example, my music could be said to be not *in* a key but *on* a key, or at least on a triadic area. Systems of relationship are set up, usually having some kind of harmonic sequence as the basis, and in that respect it follows traditional practice. But such sequences are not defined by

the old root systems with the primary duality of tonic and dominant: that doesn't exist. I'd also like to say I don't consider this a
system but a language. Somebody may eventually codify it, but
that's not my job.

My discomfort with the Darmstadt language was that it was too
systematized to be a language. Charles Rosen says somewhere that
a work of art needs a certain looseness in the language, that
imagination seizes on the looseness. It's like the E flat major chords
that begin the 'Eroica' Symphony: they have an added dimension
that raises them above the mere fact of being in E flat major.

Did Scenes and Arias *feel like the breakthrough it appears in retrospect?*
Did you discover a music you'd been looking for?

It certainly did feel like a breakthrough: indeed it was designed as
such. I'd had a rather miserable period after coming back from
Paris, when I found it difficult to write anything; and I'd just got
myself started with a piece for organ, of all things. Then I worked
on *Scenes and Arias* and *Chamber Music* at the same time – something
I've never done again in quite that way, particularly with two
pieces so different. *Scenes and Arias* was the first time that I had
considerable freedom of forces, and I've never really had that open-
handed freedom again that I was allowed by William Glock and the
BBC. Quite where the idea of setting the poem came from, I'm not
sure. I'd read quite a lot of poetry; I still do. What I had at the back
of my mind was a kind of shadowy, hypothetical action: it was
written to some degree as a study for operas, as opera was something
that I very much wished to do, and in fact my next work was my
first opera, *One Man Show*, though that was a very different sort of
piece.

I did discover things in *Scenes and Arias* that I've used ever since:
about my own musical language, about its method, about my own
style of musical rhetoric. But in fact the richness of *Scenes and Arias*
caused me a lot of trouble, because the works that I was asked to
write afterwards were of a very different order indeed: the comic
opera, a string quartet, and two works for eighteenth-century
forces (the Sonata for strings and two horns, and the Sinfonia). I
had to scale down the language.

But though it was a breakthrough for me, it didn't seem to make
much impact on anybody else at the time. It wasn't performed
again until 1968.

Where does music come from? Do you start with a thematic idea, a glimpse
of a whole form, a detailed moment or what?

These days everything I write is commissioned, so that gives you a pretty strong handle in terms of instrumentation, length, the kind of occasion that the first performance will be, the quality of the players, etc. When one is young one quite often tries to start pieces from a single idea, but as one gets older one comes round to starting off with a total view of the piece, and you then fill that out, rather like a blank canvas.

One sometimes gets ideas that come out of the blue, not within the context of a piece in progress: sometimes these ideas appear in a pure form, as if awaiting their realization. Usually, though, I hear things in terms of instrumental sound, and usually ideas come when you actually start working on the piece. Work provides ideas: ideas provide work.

What process of sketching and drafting might lead from an initial idea to a completed work?

I always sketch rather carefully, somtimes going through two or three drafts. My sketches are usually full: they contain everything that will go into the full score. And I used to work everything out in detail as I went along, but now I'm trying to get the basic bones down as rapidly as I can and then adding to the draft, or doing another draft with more detail. I hope that gives both more spontaneity and a greater sense of line. It was a revelation to me when I discovered that large parts of the *Ring* were put down on just two lines, and I've been aiming for the maximum speed of notation in the early stages.

Do you ever abandon works?

Yes I do. And I also sometimes have great difficulty in finding the direction I want a work to go in. I can't get inside a work until I've got the opening. I must have abandoned two or three large-scale works during the seventies, including two orchestral pieces; and something like that in the sixties as well. I also suppress works: I've withdrawn three early works and two largish works written in the early seventies.

How do you decide when a work is complete?

I try and answer the question to myself simply by reading it through time and again, and, as it were, timing it on my inner musical clock. Sometimes one can go spectacularly wrong, and very often it's this inner clock that's the cause of pieces not working: one hears new pieces that have very striking ideas but are unsatisfactory because they don't seem to have been put to that inner temporal test. It's one of the most difficult things to get right in composition – apart from the sheer business of getting from one note to the next.

Would you be tempted to revise works you wrote twenty or twenty-five years ago? How do you now regard those pieces?

On the whole I wouldn't want to revise them, though there are certain areas in most of them that I'm dissatisfied with. There's certainly one piece that gave me endless trouble and will never be right: that's *One Man Show*, which I did revise two or three times. It now works very well, but I wouldn't describe it as entirely satisfactory. As to other pieces, I wouldn't be tempted to revise them because my language has changed, and I'm not interested in the problems or materials of those pieces any longer. There's a sense in which one has to forget about what's one done if one's going to do anything further.

Like most composers I regard my earlier works with a mixture of dismay and affection. Some of them I'm very attached to indeed: *Scenes and Arias*, my little Flute Sonatina. Others leave me strangely cold, as if somebody else had written them. But with some pieces I'm surprised at how well they turned out. You forget the feelings that animated a piece, and the work of writing – maybe because I like pieces to have fluency, to be well made. I'm not a tombola composer, not a composer who writes an enormous number of works, and every so often comes up with a jewel. I want each piece to be made so that it will survive.

Do you enjoy performances of your music? In particular do you enjoy first performances?

There are a lot of first performances that I most certainly have *not* enjoyed: they've been very painful experiences. Happily, this gets less and less frequent, but in the past performances were sometimes inadequate or downright bad, and that's exceedingly painful. One can quickly reach a state of despair about it. If a piece has a bad first performance, it takes about five years for the piece to recover: performers are reluctant to take it up.

On the whole I don't enjoy first performances: they're too emotionally fraught.

What other music (if any!) do you hear with pleasure?

Usually music that I think I can learn from. That sounds a little sententious, but I equate the word 'pleasure' here with 'interest'. This would certainly include all the classics, and a number of the late Romantics: Brahms, Wolf, Bruckner, Strauss, Mahler, Tchaikovsky, Mussorgsky. A lot of French music I like very much: Berlioz, Debussy, Ravel, Bizet of course. I love *Tristan* and *The Mastersingers*, and most Verdi from about 1850 onwards: he's somebody I admire more and more. I like early and middle-period Schoenberg, up to about op. 22, all of Berg and not a great deal of Webern. I like most Stravinsky, most Bartók, and among English composers Elgar, early Walton, Britten of course, Tippett. Of present-day figures I most admire Lutosławski, Ligeti and Henze, and I also greatly admire Harry Birtwistle's music, possibly because it's so far removed from my own. The quality I most admire in any music is invention.

What music would you strive to avoid?

Handel operas and oratorios I don't care for very much, apart from various bits and pieces, though I love his instrumental music. At the moment the Beethoven symphonies don't mean a great deal to me, though I listen whenever I can to the string quartets and piano sonatas, which seem to me much more interesting. You'll never catch me at another opera by Bellini, and I would take some persuading to go and see something by Donizetti again. Then there's quite a lot of music from this century – particularly from the thirties, forties and fifties – that I don't care for at all. One figure from that era that I've had to change my mind about is Shostakovich: I thoroughly detested his music for a long time, but I've recently warmed to him a great deal. There's also a lot of serial and post-serial music from 1945–75 that I would go a long way to avoid; particularly where the serial language is hauled into received forms: for example, I've never heard a serial symphony that came anywhere near living up to the models of the past.

Is it still possible to compose opera? Is the art of libretto writing dead? Can operatic structures be supported without the narrative thread provided by the diatonic system?

I suppose the obvious answer, from the point of view of a composer in the mid-eighties, is that it's not possible to compose opera in the old way. But I begin to suspect that there is no new way of composing opera, and that it's only possible to compose opera in the old way. There's one simple reason for this: that opera is by and about singing, and singing implies song, which implies phrase structure, which in turn implies cadencing, which in turn implies some kind of tonality. Basically the problem is how to make a viable song – how indeed, in this day and age, to make a melody which can be apprehended as such, lodged in the memory as an entity. I don't mean to suggest that opera has to be a long string of unbroken melodies, though some of the most successful operas have been just that. It's rather that melody is one of the essential ingredients of the art form.

Of course, it's possible to write operas of a completely different kind, but I don't think it's possible to write very many of them: there's the case of *Wozzeck*, and there's the remarkable case of *Punch and Judy*. But if one's going to create an *oeuvre* of operas, one's musical language has to be sufficiently flexible, and one way of achieving that flexibility is to make use of the speech patterns of one's language; and certainly three of this century's greatest opera composers have done that: Strauss, Janáček and Britten. But of course this question of flexibility goes far beyond that: it's a matter of dramatic tensions and relaxations, of shifts in dramatic temperature.

One of the litmus tests is whether a composer can write a comic opera. There have always been remarkably few successful comic operas, but surely never as few as in the last eighty years. Comedy demands mastery in these things in a very extreme form, and it has to be an art that conceals art: the language must not draw attention to itself but be buoyant, capable of true melody, capable of considerable kinetic energy, so that the composer can write really fast music.

There's also the question of subject matter, which is another problem in the twentieth century. In the old days characters tended to be larger than life or, in comic opera, caricatures. Auden maintained that this was necessary simply because they sang: he could never imagine somebody coming on to the stage in a business suit and singing. But I don't think that's a problem in comedy, and the problem in dramatic opera is different: operatic characters tended to be heroic, and these days it's not believable or interesting to put such characters on the stage. Two of the greatest operas of the century have been concerned rather with anti-heroes: *Wozzeck* and *Peter Grimes*, both of which feature archetypally twentieth-century figures though they're both based on early nineteenth-century texts.

Until the early twentieth century opera grew directly out of the drama of its time, but in the twentieth century this has been exceedingly difficult, partly because of the question of copyright. It's very hard for a composer to use the work of a contemporary dramatist, because he's not allowed to, or it's too expensive. I had that experience when I once approached a British playwright, who was extremely enthusiastic about the idea and even gave me a copy of the play he'd prepared for television, cutting the text by half; but the project came to naught because his agents refused to allow it.

In the past operatic characters have not been noted for psychological depth, though of course there are exceptions: the Countess in *Figaro*, Leonore in *Fidelio*, Wotan, Hans Sachs, Othello, the Marschallin . . . But this does seem to be an area that the twentieth-century opera composer might apply himself to. But that brings me again to the subject of language, because it would require a language of great subtlety and elasticity.

There's also the matter of conditions of performance. I haven't written an opera now for fifteen years because I was so horrified by what happened to my last one. I should say immediately that these remarks are not addressed to theatres in England but elsewhere: I was extremely fortunate to have my last opera produced at Glyndebourne, to a very high standard. But later the opera was turned into a travesty, and it's on that kind of occasion that one's judged. There's very little you can do to get the production to match up to your intentions.

How have you selected texts for setting, or have they selected themselves?

I usually go about selecting texts with some care, and try to arrange the text in some way that is going to make a satisfying musical shape. Depending on the forces, I think carefully about the kind of poetry I might use: for example, I once set some Hardy for voice and guitar, because the plain ordinariness of the language, its slightly gauche quality, seemed appropriate to that kind of intimate setting. I once asked a friend of mine, Peter Porter, to write some verse for setting, and he produced a mini-libretto of poems. But once or twice texts have selected themselves, one example being the quite remarkable text I set in *The Ruin*: an Anglo-Saxon poem on the ruins of a Roman city. I came across that a long time ago, probably when I was a student, and it had always haunted my imagination, until finally I got the opportunity to set it.

Nowadays one area where it's very difficult to find texts is that of love poetry: most of the obvious ones have been set. My solution to that in *La vita nuova* was to set Italian texts, in which I hoped to recapture some of that freshness that it's now very difficult to get when setting English love poetry. There are certain French poets, too, that I'd like to try my hand at.

Do you like to write for particular performers, and indeed audiences?

I don't think I have any preference as far as audience is concerned, but there are always performers one would be only too happy to write for. If you're writing to commission, then almost always you have a particular performer in mind. Quite often it's somebody you've chosen, but sometimes it isn't. And there are performers I've been very happy to collaborate with: the Nash Ensemble, for instance. But I wouldn't say I must have a performer in mind. Sometimes it's been a positive assistance, particularly in the case of a singer, because one has to take very careful account of a singer's vocal qualities and expressive potential.

Do you find it more congenial, creatively, to be in the United States at the moment?

I didn't come to the United States for musical reasons: I came here initially to teach, and that's certainly been a rewarding experience. As to whether it's going to turn out well creatively, I can't really say, because I haven't been here long enough: I'm just beginning to do some work here.

Do you keep sketches from past works? Might these be useful in later ones?

I do keep sketches. In the case of works that have been published, I don't worry about that, but I have slight qualms about keeping sketches for works that are unpublished or suppressed, and I may very well destroy these at some date. Some of my sketches are already in libraries, so there's no hope of covering up one's sins there. I think Brahms's attitude in getting rid of all this preliminary material was rather admirable: keeping what went on in his kitchen to himself.

I don't think sketches are ever useful in later works: I'm not a self-quoter, with one exception. Sketches, of course, which haven't been used might indeed find their way into future works: I can think of two or three ideas that I would like to use some time, and that were originally sketched for pieces that never got completed.

Do you keep sketchbooks in which you might set down ideas independent of any particular work?

Yes, though they're just bits of paper. I try to get down ideas as they come to me, and usually I have to do it quite rapidly, or otherwise I forget them. I've also had the problem recently of dreaming musical ideas which I've then forgotten about by the morning.

Which work of yours do you most approve?

I don't think I can answer with one work: there have to be three. One has to be *Scenes and Arias*, because I discovered so much through that. Then there's my second opera, *The Rising of the Moon*, which I think I approve because I achieved what I set out to, and, much more difficult, because I think I more or less did what I was asked to do. There were fairly stiff conditions attached to the commissioning of the opera by Glyndebourne: first of all, they wanted a romantic comedy; secondly, they wanted parts for various foreign artists who appeared with the company; and thirdly, one had to take note of the dinner interval. So the first act is the longest and the remaining two get shorter; also, the first act not only sets up the action in classic fashion, it also gives the audience the feeling that they've seen something. I wanted to write a real opera in the traditional sense, and I wanted to write a comedy that was really funny; and I think I succeeded. Though I may say that if I wrote an opera again, I wouldn't be the least interested in writing one like that.

The last work I might cite is much more recent: a short orchestral work called *Spring Music*. And for similar reasons to those I put forward in connection with *The Rising of the Moon*. I'd become rather tired of being asked for an orchestral piece that would be simple, straightforward, easy to rehearse, easy to tour, not make egregious demands in the percussion department, provide a good opener. And I decided I would actually try to write such a piece. I slightly popularized my own style, and wrote something which I suppose is a rough equivalent to the *Academic Festival Overture*. One thing one wants to be as a composer is useful, and when I got down to trying to solve all these problems without writing down, or leaving whole areas of my musical personality out, I found it quite an interesting challenge. It's not the kind of piece I might write ever again, but at the moment I rather like it.

There's one other work that I'm fond of for precisely opposite reasons: *Personae*. In that case there were no constraints, and I allowed myself complete freedom of expression. I'd not been able to write for the piano in a way that hadn't already been explored, but these pieces are very much based on the feel of the keys under the hands. I'm going to write some more of them: indeed, I hope that I shall continue to write them all the way through my working life, so that they'll form a sort of ongoing record of my working practice.

19

Robert Saxton

Saxton, uniquely, will not hear of putting me to the trouble of travelling to interview him: he drives out from London to see me. And he talks with the same infinite courtesy, as well as with a suavity that deflects attention from himself to the subject of his gentle-mannered discourse. He is also a little more definite than he will later wish. Succeeding weeks bring three lots of qualifications to be inserted into the script, always accompanied by apologies for himself for being such a 'fusspot'.

You already have more than a decade of published works to look back on: how do you now see your earlier music? Is there a strong continuity?

I do see little mannerisms going through, which I may consciously try to avoid or not: that's like the style of one's handwriting. What I also see is that my older music, up to about 1979, is very decorative and somewhat static. I think I was trying to establish a sort of harmonic polyphony, but it was rather directionless, while inside me somewhere I knew I wanted to write music that was more dynamic, in the technical sense. During the last five or six years I've been working towards a much greater differentiation between foreground and background: there may be a slow harmonic background with a foreground of fast figuration, for example.

Does that mean the background comes first?

To some degree, yes, because I tend to see a work in a flash – not with all the details, but I know roughly its length and its shape, and then I work inwards to the details, finding the notes and the harmonies to make the world I want. I do nowadays work with an overall harmonic scheme, but of course it gets very altered as I work, and changes direction. So often one ends up with the difficulty that one's plan is starting to change, which is why recently I've more than once had to start a piece again. You have to be quite honest with yourself, realize there's something deep at the back of your mind, and what keeps coming to the front is still not the finished version. And yet it's inevitable that the background and the details will keep crashing into one another, which is where I think the development and transformation of ideas really comes from.

The background I start with might be some elaborate sort of passacaglia, though not with a thematic bass, because the harmony these days might not be working from the bass upwards. Then the details come intuitively: one gets into a way of thinking, though one has to try constantly to expand it. Often one thinks one's doing something dramatically different, and then when you've finished you realize there are connections with earlier pieces. When you're intensely working on a piece, then everything seems fresh every morning when you go to your desk.

Are you influenced by other composers when you're expanding your repertory?

No. I'm certainly interested in other music, partly because I have to teach: for instance, recently I've given a course of eight lectures on Messiaen. Maybe one's affected by a certain technical approach to something, but one's got the ideas already in one's head; and I don't think I'm affected on an aesthetic or philosophical level, because I find I'm less and less interested in other composers' work from that point of view. Hopefully one's absorbed those things a bit earlier. Although if I'm honest there are composers I still have as models at the back of my mind: for instance, I adore Mahler, Schumann, Bach, Stravinsky, Berg and Bartók, but I don't think you'd be aware of that from any of my pieces, except perhaps if, as an acute listener, you remembered *The Soldier's Tale* in the violin solos of *Processions and Dances* or Bach in the trumpet parts of the Concerto for Orchestra or *The Ring of Eternity*. I do, but then I wrote the pieces.

Earlier on, of course, all sorts of influences were important. I was fortunate when I was quite young, 10 or 11, to hear those old Thursday Invitation Concerts on the radio: that's how I heard Webern, and *Le marteau sans maître*, and Elisabeth Lutyens's *Wittgenstein Motet*, which knocked me out. I remember creeping off and trying to write a motet, though I didn't even know what a motet was. I was very excited by that sort of music.

But then I got under the spell of Britten, and he helped me when I was a boy, mostly by correspondence, though I did have one lesson at his house. Afterwards, when I went to Elisabeth Lutyens, she said she wasn't going to ram serialism down my throat, but I did want to investigate all those things, so then from about the age

Robert Saxton   *photo: Malcolm Crowthers*

of 16 my ears were going in a certain direction. Boulez was a great influence, but at a particular level: now I'm a bit older I can see how much there is in Boulez that comes from Messiaen – the cellular writing, the chord groups – whereas then I was trying to tackle the problem of harmonic counterpoint, so Webern's cantatas would probably have been more relevant models. But when you're a student you don't always see the wood for the trees. What attracted me to Webern at that time was the distilled Mahlerian world of the op. 6 and op. 10 orchestral pieces. I was also completely seduced by Debussy's music.

Are you very conscious when you're composing not just of how it will sound but how it will be heard?

Absolutely. Some years ago, when I was even more naive, I really couldn't understand how people should be unable to hear how a piece of mine worked. And people said it was all very French, whereas I was and am concerned with harmonic and polyphonic coherence, and all my pieces work material in a way which is actually not French at all in its methods. So I think there was a gap between objective observation and my subjective intentions. I presume that's far less now that I'm writing the sort of music that I couldn't write ten years ago, though I wanted to.

I'm beginning to think, without getting too Jungian about it, that there are certain archetypes that are necessary shapewise. My shapes have got much less abstract and much simpler, which came about partly through a desire to make my structures grow more, and partly because of head-on collision with Carter's music. What interested me about Carter was the way he could get big gestures that are really quite simple, the way Berg could, and yet the details are all complex and their interactions are complex. That did have an effect on me. I started wanting to make my structures more directional: it's not just the harmony but also the large-scale rhythm one's trying to organize, and I learned a lot from Carter in that direction – not detailed technical points, but a way of thinking. It made me realize when I first heard it that there were things inside me that were very similar to that: not so much the surface sound of the music, which is what attracted me to Boulez or Webern, but the way the processes are working.

My more recent pieces make broader, less abstract gestures, which people seem to grasp more quickly – but the reasons for making the music work that way are purely musical and subjective, and have nothing whatever to do with simplicity of gesture for an audience's sake. After all, when I'm composing I am the audience.

This is something quite general, isn't it: the renewed concern with big gestures, big shapes, long-range coherence?

Definitely it's in the air. I'm very aware of that when I'm teaching students who weren't even born when Britten's *War Requiem* was first performed, and I remember very well listening to the first performance on the radio. Their experiences are very different: *Gruppen* is as old to them as *The Rite of Spring* to me, and, rather horrifyingly I think, they don't have it in their bloodstream. But all the way from those students to Stockhausen, composers are interested nowadays in notes and intervals, and worrying where they're going, trying to create a coherent harmonic world capable of articulating large time structures and dealing with problems of metre. You seem to have these vast differences between Carter and Steve Reich, but maybe people will look back and see them both as opposite sides of the same coin: they both write things that go from A to Z.

Obviously it's very hard to see one's own work clearly: I suppose that's why composing is so difficult. But there seem to be certain fundamental gestures which composers need to write and audiences want, in terms of articulating time. Though then you have to look at medieval music, which doesn't necessarily work that way.

Or Oriental music.

But – and this isn't something I just think: I actually feel it in my bones – one of the things one's learned from the 1960s is that if one's Occidental one just isn't Oriental. It's no good thinking that one can get inside another culture with the understanding that any creative artist must have in order to create a vibrant and living world which works on all levels. One can't afford just to half-adopt something. Of course a quasi-Oriental understanding of the movement, of the quality of the individual sound, is important in some Debussy and Webern for instance. But there are things a composer can't change: that we have concerts in the West, that art music is to some degree artificial, that we've had a harmonic tradition. It's very difficult to take the post-war attitude of starting again from scratch. Which may be why some people feel disillusioned at the moment, though I feel very optimistic: the century's been so rich, not just in music, but in philosophy and painting and literature. We may be in a period of relative consolidation, but it's tremendously hopeful.

Does your hopefulness extend to electronic music, which you haven't been involved in, as far as I'm aware?

I used a tape at the end of my tiny Mallarmé piece *Brise marine* so that the singer has a duet with herself: that was for poetic-musical reasons to do with the end of the poem.

But I have used electronics properly once, in a piece for two sopranos and tape delay, and I had a text specially written which began with discussion of the ends of things and finished with beginnings, so that the piece could create a big circle. That seemed to suit the tape-delay idea. But though certain things pleased me about the piece – I was able to control the delay channels very strictly so that the harmony always accumulated the right way over about thirteen minutes – I'm not satisfied with it, and I'd very much like to realize it again, get much more sound material out of the text.

For a very long time I've wanted to use electronics. When I was a student I sketched a piece based on a rather post-Günter Grass text that I wrote myself, which is one of the reasons I scrapped the piece. That was going to have tapes and all sorts of things, and I just couldn't realize it. There are ideas at the back of my mind for one or two pieces that would involve live performers and electronics: I found with the tape-delay piece that I could bring out things from the recesses of my brain.

Normally I tend to be very conscious of detail, which I'm sure one's got to be, because I see composition like nature: the tree will fall down if the roots aren't right. But with electronics one can work in quite big splashes, and I find that very exciting, although there's obviously an enormous amount of detailed studio work involved.

And perhaps one can work in big splashes too in the theatre.

When I was at school I was always involved in the theatre: I even acted the Captain in Büchner's *Woyzeck*. I wrote a very bad musical, and incidental music for plays. Then when I got to university I started running a contemporary music ensemble with fellow students and I just went in a different direction. But recently I've been working on an idea for a possible television programme about Paul Klee's painting technique in connection with music. And often I'll get an idea from going to a play: certain structural things, or just an atmosphere. I find it very relaxing to go to the theatre, because I can't relax at a concert or opera. Within ten seconds I'm thinking: God, how did he do that? And though one's also thinking like that at an art exhibition or at the theatre, it's not one's professional medium.

Literature, too, has surely been a vital influence?

Yes, that is evident. Sources tend to be viewed and interpreted rather subjectively, though I hope as a composer one gets to the essence of something, because one is reacting to what an artist has imagined, even if in a different medium. For instance, in my last 'official' student work, *Reflections of Narziss and Goldmund* there were two aspects of the Hesse novel that attracted me: that fairy-tale medieval Germany that Schumann and Mahler also liked to escape to, and the structural matter of Narziss and Goldmund being opposites but also identical. Or in a more recent piece, *The Sentinel of the Rainbow*, I was concerned that the musical processes, and indeed the ideas themselves, should not be just pictorial and so in a sense passive, but should re-create in time the fundamental concepts behind the myth.

What about the world of nature: does that spark off ideas?

Yes. I have an odd relationship with the natural world: I can easily forget which flower is which, but just looking at things is important. I spent nearly all my childhood holidays on the Norfolk coast, where the sky goes on for ever, and I also came to love the Italian Dolomites, where I went for three years consecutively, and where one can sense the world of Berg, Dallapiccola, Webern and Mahler so strongly. Then – a very different landscape – I was at school in Dorset, among those rolling hills: it was like living in the set of *The Midsummer Marriage* for five years. I suppose it's quite an English thing, this visionary experience you get with extraordinary land-scapes. That certainly has affected me. And I'm also interested in the way that a landscape can appear so still, yet you know that inside everything's moving and working, and that what you see is only a tiny part of the whole. That seems to me a complete mirror of what creative art is.

And it leads on to something else in my personality that I am very aware of: that my family are East European Jews. My mother's father was Polish, my great-grandfather on my father's side was Russian, and part of the family was Lithuanian. Yet I've been brought up here: I played cricket and did everything else, and of course was helped by Britten and in my mid-teens knocked absol-utely flat by *The Midsummer Marriage*. Inside there's a whole melting pot going on, and there are certain pieces of mine that flicker in this odd way between the two completely different traditions. *Processions and Dances*, for instance, is very East Euro-pean in its references, whereas *The Ring of Eternity* is a realization of certain ideas from seventeenth-century English metaphysical poetry – though I know Henry Vaughan was Welsh!

Do you think your music may be becoming more East European?

It may be I'm finding my roots. I had a relative who died recently and left me an album: he went back to Lithuania in 1921 to visit the family, and I've got these sepia photographs of them all with long beards and pails on sticks. It all looks like the set of *Fiddler on the Roof*. So if history had been slightly different, I would have been in that situation, which makes it very real to me. Although I feel very much that I'm an English composer, and although being a com-poser in England is different from being a composer in France, Germany or Italy, in the end a real composer embraces concepts that are not national but of the world. After all, that's what musical language and musical communication are about – that is music's domain.

20

Harrison Birtwistle

There is, as he keeps saying, no time. Interviewing Birtwistle is like trying to mate pandas. The creature is friendly but on the surface ponderous, though capable of sudden grace, exactness and surprise. To encourage such moments one has to get the conditions right: the appropriate question at the appropriate time in the appropriate terms. I cannot claim to have scored many times in what follows, recorded, during one of his now rare visits to England, in the offices of his agent in London.

You've said that what you were composing before you went to Manchester was 'sub-Vaughan Williams'. How did that come about?

It was a question of what the current activity was, what was creative at the time. Schoenberg was a name, Stravinsky was a name, but nobody performed their music, and I only knew some of those pieces by looking at them; then I had one or two recordings (I remember I had a recording of *The Rite of Spring*).

When you went to Manchester did you go as a composer or as a clarinettist?

I went as a clarinettist.

Did you think that was how you were going to be earning your living?

Yes. Nobody was composing. Nobody went to Manchester to do composition. So in a sense I never had an education as a composer because I was taught to be a clarinettist.

Did you not have composition lessons with Richard Hall?

Yes, I did, but I didn't know what it meant. I didn't know how to identify the music I wrote with what I was being taught.

Then as soon as you had a piece performed you sold your clarinets.

Yes, I always had this struggle that when I was writing music I ought to be practising the clarinet, and when I was playing the clarinet I ought to be writing music. So I eliminated that problem. I

Harrison Birtwistle   *photo: Malcolm Crowthers*

think what I'd always wanted to do, right from the beginning, was write music.

Though you've kept a personal relationship with the clarinet in writing so much for it, or is that just the accident of having Alan Hacker to play your music?

I think it's Alan. I've found it quite difficult to write for the clarinet, actually. If you have this physical relationship with an instrument, knowing how to play it, then that can be the odd one out, and it's the one that you want to reject: you want an equal relationship with all the instruments. I think that's how I think about it. Something like that.

But the physical idea of performing is very important, isn't it? You must see the instrumentalists on the stage almost before you put pen to paper.

Oh yes, absolutely. Like voices in an abstract play, the voices of the instruments are important.

How do pieces start?

Pieces don't really start: they're part of a continuous process. There are certain things thrown up in the course of composition. Arriving at a certain place I can see another point that I might try to get to, but I'll never get there.

Do you mean an actual musical sound?

No, a point. I can see how it could logically arrive there, but very often it doesn't. For instance, for *Secret Theatre* I drew up a lot of pre-compositional ideas about how things could progress, how they could get from point to point; I constructed a whole map, as it were. But then in the process of composition, in the journey, I went in other ways, so those original journeys are still there. I'm now writing an orchestral piece which will be a different facet of the same thing. But then again, it'll be a different sort of piece.

What form did your map take? Were there harmonic processes?

No, they were . . . I don't know, it's difficult . . . They were like a set of rules: constructing a world with its paths, its journeys, its directions . . . it's hard to talk about.

The new orchestral piece is going to be for a large orchestra?

Yes.

What sort of length will it be?

Half an hour. It's quite ambitious, I think.

Does it have a title?

No.

Do titles arise during the course of composition?

Yes. I've got ideas for the title: there's something in Günter Grass where he talks about 'geometria', so it's something to do with that. It's a geometrical piece, like a geometric labyrinth.

Is it going to have soloists, like Secret Theatre?

It does and it doesn't. They're not specific like that, but it has two layers. That was one thing I thought about in *Secret Theatre*, to make the layers asynchronous; but when I did it they did start to change at the same time. In the orchestral piece there's the possibility that it'll be more contrapuntal, so that sometimes the blocks are together and sometimes they're not. I don't actually know, because I'm still writing it.

If it's difficult to know how pieces begin, is it difficult to know when they're finished?

No. I've always thought of my pieces as starting from germs: there was something with which you built. That's not the same now. What I do is write pieces in which the world is completely formed, and then you dissect it: it's not put together.

In what sense is it completely formed?

It's as though it already existed. It just begins. That's what *Secret Theatre* does: the most complex music is about five pages in, and it just opens out, like the needle of a syringe going right to the centre.

Do you ever abandon works?

I've thrown a lot of music out, yes. I threw an orchestral piece away, *The Triumph of Time*, before I wrote the one that exists. I knew more or less what I wanted to do, but I couldn't find it.

You've said that when you're composing you're concerned with the structure and not with what it's . . .

. . . saying. No, because I can't control that, can I? I don't see how one can.

But when you're writing incidental music it must be required that you know what it's saying?

Yes, that's a different activity.

But there must be something of that too in opera?

Yes, but I've got a feeling that my operatic efforts are in some degree on the side. They're occasional pieces.

Even though Punch and Judy *had so much to do with other music you were writing in the mid-sixties?*

I think *Tragoedia*'s more of a statement: to me it is. I discovered a world in *Tragoedia*; then in *Punch and Judy* I exploited it.

I'm reminded of what you said about Agon *as being a world, one that had seemed to exist for ever.*

Yes. Before that I knew Schoenberg's twelve-tone pieces, but in *Agon* I realized that you could have a world that was archetypal, that was serial but had nothing to do with Schoenberg. Somebody said it was a piece that Britten was very worried by, because he'd thought that you couldn't compose music serially until he heard *Agon*.

Had you felt that? Because you had been worried by serialism . . .

Well, it seemed that what he'd done was to make a kind of music that I'd been doing intuitively. But he'd formalized it – though the intuition does have to come first. For instance, I will improvise chords on the piano, find things I like, and then examine them to see what they're made of. It's like finding something and then seeing how it works.

Is that the way a lot of your music starts, from improvising?

It's not improvising in that sense, but finding things to do with voicing and so on that I can actually feel. That's why working in an electronic studio has been of great importance to me, because there you're dealing with the material at first hand.

But presumably you work with a technician?

Yes, though the technician's only the peformer.

What were you achieving in the electronic component of Orpheus?

There are three parts to it. One part is what I call 'auras' or 'veils': they're backdrops, canvases within which things can exist. Another part consists of 'signals': they're the voice of Apollo; they can stop the orchestra; they're huge interjections, punctuations. And then there are pieces that are made up of these signals, but are through-composed: they're longer, around three minutes, and they're another part of the drama.

You were talking about finding material by improvising, and yet the few examples given in Michael Hall's book suggest a different approach, starting out from something very abstract.

I can't remember what they are.

There was one from Verses for Ensembles, *one from . . . agm . . .*

Yes, I can't say. The example from . . . *agm* . . . was a bit interesting for me because . . . It would take a long time to explain, and
you haven't got time, have you?

Do, see how we go.

For instance, if you take a piece of mine like *Verses for Ensembles*
there are ritornellos in it. There are some brass ritornellos in four
parts which can be played in many, many ways. I was interested in
the notion that you could have a piece of music which only existed
in the abstract. It's like looking at an object: every view is unique,
but the object exists irrespective of the way it's viewed. So it's the
notion that this piece of music exists, just like an object, and what
you can do is perform certain facets of it, examine it in different
ways. In *Verses* that works in rather a conventional way, but then I
started working on smaller forms to do with varied ostinati, in
which an ostinato can consist of, say, five increments, but on each
repeat you can only have four of them: so you never actually hear
the thing as a whole. You can do the same thing with a chord – this
was something I took directly from electronics – where you have a
complex number of notes, and filter it at every repeat so that it's
never the same.

There are things that keep repeating, but if you listen to them or
look at them closely, they're not repeating. It's like the leaves of a
tree. You know what an oak leaf looks like, but if you take one,
then look at the next one, they're all different. The total object is
never sounded, but through time you build up a memory picture of
what it is. Consequently the order in which these things appear
doesn't actually matter, but they're very carefully composed. It's
like shells on a shore: I compose each shell, but they're all slightly
different, and they're thrown by circumstance on the shore, by
what the sea does to them.

But you don't in fact allow the bits to be put together in different ways.

No, I decide what the order is, through my ears, through my
intuition, through whatever composition is.

Do you allow the possibility that it could be otherwise?

No. It's a funny double standard, but once it's there it becomes a
fact. You take a photograph of the seashore, to continue the
analogy: when I click the camera, that's my photograph.

You used the phrase 'varied ostinati', which suggests a strong degree of continuity but also an absence of goal direction.

That's right. It comes from identifying the nature of my material and then trying to understand it for what it is. I've never tried to fight it; I've tried to understand it. To understand the nature of your material is the most important thing for creativity, I think. Because if I felt I had an obligation to tonality or wanted to use sonata forms it would be pointless.

It's not easy to know what a composer means by his 'material'.

I know what my material is. I don't think I always did, but I do now. I'm not trying to carve out of stone when I have a piece of wood.

But it might be interesting to go against the nature sometimes.

Yes, but I do that in other ways. Of course.

After the experience with Orpheus *are you going to use electronics in another piece?*

I'd like to, but there's no time, is there? I've got an idea for an electronic piece – I've had it for years – but I know that somebody's going to do it. I know that it's possible. I'd like to get involved, but it takes so much time.

Are there many composers you try to keep in touch with?

Not really. It becomes more and more difficult to talk to other composers. There's nothing to say, after a while.

Do you go to performances of your pieces?

Yes. Not a lot.

Is that an enjoyable experience?

Not particularly. I very much like a first performance, when it's coming to life. Once I know that it has a life to exist, then it's OK. I have to come to terms with how it's worked; I have a little slot, and I know what that piece is. There's not much you can do about it then: it's too late. Like having children.

Are you interested in seeing how pieces are done differently?

With operas I would be, if I had enough time. Because when I write for the theatre I have very specific ideas about how they should be done. *Punch and Judy*, for instance, I've never seen done the way I would like to see it: and that's the very point of why I wrote it in the first place.

How would you like to see it?

A very controlled physical world, rather like Japanese theatre: not mimicking that, but with a real vocabulary of movement, and mask work. Totally artificial. And very formal.

Do you ever change pieces after you've heard them?

Not a lot, no.

Do they ever surprise you?

Yes. The vertical never surprises me, but what you can only calculate is how a thing exists in time. I've often thought about whether it was possible to produce a sort of shorthand, and make a piece so that it moves faster, and then work into the detail, but then I found that the detail was making the decisions in the end, pointing into directions that the shorthand had gone but I didn't want to go. So that doesn't work.

Do you start at page 1 and go through to the end?

Yes.

Do you keep regular hours for composition?

Yes. At the beginning of pieces I don't, but once they get going I do. I work very hard.

Do you work on more than one piece at a time?

No I can't. I can't do anything. I find it very hard to write letters.

Would you have been surprised by the music you're writing now if you'd seen it, say, ten years ago?

I think it's going in the direction in which I want it to go. It's better than it was.

How much control do you have over its direction?

This is an interesting point. It's something I think about a great deal. The creative process to me is like a sort of wedge, into which people drive themselves, and it gets drier and drier as you get towards the point. The older you get the less free you are.

Stravinsky?

But then he made very self-conscious choices to change direction.

Would you do that?

No. I suddenly am aware of another dimension, or of something that's come to the fore. I think I'm fairly unique in the way that I work.

There's certainly that homogeneity . . .

Could be.

Note: the lists of works and recordings are not comprehensive. Full information is available from the relevant publishers.

Bainbridge, Simon   *b* London, 30 Aug 1952; *educ* Highgate School, RCM (1969–72, Lambert), Tanglewood (1973, 1974); *works* Heterophony for orchestra (1970), Spirogyra for septet (1971), Wind Quintet (1971), String Quartet (1972), Flugal for ensemble (1973), Wind Quartet (1974), People of the Dawn for soprano and quintet (1975), Viola Concerto (1976), Music for Mel and Nora (1979), Landscapes and Magic Words for soprano and ensemble (1981), Voicing for ensemble (1982), Path to Othona for ensemble (1982), Concertante in moto perpetuo for oboe and nonet (1983), Fantasia for two orchestras (1983–4), A cappella for six voices (1984–5); *pub* United Music Publishers; *rec* Viola Concerto (Unicorn RHD 400)

Benjamin, George   *b* London, 31 Jan 1960; *educ* privately (Peter Gellhorn), Paris Conservatoire (Messiaen, Loriod), Cambridge (1978–82, Goehr); *works* Altitude for brass band (1977), Piano Sonata (1977–8), Octet (1978), Flight for flute (1979), Ringed by the Flat Horizon for orchestra (1979–80), Duo for cello and piano (1980), A Mind of Winter for soprano and small orchestra (1981), Sortilèges for piano (1981), Meditations on Haydn's Name for piano (1982), At First Light for chamber orchestra (1982), Fanfare for Aquarius for ensemble (1983), Relativity Rag for piano (1984); *pub* Faber Music; *rec* Altitude (Green Records), Piano Sonata + Flight + Duo (Nimbus 45009)

Birtwistle, Harrison   *b* Accrington, 15 July 1934; *educ* Royal Manchester College of Music (1952–5, Hall); *post* musical director of National Theatre (1975–); *works* Refrains and Choruses, for wind quintet (1957), Monody for Corpus Christi, for soprano and trio (1959), Chorales for orchestra (1960–3), Entr'actes and Sappho Fragments, for soprano and sextet (1964), Tragoedia for wind

quintet, harp and string quartet (1965), Punch and Judy, chamber
opera (1966–7), Nomos for amplified wind quartet and orchestra
(1967–8), Verses for Ensembles, for small orchestra (1968–9),
Down by the Greenwood Side, music theatre (1968–9), Meridian
for voices and instruments (1970–1), An Imaginary Landscape for
orchestra (1971), Chronometer on tape (1971–2), The Triumph of
Time for orchestra (1971–2), Melencolia I for clarinet, harp and
strings (1976), Silbury Air for small orchestra (1977), . . . agm . . .
for sixteen voices and small orchestra (1978–9), Clarinet Quintet
(1980–1), The Mask of Orpheus, opera (1973–83), Secret Theatre
for small orchestra (1984); *pub* Universal; *rec* Refrains and Choruses
(Philips SAL 3669), Tragoedia (HMV ASD 2333, Argo ZRG 759),
Punch and Judy (Decca HEAD 24–5), Verses for Ensembles + Nenia
+ The Fields of Sorrow (Decca HEAD 7), The Triumph of Time
(Argo ZRG 790), . . . agm . . . (Erato STU 71543); *bib* M. Hall: HB
(London, Robson, 1984)

Bryars, Gavin *b* Goole, Yorkshire, 16 Jan 1943; *educ* Goole
Grammar School (1954–61), Sheffield U. (philosophy 1961–4),
privately (Cyril Ramsey 1954–61, George Linstead 1961–6); *posts*
lecturer at Portsmouth College of Art (1969–70) and Leicester
Polytechnic (1970–); *works* Mr Sunshine for keyboards (1968),
Made in Hong Kong, indeterminate (1968), Marvellous aphorisms
are scattered richly throughout these pages, solo theatre piece
(1969), The Sinking of the Titanic, indeterminate (1969), Golders(as)
Green by Eps(ups)om('n) Downs, indeterminate (1969), Pre-
Medieval Metrics for ensemble (1970), The harp that once through
Tara's halls, instructions for low-fidelity recording (1970), Serenely
beaming and leaning on a five-barred gate, private piece (1970),
Ouse for two singers (1970), The ride cymbal and the band that
caused the fire in the sycamore trees, for one or more prepared
pianos (1970), To gain the affections of Miss Dwyer even for one
minute would benefit me no end, for electronic equipment (1970),
A Game of Football, in large spaces (1970), 1, 2, 1–2–3–4 for
ensemble (1971), The Squirrel and the Ricketty-Racketty Bridge
for players each with two guitars (1971), Jesus' blood never failed
me yet, for recorded voice and chamber orchestra (1971), The Heat
of the Beat, indeterminate (1972), A Place in the Country, for fifty-
three or twenty-four similar instruments in a large outdoor space
(1972), Far Away and Dimly Pealing, indeterminate (1972), Long
Player for piano and violin and/or cello (1975), Ponukelian Melody
for ensemble (1975), White to Play and Win, for percussion trio and

music box (1976), Tra-la-la-lira-lira-lay for ensemble (1976), Irma, realization of opera by Tom Phillips (1977), The Perfect Crime for ensemble (1977), White's SS for ensemble (1977), R + 7 for percussion duo (1977), Poggioli in Zaleski's Gazebo for ensemble (1977), Out of Zaleski's Gazebo for two pianos (1977), Danse dieppoise for ensemble (1978), My First Homage for ensemble (1978), Ramsey's Lamp for two pianos (1979), Epsom Downs for percussion quartet (1979), Sforzesco Sforzando for four pianos (1979), Epsom Downs Mark 2 for percussion duo (1979), The Cross-Channel Ferry for ensemble (1979), The Vespertine Park for percussion ensemble (1980), The English Mail-Coach for percussion quartet (1980), After Mendelssohn for piano duet (1980), Sidescraper for piano duet (1980), Hi-Tremolo for percussion ensemble (1980), Sixteen for tape and two organs (1981), Medea, opera (1981–2), Act 2 Scene B from Civil Wars, for percussion ensemble (1983), Allegrasco for soprano saxophone and piano (1983), Les fiançailles for ensemble (1983), Effarene for two voices, four pianos and percussion sextet (1984), Act 3 Scenes A and B from Civil Wars, for voices and orchestra; *pub* composer; *rec* The Sinking of the Titanic + Jesus' blood never failed me yet (Obscure OBS 1, Editions EG EGED 21), Irma (Obscure OBS 9, Editions EG EGED 29), My First Homage + The Vespertine Park + The English Mail-Coach + Hi-Tremolo (Crépuscule TWI 027); *bib* article by K. Potter in *Contact*, 22 (1981), 4

Casken, John *b* Barnsley, 15 July 1949; *educ* Birmingham U. (1967–71, Joubert, Dickinson), Warsaw (1971–3, Dobrowolski, Lutosławski); *posts* lecturer at Birmingham U. (1973–9), Huddersfield Polytechnic (1979–81) and Durham U. (1981–); *works* Music for cello and piano (1971–2), Kagura for thirteen wind (1972–3), Jadu for two cellos (1973), Fluctus for violin and piano (1973–4), Music for the Crabbing Sun for quartet (1974), Music for a Tawny-Gold Day for quartet (1975–6), Arenaria for flute and ensemble (1976), Thymehaze for recorder and piano (1976), Tableaux des trois âges for orchestra (1976–7), Amarantos for nonet (1977–8), Ligatura for organ (1978), Ia Orana, Gauguin for soprano and piano (1978), Melanos for tuba and nonet (1979), Firewhirl for soprano and septet (1979–80), A Belle Pavine for violin and tape (1980), Quatédrale on tape (1980), Piano Concerto (1980), String Quartet (1981–2), Fonteyn Fanfares for twelve brass (1982), Masque for oboe and chamber orchestra (1982), Eructavit for decet (1982), Taerset for clarinet and piano (1982–3), Erin for double-bass and chamber orchestra (1982–3), To Fields we do not Know for chorus (1983–4), The Piper's Linn for Northumbrian small pipes and tape (1983–4), Orion over Farne for orchestra (1984), Clarion Sea for brass quintet (1984–5), Vaganza for ensemble (1985); *pub* Schott; *rec* Ia Orana, Gauguin + Firewhirl + String Quartet (Wergo WER 60096); *bib* article by JC in *Contact*, 12 (1975), 3

Davies, Peter Maxwell   *b* Manchester, 8 Sept 1934; *educ* Leigh Grammar School, Manchester University, Royal Manchester College of Music (1952–7, Hall), Rome (1957–9, Petrassi), Princeton (1962–4, Sessions, Kim); *works* Trumpet Sonata (1955), Prolation for orchestra (1957–8), String Quartet (1961), First Taverner Fantasia for orchestra (1962), Second Taverner Fantasia for orchestra (1964), Revelation and Fall for voice and large ensemble (1966), Taverner, opera (1962–8, Covent Garden 1972), Worldes Blis for orchestra (1966–9), Eight Songs for a Mad King, for voice and sextet (1969), St Thomas Wake for orchestra (1969), Vesalii icones for dancer, cello and quintet (1969), Blind Man's Buff, music theatre (1972), Stone Litany for soprano and orchestra (1973), Ave maris stella for sextet (1975), Symphony no. 1 (1973–6), The Martyrdom of St Magnus, chamber opera (1976), A Mirror of Whitening Light for small orchestra (1976–7), Salome, ballet (1978), The Lighthouse, chamber opera (1979), Symphony no. 2 (1980), Image, Reflection, Shadow for sextet (1982), Symphony no. 3 (1984); *pub* Boosey & Hawkes, Chester, Schott; *rec* Trumpet Sonata (Nonesuch H 71275), O magnum mysterium (Argo ZRG 5327), Second Taverner Fantasia (Argo ZRG 712), Revelation and Fall (HMV ASD 2427, Angel S 36558), Antechrist + Hymnos + Missa super 'L'homme armé' + From Stone to Thorn (Oiseau-Lyre DSLO 2), Eight Songs for a Mad King (Nonesuch H 71285, Unicorn UNS 261), Vesalii icones (Nonesuch H 71295, Unicorn KPM 7016), Renaissance and Baroque Realizations (Unicorn KP 8005), Dark Angels (Nonesuch H 71342), Ave maris stella (Unicorn KP 8002), Symphony no. 1 (Decca HEAD 21), Salome (EMI 157–39270/2), Piano Sonata (Auracle AUC 1005), Image, Reflection, Shadow (Unicorn DKP 9033); *bib* PMD: Studies from Two Decades, ed. S. Pruslin (London, Boosey, 1979), P. Griffiths: PMD (London, Robson, 1982)

Ferneyhough, Brian   *b* Coventry, 16 Jan 1943; *educ* Birmingham School of Music (1961–3), RAM (1966–7, Berkeley), Amsterdam Conservatory (1968–9, de Leeuw), Basle Academy (1969–71, Klaus Huber); *posts* lecturer at Freiburg Musikhochschule (1973–)

and Darmstadt; *works* Sonatina for three clarinets and bassoon (1963), Four Miniatures for flute and piano (1965), Coloratura for oboe and piano (1966), Epigrams for piano (1966), Sonata for Two Pianos (1966), Three Pieces for piano (1967), Prometheus for wind sextet (1967), Sonatas for String Quartet (1967), Epicycle for twenty strings (1968), Missa brevis for twelve voices (1969), Firecycle Beta for orchestra (1969–71), Cassandra's Dream Song for flute (1971), Sieben Sterne for organ (1971), Transit for six amplified voices and chamber orchestra (1972–5), Time and Motion Study I for bass clarinet (1971–7), II for cello and tape (1973–⟨), III for sixteen voices, percussion and tape (1974), Unity Capsule for flute (1975–6), Funérailles for string septet and harp (1969–77), La terre est un homme for orchestra (1976–9), String Quartet no. 2 (1980), Lemma-Icon-Epigram for piano (1981), Superscriptio for piccolo (1981), Carceri d'invenzione I for chamber orchestra (1982), II for flute and chamber orchestra (1984), Adagissimo for string quartet (1983), Etudes transcendantales for soprano and quartet (1984–5), Kurze Schatten II for guitar (1985); *pub* Peters; *rec* Sonatas (RCA RL 25141), Transit (Decca HEAD 18), String Quartet no. 2 (RCA RS 9006); *bib* articles by J. Harvey in *Musical Times*, cxx (1979), 723, and by K. Potter in *Contact*, 20 (1979), 4

Goehr, Alexander *b* Berlin, 10 Aug 1932; *educ* Royal Manchester College of Music (1952–5, Hall), Paris (1955–6, Messiaen, Loriod); *posts* BBC producer (1960–8), professor at Leeds (1971–6) and Cambridge (1976–); *works* Piano Sonata op. 2 (1951–2), Fantasias for clarinet and piano op. 3 (1954), Fantasia for orchestra op. 4 (1954), Capriccio for piano op. 6 (1957), The Deluge for two voices and octet op. 7 (1957–8), Variations for flute and piano op. 8 (1959), Four Songs from the Japanese for high voice and piano or orchestra op. 9 (1959), Sutter's Gold for bass, chorus and orchestra op. 10 (1959–60), Suite for sextet op. 11 (1961), Hecuba's Lament for orchestra op. 12 (1959–61), Violin Concerto op. 13 (1961–2), Two Choruses op. 14 (1962), Little Symphony op. 15 (1963), Little Music for strings op. 16 (1963), Five Poems and an Epigram of William Blake for chorus and trumpet op. 17 (1964), Three Pieces for piano op. 18 (1964), Pastorals for orchestra op. 19 (1965), Piano Trio op. 20 (1966), Arden Must Die, opera op. 21 (1966, Hamburg 1967), Warngedichte for low voice and piano op. 22 (1967), String Quartet no. 2 op. 23 (1967), Romanza for cello and orchestra op. 24 (1968), Naboth's Vineyard, music theatre op. 25 (1968), Konzertstücke for piano and orchestra op. 26 (1969), Nonomiȳa for piano op. 27 (1969), Paraphrase for clarinet op. 28 (1969), Symphony in One Movement op. 29 (1969–70), Shadowplay, music theatre op. 30 (1970), Sonata about Jerusalem, music theatre op. 31 (1970), Concerto for Eleven op. 32 (1970), Piano Concerto op. 33 (1971–2), Metamorphosis/Dance for orchestra op. 34 (1973–4), Chaconne for nineteen wind op. 35 (1974), Lyric Pieces for octet op. 36 (1974), String Quartet no. 3 op. 37 (1975–6), Psalm 4 for female voices, viola and organ op. 38a (1976), Fugue on Psalm 4 for string orchestra op. 38b (1976), Romanza on Psalm 4 for string orchestra op. 38c (1976), Prelude and Fugue for three clarinets op. 39 (1978), Babylon the Great is Fallen for chorus and orchestra op. 40 (1979), Das Gesetz der Quadrille for low voice and piano op. 41 (1979), Sinfonia for chamber orchestra op. 42 (1979), Deux études for orchestra op. 43 (1981), Behold the Sun, opera op. 44 (1981–4, Duisburg 1985); Behold the Sun, concert aria op. 44a (1981), Sonata for cello and piano op. 45 (1984), A Musical offering: J. S. Bach 1685–1750 for ensemble op. 46 (1985), *pub* Schott; *rec* Piano Sonata (HMV ASD 645), Capriccio + Nonomiÿa (Auracle AUC 1005), Four Songs from the Japanese (Pye GSGC 14105), Violin Concerto (HMV ASD 2810), Two Choruses (HMV ASD 640), Little Symphony (Philips SAL 3497), Three Piano Pieces (HMV ASD 2551), Piano Trio + String Quartet no. 2 (Argo ZRG 748), Cello Romanza + Metamorphosis/Dance (Unicorn DKP 9017), Paraphrase (Oiseau-Lyre DSLO 1), String Quartet no. 3 + Das Gesetz der Quadrille (Wergo WER 60093); *bib* B. Northcott, ed.: The Music of AG (London, Schott, 1980)

Harvey, Jonathan   *b* Sutton Coldfield, 3 May 1939; *educ* St Michael's College, Tenbury, Cambridge, privately (Stein, Keller), Glasgow (PhD 1964), Princeton (1969–70, Babbitt); *posts* lecturer at Southampton U. (1964–77) and Sussex U. (1977–); *works* Ludus amoris, cantata (1969), Persephone Dream for orchestra (1972), Inner Light 1 for sextet and tape (1973), 2 for five voices, ensemble and tape (1977), 3 for orchestra and tape (1975), Smiling Immortal for chamber orchestra (1977), String Quartet (1977), Veils and Melodies on tape (1978), Magnificat and Nunc dimittis for chorus and organ (1978), Album for wind quintet (1978), Hymn for chorus and orchestra (1979), Be(com)ing for clarinet and piano (1979), Concelebration for quintet (1979), O Jesu, nomen dulce for chorus (1980), Toccata for organ and tape (1980), Mortuos plango, vivos voco on tape (1980), Passion and Resurrection, church opera (1981), Resurrection for chorus and organ (1981), Modernsky

Music for quartet (1981), Whom ye Adore for orchestra (1981), Curve with Plateaux for cello (1982), Bhakti for ensemble and tape (1982), Easter Orisons for chamber orchestra (1983), Nataraja for flute and piano (1983), The Path of Devotion for chorus and chamber orchestra (1983), Flight–Elegy for violin and piano (1984), Nachtlied for soprano, piano and tape (1984), Come, Holy Ghost for chorus (1984), Gong-Ring for ensemble and electronics (1984), Ricercare una melodia for trumpet and tape (1985), Song Offerings for soprano and octet (1985); *pub* Faber Music, Novello; *rec* String Quartet (RCA RS 9006), Mortuos plango (Erato STU 71544); *book* The Music of Stockhausen (London, Faber, 1975); *bib* articles by JH in *Tempo*, 140 (1982), 2, and in *Contemporary Music Review*, i/1 (1984), 111, and articles by D. Brown in *Musical Times*, i (1968), 808, and by P. Evans in *Musical Times*, cxvi (1975), 616

Holloway, Robin *b* Leamington Spa, 19 Oct 1943; *educ* St Paul's Cathedral (1952–7), privately (Goehr 1959–63), Cambridge (1961–4), Oxford (1965–7); *posts* research student and later fellow at Gonville and Caius College, Cambridge (1967–); *works* Garden Music op. 1 for octet (1962), Concertino no. 1 op. 2 for small orchestra (1964), Three Poems of William Empson op. 3 for mezzo and quintet (1964–5), Music for Eliot's 'Sweeney Agonistes' op. 4 for quintet (1965), In Chymick Art op. 5 for soprano, baritone and nonet (1965–6), Concerto op. 6 for organ and wind (1965–6), Four Housman Fragments op. 7 for soprano and piano (1965–6), First Concerto for Orchestra op. 8 (1966–9), Melodrama op. 9 for speaker, male chorus and ensemble (1967), Concertino no. 2 op. 10 for small orchestra (1967), Divertimento no. 1 op. 11 for amateur orchestra (1968), Four Poems of Stevie Smith op. 12 for soprano (1968–9), Scenes from Schumann op. 13 for orchestra (1970), The Wind Shifts op. 14 for high voice and strings (1970), Banal Sojourn op. 15 for high voice and piano (1971), Fantasy-Pieces op. 16 for ensemble (1971), Evening with Angels op. 17 for ensemble (1972), Divertimento no. 2 op. 18 for wind nonet (1972), Georgian Songs op. 19 for baritone and piano (1972), Cantata on the Death of God op. 20 for soloists, chorus and orchestra (1972–3), Five Little Songs about Death op. 21 for soprano (1972–3), Five Madrigals op. 22 (1973), Domination of Black op. 23 for orchestra (1973–4), Lights Out op. 24 for baritone and piano (1974), In the Thirtieth Year op. 25 for tenor and piano (1974), Author of Light op. 26 for contralto and piano 1974), The Leaves Cry op. 27 for soprano and piano (1974), Sea Surface Full of Clouds op. 28 for soloists, small chorus and chamber orchestra (1974–5), Concertino no. 3 op. 29 for ensemble (1975), Clarissa op. 30, opera (1976), Romanza op. 31 for violin and small orchestra (1976), This is Just to Say op. 32 for tenor and piano (1977), Divertimentos no. 3 op. 33a and no. 4 op. 33b for soprano and wind quintet (1977 and 1979), The Rivers of Hell op. 34 for septet (1977), The Blue Doom of Summer op. 35 no. 1 for voice and harp (1977), Willow Cycle op. 35 no. 2 for voice and harp (1977), Hymn for Voices op. 36 for chorus (1977), From High Windows op. 37 for baritone and piano (1977), The Consolation of Music op. 38 no. 1 for chorus (1977), He-She-Together op. 38 no. 2 for chorus (1978), Killing Time for soprano (1978), Three Slithy Toves for two clarinets (1978), The Noon's Repose op. 39 for tenor and harp (1978–9), Second Concerto for Orchestra op. 40 (1978–9), Serenade in C op. 41 for octet (1979), Idyll op. 42 for small orchestra (1979–80), Sonata, Adagio and Rondo op. 43 for horn and orchestra (1979–80), Aria op. 43 for ensemble (1979–80), Ode op. 45 for wind quartet and strings (1980), Wherever We May Be op. 46 for soprano and piano (1980–1), Sonata op. 47 for violin (1981), Brand op. 48, dramatic ballad for soloists, chorus and orchestra (1981), The Lover's Well op. 49 for bass-baritone and piano (1981), Men Marching op. 50 no. 1 for brass band (1981–2), From Hills and Valleys op. 50 no. 2 for brass band (1981–2), Women in War op. 51 for four voices and piano (1982), Suite for saxophone (1982), Anthem for chorus (1982), Serenata notturna op. 52 for four horns and small orchestra (1982), Showpiece op. 53 for ensemble (1982–3), Second Idyll op. 54 for small orchestra (1983), Viola Concerto op. 56 (1983–4), Serenade in E flat op. 57 for decet (1983–4), Moments of Vision op. 58 for speaker and quartet (1984), Romanza op. 59 for oboe and strings (1984), On Hope for soprano, mezzo and string quartet (1984), Bassoon Concerto (1984), Ballad for harp and orchestra (1985); *pub* Boosey & Hawkes; *rec* Sea Surface Full of Clouds + Romanza for violin (Chandos ABRD 1056); *bib* special issue of *Tempo*, 129 (1979)

Knussen, Oliver   *b* Glasgow, 12 June 1952; *educ* privately (Lambert), Tanglewood (Schuller); *works* Processionals for nonet op. 2 (1968), Concerto for Orchestra op. 5 (1968–70), Hums and Songs of Winnie-the-Pooh for soprano and quintet op. 6 (1970), Three Little Fantasies for wind quintet op. 6a (1970), Symphony no. 2 for soprano and small orchestra op. 7 (1970–1), no. 3 op. 18 (1973–9), Choral for orchestra op. 8 (1970–2), Rosary Songs for soprano and trio op. 9 (1972), Océan de terre for soprano and ensemble op. 10

(1972–3), Music for a Puppet Court for orchestra op. 11 (1972), Trumpets for soprano and three clarinets op. 12 (1975), Ophelia Dances: Book 1 for nonet op. 13 (1975), Autumnal for violin and piano op. 14 (1976–7), Cantata for oboe quartet op. 15 (1977), Sonya's Lullaby for piano op. 16 (1977–8), Coursing for chamber orchestra op. 17 (1979), Where the Wild Things Are, opera op. 20 (1979–81), Higglety Pigglety Pop!, opera (1984–5); *pub* Faber; *rec* Symphony no. 2 + Trumpets + Cantata + Coursing (Unicorn-Kanchana DKP 9027), Ophelia Dances + Symphony no. 3 (Unicorn RHD 400), Where the Wild Things Are (Unicorn-Kanchana DKP9044)

Matthews, Colin *b* London, 13 February 1946; *educ* Nottingham U. (classics), privately (Whittall, Maw); *works* Ceres for nonet op. 4 (1972), Five Studies for piano op. 5 (1974–6), Sonata no. 4 for orchestra op. 6 (1975), Partita for violin op. 7 (1975), Five Sonnets to Orpheus for tenor and harp op. 8 (1975–6), Specula for quartet op. 9 (1976), Night Music for small orchestra op. 10 (1976–7), Piano Suite op. 11 (1977–9), Rainbow Studies for quintet op. 12 (1977–8), Un colloque sentimental for medium voice and piano op. 14 (1971–8), Shadows in the Water for tenor and piano op. 15 (1978–9), String Quartet no. 1 op. 16 (1979), Sonata no. 5 'Landscape' for orchestra op. 17 (1977–81), Little Suite no. 1 for small orchestra op. 18a (1979), no. 2 op. 18b (1979), Little Suite for harp op. 18c (1979), Oboe Quartet op. 19 (1981), Secondhand Flames for five voices op. 20 (1982), Divertimento for string octet op. 21a or string orchestra op. 21b (1982), The Great Journey: Part 1 for baritone and ensemble op. 22 (1981–3), Canonic Overture: Arms Racing op. 24a (1983), Toccata mechanica for orchestra op. 24b (1984), Triptych for piano quintet op. 25a (1984), Night's Mask for soprano and septet op. 26 (1984), Cello Concerto op. 27 (1983–4); *pub* Faber Music, Novello

Matthews, David *b* London, 9 March 1943; *educ* Nottingham U. (classics), privately (Milner); *works* Three Songs for soprano and orchestra op. 1 (1968–71), Three Songs for baritone and piano op. 2 (1969–70), Stars for chorus and orchestra op. 3 (1970), String Quartet no. 1 op. 4 (1969–70), no. 2 op. 16 (1974–6), no. 3 op. 18 (1977–8), no. 4 op. 27 (1981), no. 5 op. 36 (1984), Fantasia for viola op. 5 (1970), Little Concerto for chamber orchestra op. 6 (1970–1), Upon Time, four songs for medium voice and piano op. 7 (1970–1), Fantasia for cello op. 8 (1971), Symphony no. 1 op. 9 (1975–8), no. 2 op. 17 (19761–8) no. 3 op. 37 (1983–5), The Book of Hours, six songs for high voice and piano op. 10 (1975–8), Music of Evening for quintet op. 11 (1976), Songs and Dances of Mourning for cello op. 12 (1976), Toccatas and Pastorals for quartet op. 13 (1976), Eclogue for soprano and septet op. 14 (1975–9), Three Preludes for piano op. 15 (1976–9), Etude for piano op. 21 (1978), Ehmals und Jetzt, six songs for soprano and piano op. 22 (1972–9), Four Yeats Songs for tenor and piano op. 23 (1976–9), September Music for small orchestra op. 24 (1979–82), The Company of Lovers, five choral songs op. 25 (1980), White Nights for violin and small orchestra op. 26 (1980), Introit for two trumpets and strings op. 28 (1981), Serenade for chamber orchestra op. 29 (1982), Duet Variations for flute and piano op. 30 (1982), Violin Concerto op. 31 (1980–2), Winter Journey for violin op. 32 (1982–3), The Golden Kingdom, nine songs for high voice and piano op. 33 (1978–83), Piano Trio op. 34 (1983–4), Clarinet Quartet op. 35 (1984), In the Dark Time for orchestra op. 38 (1984–5); *pub* Faber Music, Boosey and Hawkes; *rec* The Company of Lovers (Arika AR002)

Maw, Nicholas   *b* Grantham, 5 Nov 1935; *educ* Wennington School, Yorkshire (1945–54), RAM (1955–8, Berkeley, Steinitz), Paris (1958–9, Boulanger, Deutsch); *works* Sonatina for flute and piano (1957), Nocturne for mezzo and chamber orchestra (1957–8), Five Epigrams for chorus (1960), Our Lady's Song for chorus (1961), Essay for organ (1961), Chamber Music for wind quartet and piano (1962), Scenes and Arias for three female voices and orchestra (1962), Round for voices and piano (1963), The Angel Gabriel for chorus (1963), Balulalow for chorus (1964), One Man Show, opera (1964), String Quartet (1965), Sinfonia for small orchestra (1966), The Voice of Love for mezzo and piano (1966), Six Interiors for tenor and guitar (1966), Double Canon for Igor Stravinsky (1967), Sonata for strings and two horns (1967), The Rising of the Moon, opera (1967–70, Glyndebourne 1970), Epitaph-Canon in Memory of Igor Stravinsky for flute, clarinet and harp (1971), Concert Music for orchestra (1972), Five Irish Songs for chorus (1973), Serenade for small orchestra (1973), Life Studies for strings (1973–6), Personae for piano (1973), Te Deum (1975), Reverdie for male chorus (1975), Annes! for chorus (1976), Nonsense Rhymes for children's voices and piano (1976), La vita nuova for soprano and ensemble (1979), The Ruin for chorus and horn (1980), Flute Quartet (1981), Summer Dances for youth orchestra (1981), Night Thoughts for flute (1982), String Quartet no. 2 (1982),

Spring Music for orchestra (1982–3); *pub* Boosey & Hawkes, Chester, Faber Music; *rec* Chamber Music (Argo ZRG 536), Scenes and Arias (Argo ZRG 622), String Quartet (Argo ZRG 565), Sinfonia + Sonata (Argo ZRG 676), The Voice of Love + La vita nuova (Chandos ABR 1037), Life Studies (Argo ZRG 899); *bib* articles in *Tempo*, 68 (1964), 71 (1964–5), 92 (1970), 106 (1973), 125 (1978)

Muldowney, Dominic *b* Southampton, 19 July 1952; *educ* Taunton's Grammar School, Southampton, Southampton U. (Harvey), privately (Birtwistle), York U. (1971–4, Rands, Blake); *posts* composer-in-residence for Southern Arts (1974–6), music director at National Theatre (1976–); *works* Bitter Lemons for chorus (1970), An Heavyweight Dirge, music theatre (1971), Driftwood to the Flow for eighteen strings (1972), String Quartet no. 1 (1973), no. 2 (1980), Klavier-Hammer for one or more pianos (1973), Music at Chartres for ensemble (1974), Lovemusic for Bathsheba Evergreen and Gabriel Oak for ensemble (1974), Solo/Ensemble for sextet (1974), Da capo al fine, ballet on tape (1975), Cantata for voices and instruments (1975), Perspectives for orchestra (1975), The Earl of Essex's Galliard, music theatre (1975–6), Three-Part Motet for orchestra (1976), From Arcady (1) for violin (1976), (2) for basset horn and tuba (1978), (3) for cor anglais, viola and cello (1976), (4) for four oboes (1977), Double Helix for octet (1977), Five Melodies for saxophone quartet (1978), Garland of Chansons for six oboes and three bassoons (1978), Three Hymns to Agape for three oboes (1978), A First Show for percussion and tape (1978), Six Psalms for voices and instruments (1979), Macbeth, ballet for orchestra (1979), . . . In a Hall of Mirrors . . . for saxophone and piano (1979), A Little Piano Book (1979), Piano Trio (1980), From 'Little Gidding' for baritone, treble and piano (1980), Five Theatre Poems (Brecht) for voice and piano or sextet (1980–1), In Dark Times (Brecht) for four voices and quintet (1981), The Duration of Exile (Brecht) for voice and septet (1983), A Second Show for voice, trio and tape (1983), Piano Concerto (1983), Saxophone Concerto (1984); *pub* Universal; *rec* two of Five Theatre Poems (EMI EL 27 0049 1)

Oliver, Stephen *b* Liverpool, 10 March 1950; *educ* Oxford (1968–72, Johnson); *operas* The Duchess of Malfi (1971), The Dissolute Punished (1972), The Three Wise Monkeys (1972), A Furcoat for Summer (1973), Three Instant Operas (1973), The Donkey (1973), Perseverance (1974), Tom Jones (1974–5), Bad

Times (1975), The Girl and the Unicorn (1978), The Dreaming of the Bones (1979), Euridice (after Peri, 1981), Sasha (1982), Brittania Preserv'd (1984), Beauty and the Beast (1984), Waiting (1985); *short operas* Sufficient Beauty (1973), Past Tense (1973), The Waiter's Revenge (1976), The Garden (1977), A Stable Home (1977), Jacko's Play (1979), A Man of Feeling (1980), The Ring (1984); *other theatre works* Blondel, musical (1983), ballets, incidental music; *instrumental music* Ricercare no. 1 for four instruments (1974), no. 2 for wind band (1981), no. 3 for three instruments (1983), Luv for orchestra (1975), Symphony for small orchestra (1976), O no for brass band (1976), Kyoto for organ duet (1977), Sonata for guitar (1978), Study for piano (1979), Nicholas Nickleby Suite for brass quintet (1980); *choral music* Magnificat and Nunc dimittis (1976), The Child from the Sea, cantata (1980), A String of Beads, cantata (1980), Namings, cantata (1981), Trinity Mass (1981), Seven Words, cantata (1985); *pub* Novello; *rec* Jacko's Play (Delyse 7DS 1), Nicholas Nickleby (That's Entertainment TER 1029), Blondel (MCA PBL 1), Peter Pan (RSC 1)

Osborne, Nigel *b* Manchester, 23 June 1948; *educ* Oxford (1966–70, Leighton, Wellesz), Warsaw (1970–1, Rudziṅksi); *post* lecturer at Nottingham U. (1978–); *works* Seven Words for soloists, chorus and orchestra (1971), Heaventree for chorus (1973), Remembering Esenin for cello and piano (1974), Kinderkreuzzug for children (1974), The Sickle for soprano and orchestra (1975), Chansonnier for chorus and ensemble (1975), Prelude and Fugue for ensemble (1975), Musica da camera for violin, tape delay and audience (1975), Passers By for trio, synthesizer and slides (1976), Cello Concerto (1977), I am Goya for bass-baritone and quartet (1977), Vienna.Zurich.Constance for soprano and quintet (1977), After Night for guitar (1977), Two Spanish Songs for soprano (1977), Figure/ Ground for piano (1978), Kerenza at the Zawn for oboe and tape (1978), Orlando furioso for chorus and ensemble (1978), Songs from a Bare Mountain for women's chorus (1979), In Camera for ensemble (1979), Under the Eyes for voice and quartet (1979), Quasi una fantasia for cello (1979), Madeleine de la Ste-Baume for soprano and double-bass (1979), Flute Concerto (1980), Gnostic Passion for chorus (1980), Poem without a Hero for four voices and electronics (1980), Mythologies for sextet (1980), For a Moment for women's chorus and cello (1981), The Cage for tenor and ensemble (1981), Piano Sonata (1981), Choralis I–III for six voices (1981–2), Sinfonia I (1982), II (1983), Cantata piccola for soprano and string quartet (1982), Fantasia for ensemble (1983), Wildlife for ensemble (1984), Alba for mezzo, ensemble and tape (1984), Zansa for ensemble (1985), Pornography for mezzo and ensemble (1985); *pub* Universal; *rec* Remembering Esenin + The Sickle + I am Goya + Flute Concerto (Unicorn DKP 9031), After Night (Bedivere BVR 316); *bib* article by N. O'Loughlin in *Musical Times*, cxxi (1980), 307

Saxton, Robert *b* London, 8 October 1953; *educ* Bryanston, privately (Lutyens 1970–4, Berio), Cambridge (1972–5, Holloway), Oxford (1975–6, Johnson); *posts* lecturer at Goldsmiths College and Bristol U. (1984–); *works* Ritornelli and Intermezzi for piano (1972), La promenade d'automne for soprano and septet (1972), Krystallen for flute and piano (1973), Where are you going to my pretty maid? for soprano and sextet (1973), What does the song hope for? for soprano, septet and tape (1974), Echoes of the Glass Bead Game for wind quintet (1975), Reflections of Narziss and Goldmund for ensemble (1975), Two Pieces for piano (1976), Brise marine for soprano, piano and tape (1976), Poems for Mélisande for flute and piano (1977), Sonatas for Two Pianos (1977), Arias for oboe and piano (1977), Study for a Sonata for quartet (1977), Toccata for cello (1978), Canzona for octet (1978), Cantata no. 1 for tenor, counter-tenor and piano (1979), no. 2 for tenor, oboe and piano (1980), no. 3 for two sopranos and tape delay (1981), Eloge for soprano and nonet (1980), Choruses to Apollo for orchestra (1980), Traumstadt for small orchestra (1980), Piano Sonata (1981), Processions and Dances for octet (1981), Piccola musica per Luigi Dallapiccola for quintet (1981), Chiaroscuro for percussion solo (1981), Chaconne for double choir (1981), Fantasiestück for accordion (1982), The Ring of Eternity for chamber orchestra (1982–3), Concerto for Orchestra (1983–4), The Sentinel of the Rainbow for sextet (1984); *pub* Chester

Souster, Tim *b* Bletchley, 29 Jan 1943; *educ* Bedford Modern School (1952–61), Oxford (1961–5, Rose, Lumsden, Wellesz), privately (Bennett), Darmstadt (1964); *posts* BBC producer (1965–7), composer-in-residence at King's College, Cambridge (1969–71), teaching assistant to Stockhausen at the Cologne Musikhochschule (1971–3), research fellow at Keele U. (1975–9); *works* Songs of Three Seasons for soprano and viola (1965), Metropolitan Games for piano duet (1967), Titus Groan Music for wind quintet and electronics (1969), Waste Land Music for quartet with electronics

(1970), Triple Music II for three orchestras (1970), Spectral for viola and electronics (1972), World Music for octet with electronics (1974), Song of an Average City for small orchestra and tape (1974), Zorna for soprano saxophone, tape delay and drums (1974), The Music Room for trombone and tape (1976), Afghan Amplitudes for trio with electronics (1976), Arcane Artefact for trio with electronics (1977), Song for trio with electronics (1977), Arboreal Antecedents for trio with electronics (1977–8), Driftwood Cortège on tape (1978), Sonata for cello and ensemble (1978–9), Equalisation for brass quintet and electronics (1980), Mareas for four amplified voices and tape (1981), The Transistor Radio of St Narcissus for flugelhorn and electronics (1982), Curtain of Light for metal percussion and tape (1984), Le souvenir de Maurice Ravel for septet (1984), Paws 3D for orchestra (1984), Work for pianist with computer (1985); *pub* composer; *rec* Spectral + Afghan Amplitudes + Arcane Artefact + other works (Transatlantic TRAG 343), Sonata + Equalisation (Nimbus 45020); *bib* article by TS in *Contact*, 17 (1977), 3

Tavener, John Kenneth   *b* London, 28 Jan 1944; *educ* Highgate School, RAM (1961–5, Berkeley, Lumsdaine); *works* The Whale, dramatic cantata (1965–6), Celtic Requiem (1969), Ultimos ritos, meditation for large forces (1969–72), Thérèse, opera (1973–6, Covent Garden 1979), A Gentle Spirit, chamber opera (1977), The Liturgy of St John Chrysostom (1978), Akhmatova Rekviem, for soprano and baritone with orchestra (1979–80), Prayer for the World, for sixteen voices (1981), Ikon of Light, for choir and string trio (1983), Sixteen Haiku of Seferis, for soprano, tenor, percussion and strings (1984); *pub* Chester; *rec* The Whale (Apple SAPCOR 15, Ringo 2320 104), Celtic Requiem (Apple SAPCOR 20), The Liturgy of St John Crysostom (Ikon IKOS 8E), The Great Canon of the Ode to St Andrew of Crete (Gimell 1585–02), Ikon of Light + Funeral Ikos + The Lamb (Gimell 1585–05); *bib* articles by P. Griffiths in *Musical Times*, cxv (1974), 468 and cxx (1979), 814, and by P. Phillips in *Contact*, 26 (1983), 29

INDEX